JOE COLTON'S JOURNAL

Wyatt Russell has come a long way since he and his poor-as-dirt family stayed at our Hopechest Ranch years ago. But my son Rand tells me that his boyhood chum's big salary and prestigious job aren't exactly keeping him warm at night. In fact, Wyatt's looking to settle down. So when Wyatt offered to do Rand a favor and send some sensitive information to my foster daughter, Emily—who is hiding out in Keyhole, Wyoming, because of the danger looming over the Coltons—it became crystal clear that his real reason for making a pit stop in that dinky little town was to see his former sweetheart, Annie Summers, again. However, things sure have changed since their relationship fell apart years ago. Annie is now a single mom struggling to raise rambunctious twin boys. She's disillusioned by love, thanks in no small part to Wyatt.... Still, being with Annie again has stirred up some mighty intense feelings in Wyatt. And Wyatt is hardly the type to back down from a challenge!

About the Author

CAROLYN ZANE

lives with her husband, Matt, and their two little daughters—Madeline and Olivia—in the scenic countryside near Portland, Oregon's Willamette River.

In 1992, as part of her New Year's resolution, Carolyn began writing her first novel. After completing *The Wife Next Door* in 1993, she was fortunate enough to sell that book to Silhouette. In the years that followed, Carolyn has written and sold nearly thirty books to Silhouette Romance and to two inspirational publishers, and has well over a million books in print, around the world.

Taking on Twins

Carolyn
Zane

Published by Silhouette Books

America's Publisher of Contemporary Romance

Special thanks and acknowledgment are given to Carolyn Zane for her contribution to THE COLTONS series.

SILHOUETTE BOOKS
300 East 42nd St.,
New York, N.Y. 10017

ISBN 0-373-38711-3

TAKING ON TWINS

Copyright © 2001 by Harlequin Books S.A.

Visit Silhouette at www.eHarlequin.com

Printed in U.S.A.

THE COLTONS

Meet the Coltons—
a California dynasty with a legacy of privilege and power.

Wyatt Russell: *Hotshot lawyer.* He's come a long way from his dirt-poor childhood, but Wyatt's high-flying life now feels empty. Could his happiness lie in the town he'd left behind?

Annie Summers: *Struggling single mom.* Although Annie thought she was happy with the new life she'd made for herself and her twin sons, her reunion with Wyatt has suddenly made her question the choices she's made...and wish for the impossible.

Graham Colton: *The black sheep.* When news of his being blackmailed comes out, Joe's brother is only too willing to confess his sins—sins that could topple this family dynasty by pitting brother against brother!

THE COLTONS

Theodore Colton m. 1940 Kay Barkley
1908–1954   1919–1954

Ed Barkley m. 1916 Betty Barkley
1895–1966   1899–1970

Edna Kelly m. 1945 George Portman
1920–1970   1915–

Meredith Portman
1949–

m. 1969 Joseph Colton
1941–

Graham Colton
1946–

m. 1970 Cynthia Turner
1941–

Jackson, 1973–
Liza, 1975–

Patsy
1949–

Natural Children
- Rand, 1970–
- Drake, 1972–
- Michael, 1972–1980
- Sophie, 1974–
- Amber, 1976–

Foster Children
- Chance Reilly, 1967–
- Tripp Calhoun, 1968–
- Rebecca Powell, 1968–
- Wyatt Russell, 1969–
- Blake Fallon, 1969–
- River James, 1970–
- *Emily Blair, 1980–

- Jewel, 1969– (by Ellis Mayfair)
- *Joe, Jr., 1991–
- *Teddy, Jr., 1993–

THE McGRATHS

Jack McGrath
1906–1988

m. 1935

Maureen O'Toole
1915–1989

Liam, 1936–
Collin, 1938–
Maude, 1940–
Francis, 1942–
Peter m. 1970 Andie Clifton
1949–   1951–

Austin, 1971–
Heather, 1976–

LEGEND
- - Child of Affair
━ Twins
• Adopted by Joe Colton

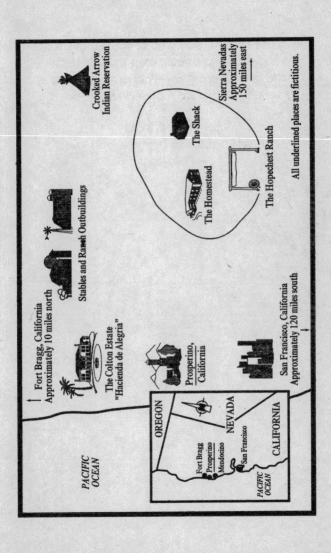

Crooked Arrow
Indian Reservation

Sierra Nevadas
Approximately
150 miles east →

The Shack

Stables and Ranch Outbuildings

The Homestead

The Hopechest Ranch

All underlined places are fictitious.

← Fort Bragg, California
Approximately 10 miles north

The Colton Estate
"Hacienda de Alegria"

Prosperino,
California

San Francisco, California
Approximately 120 miles south ↓

PACIFIC
OCEAN

OREGON

NEVADA

CALIFORNIA

Fort Bragg
Prosperino
Mendocino

San Francisco

PACIFIC
OCEAN

One

"Wyatt?"

Wyatt Russell glanced up to see his foster cousin and bride-to-be Liza Colton burst through the front doors of her uncle Joe's massive Spanish-style ranch house. In her tail-wind she dragged some hapless devil that he could only guess to be her fiancé. Liza's giddy laughter rang out and a grin started in Wyatt's belly and flared into his cheeks. Man, it was good to be back. As he pulled his bags out of the trunk of the idling cab, Wyatt inhaled a deep lungful of home.

Ah, Prosperino, California. Just standing in this fertile valley was rejuvenating.

The day was typically sunny, the sweeping vista filled with rolling hills and endless blue sky.

Yes, this was paradise on earth. Even more so, because of the people who waited here for his return.

"Yes! Nick, honey, it *is* Wyatt! Sweetheart, come on, hurry!"

"Nick," as it were—wearing an indulgent smile—allowed himself to be yanked by the wrist as Liza rushed down the aggregate steps that led from the Hacienda de Alegria and to the cab parked beneath the sprawling portico. "Wyatt Russell, you sneaky—and terminally late might I add—rascal! I can't believe you are actually here in time for my wedding! And a week early? Nick, honey, get ready to catch me, I may faint."

"Liza!" Wyatt dropped his suitcases in favor of a hug and swept the willowy woman into his arms.

After they rocked and exclaimed over each other for a moment, Wyatt set Liza back on her feet and looked her up and down. Now slender and sophisticated, cousin Liza's baby fat had migrated to all the right places, leaving her a beautiful woman. Wyatt let out a low whistle.

"Good grief. My little Lizard's gone and grown up on me."

"So have you, Beevis." Liza preened under his scrutiny. She reached up and lightly touched the cleft in his chin with a forefinger. "Handsome as ever I see, ya big heartbreaker."

Wyatt rolled his eyes. "How long has it been?"

"Too long." She pouted. "Now that you're a big-time Washington lawyer, you don't have time for us little people."

"This from the diva of the hoi polloi."

"Don't tell me you pay any attention to my career."

Wyatt snorted. "Only every time I go through the checkout line. Did you know that you and Elvis are expecting an alien baby?"

"That is *so* yesterday. You obviously haven't heard that Nick and I are divorcing."

"Before the wedding?"

"Saves all kinds of time, don't you agree?"

"Always thinking. And, speaking of your career, congratulations on getting your voice back. You sound better than ever."

She lifted a palm of supplication to the heavens. "Thanks to Nick." Liza tugged her fiancé from where he stood in the shadows behind her. "That's how we met. He was my doctor."

"Nick, music fans everywhere are indebted to you, man."

Nick chuckled. "She makes me look good."

"Wyatt, I want you to meet the man I love—" her sigh was content as she circled his biceps with her arms "—Nick Hathaway. Nick, Wyatt Russell was one of Uncle Joe's many foster sons and—" she grinned "—my nemesis growing up."

As Wyatt held his hand out to Nick, he could see the love sparkling in Liza's eyes and knew that she was happy. He felt a tiny stab of envy and exhaled in a world-weary way. If only he could get his caseload to cooperate, maybe he could start penciling in a social life. A special someone. The bachelor deal was growing tedious and he longed for the type of connection with a woman that he saw radiating between these two.

He raked a hand through his hair. Weddings. They always made him go soft in the head.

"Good to know you, Nick," he said, gripping the other man's hand and clapping him on the back. And he meant it. There was something about Nick that immediately inspired trust. Wyatt liked him already.

"Good to meet you, too. Liza has told me all about you."

"All?" Wyatt bent to retrieve his bags. "Has she told

you that if you want to hear her really hit those high notes, a well-placed pile of plastic barf will do the trick? I recommend her sock drawer, although her shoes and her closet are both good.''

Nick cast a thoughtful look upon his intended. "I'll keep this in mind.''

"You will do no such thing! Wyatt, leave your luggage here. We'll get it later.'' Flitting like a delicate butterfly, Liza moved between the men and, slipping her hands into the crooks of their elbows, urged them toward the house. "Right now everyone is wanting to see you. Especially Uncle Joe.''

Just as Liza had predicted, the welcoming committee was waiting in the parlor just off the breezy foyer.

"Wyatt, my boy!'' Family patriarch Joe Colton's affectionate voice reverberated off the endless expanse of slate flooring, and Wyatt was summarily joggled and jostled and pounded on the back. "You made it, son! Good deal. Just in time for dinner, too. Nothing has changed, I see.''

The poignancy of belonging burned the back of Wyatt's throat as he returned Joe's manly displays of affection. It was such a relief to see Joe standing there, safe and sound considering what he'd been through last year. The older man carried only a light scar on his cheek as a somber reminder of the attempt made on his life at his sixtieth birthday party.

"You're looking good, Joe.''

Joe snorted and waved the compliment away.

Wyatt grinned. Joe never could take a compliment. He never seemed comfortable with the fact that, even in middle age, he was still a handsome guy, commanding the ladies' attention with dark good looks and the physical build he hammered into shape every morning. Even though he'd just entered his seventh decade, his hair was only now beginning to silver at his temples, which only added to his distinguished appeal.

But none of that stuff mattered to Joe.

No. To Joe, family love and a good moral character were of utmost importance. And that was why, Wyatt noted with admiration, Joe Colton was the man he was today.

As Joe steered him into the parlor, Wyatt heard his name ring out. Soon, he was enveloped in hugs and memories of happy times that began in the bosom of this family and he laughed with unbridled joy at each familiar face that came forward to greet him. This family was his heart and soul.

But even so, he was suddenly feeling a tad fifth-wheelish.

As he looked over the crowd of faces that helped to shape his youth, everyone, it seemed to Wyatt, had a partner in this old life. Everyone but him. Odd how he'd never really noticed this feeling before today. Then again, there *had* been a rash of weddings recently. His gaze slowly swept the crowd as he made note of the many couples.

Besides Joe and Meredith, there were the parents of the bride, Uncle Graham and Aunt Cynthia, Wyatt's foster brother Rand and his wife, Lucy, Joe's daughter Sophie and her husband, River, Joe's son, Drake and his wife, Maya, and family friend, Heather, and her husband, Thad.

And, of course, there were the bride and groom, Liza and Nick.

And these were just the people in the parlor at the moment. Damn. Wyatt passed a palm over his jaw. When had everyone gone and paired off? Over the next hour, more of the family moved in and out to extend their greetings, all married, or at the very least, engaged.

"Hey brother, how was your flight?" Rand—Wyatt's foster brother and newest partner in their Washington D.C. law practice—inquired as he pressed a cold drink into Wyatt's hand.

"Smooth as glass. Yours?"

"Same." Rand lowered his voice and darted a covert glance over his shoulder at Meredith. "Have you seen Austin yet?" Austin McGrath was a shirttail foster cousin of his and Rand's and a private investigator of growing renown.

Wyatt shook his head. "Last time we spoke on the phone, he'd hit a dead end. But he said he was close and should be sending over some sensitive information as soon as it comes in."

"Good. I'm anxious to see if he has anything new on the situation with—" he glanced over his shoulder at Meredith "—*Mom*. If he sends news, I want to meet with you in private and bring you up to speed."

Wyatt nodded. "Sure."

"By the way, brother, thanks for staying behind and wrapping up so many loose ends back at the office. Lucy and I needed the family time."

"No sweat. How was San Francisco?"

Rand crossed his eyes for a brief, yet meaningful moment. "We spent a few days…er, enjoying Lucy's relatives. At her second cousins insistence, young Max will be staying there, until the wedding. Wouldn't take no for an answer."

"Ah. In-laws. How is that?"

"You're a lucky man, Wyatt. Don't take your bachelorhood for granted."

"In-laws are that bad?"

Brow arched, Rand's grin was weak.

Wyatt's shrug was philosophical. "Yeah, well, at least you have a date to the wedding."

Turning from her conversation with the bride, Lucy stepped between them and looked from her husband to Wyatt and back again and, as if she knew what they'd been talking about, said, "Rand, we've got to get Wyatt a date to the wedding."

Wyatt laughed. "Can't you turn her off for a minute?"

Rand shook his head. "Are you kidding?"

"Lucy—" Wyatt dragged her against his chest and ruffled her hair "—give it a rest. It's bad enough that I have to put up with your incessant matchmaking on a daily basis back home."

"Some day you'll thank me."

"I'll thank you to shut up."

Lucy pretended to pout. "Okay, Mr. Grinch. Come on, I'll show you your suite. It's right across from ours. Lucky you. I can matchmake all weekend."

"Lucky me."

As Wyatt unpacked his bags and stowed them in the closet of his luxurious suite, he couldn't help but wonder if there would ever be a wedding in his own future.

He gave his head a sharp shake. Nah. He'd blown his chance, back in college with Annie.

Annie.

Not a day went by that he didn't think of her. Even the mere thought of her name had his guts roiling with regret. A muscle worked in his jaw and he ground his back teeth in a way that was becoming second nature. What an idiot.

He could have been happily married by now, with a couple of kids to wrestle if he hadn't been so self-focused. Wyatt rolled his shoulders and rotated his head from side to side to ease the tension.

Something about Liza's impending marriage made him reflective. Maudlin. Short-tempered. And he knew it had a lot to do with his own sorry, lackluster personal life. Oh, his career path was very fulfilling and had been since college. But now that he had hit—and passed—thirty, he harbored a yearning for something he'd felt very strongly the moment he stepped from the cab.

Family. Home. Belonging to a unit. There was nothing like it.

A knock sounded at his door. "Wyatt? It's me, Lucy."

Then again, along with family came the hassles.... With a mock frown, Wyatt yanked open his door and barked, "I can find my own damned dates."

"Yeah, right. Come on, Rand," Lucy called. "He's decent." She scowled and moved into Wyatt's room and perched on the bench at the end of his bed. "Well, he's dressed anyway."

Rand, reading as he walked, moved into the room and dropped down to sit next to his wife.

Noticing the sober look on his foster brother's face, Wyatt stopped unpacking. "What is it?"

"The information Emily's been wanting for so long finally came in."

"Have you spoken with Emily?" Wyatt couldn't help but worry and wonder about their young sister. Though she was of age, she was still just a kid in his mind.

"Not yet. But I will. Listen. Austin had a courier drop this by so that we could take a look."

Wyatt moved to the end of his bed and dropped on the bench next to Lucy, sandwiching her between himself and Rand. "What does it say?"

"More evidence that Meredith isn't Meredith anymore." Rand's tone was wry.

Wyatt's exhale was long and slow. "What now?"

Rand tapped the pages he held. "Okay. So far we've all suspected that the woman out there we've known as 'Mom' might not be mom at all, but instead, her twin sister."

"Patsy Portman," Lucy murmured.

"Right."

"That's just...so hard to *believe*. I mean, come on. It's wacky." Wyatt raked a hand through his hair. "

"True. But Emily believes it," Rand drawled. "And she was traumatized enough to run away last September."

"We should have listened to Emily." To stem his agitation, Wyatt stood and moved to the wet bar. He pulled bottles of sparkling water from the refrigerator and passed them out.

"Don't be so hard on yourselves," Lucy murmured as she popped the top to her bottle. "Sometimes people change after severe trauma to the head. Act completely different. Besides, you had no way of knowing that Meredith had a twin. Obviously, she didn't want any of you to know about Patsy. And can you blame her?"

Wyatt took a long pull on his water bottle, hoping to rinse the acid taste from his mouth. "No. Except that now that Em's run away, it might have been helpful."

"Considering what Emily's been saying about Meredith, she may be better off out of this house." Rand held up the documents in his hand. "Austin's report confirms her worst suspicions." He snapped the pages with his thumb and forefinger.

As understanding dawned, Wyatt leaned against the wet bar and gave his head a kind of backward nod. "It's confirmed. Patsy Portman is here."

"Right."

Lucy twisted her fingers together. "Then it's true. That wacko is here. In the house. With us. Now."

Wyatt arched a brow. "We knew there was that possibility."

"Yes, I knew it up here," Lucy gestured to her head, "but deep down, I couldn't really believe it. I mean it's so...so...I mean, how can one woman take another's place and fool everyone for ten years?"

Tipping his chin to his shoulder, Rand looked over at Wyatt. "Which also begs the question, if she's not Mom, then where is Mom?"

Wyatt chose not to mince words. "You think she may be dead?"

"Could be. Drake thinks so. Hell, practically the whole family does."

"Murdered?"

"Probably. Patsy's done it before."

Lucy glanced between the two men. "Why would Patsy do that to her own sister?"

"Jealousy, most likely." Wyatt was becoming more certain with every bit of information revealed. "Taking Meredith's identity would also keep her from facing another murder rap."

Lucy let her head flop back on her shoulders. "Okay, so my mother-in-law is a murderer."

Wyatt held up a finger. "Actually, she's your aunt-in-law."

Lolling her head from Wyatt to Rand, she stared pointedly at her husband. "I don't ever want to hear you complain about my family again."

"So far, Mom's murder is still conjecture." Rand tipped back his water bottle and drank, then wiped his mouth on his sleeve. "Right now, we don't have any hard evidence that she is indeed dead. Without a body, we can't prove anything yet."

"But until we do, we have to pretend that Patsy is Meredith, and that her bizarre behavior is normal?" Lucy wondered.

Wyatt shrugged. "Nothing we haven't been doing for years now."

Lucy looked back and forth between the men and shivered. "The only difference is that now we know for sure."

* * *

Later that evening, dinner with his family sent memories cascading through Wyatt, making him feel more alive than he'd felt in years. There was nothing like the praise—and good-natured insults—of family. It was too bad that "Meredith" had pleaded headache and missed most of the festivities. When she'd made her excuses and stepped from the room, he'd exchanged meaningful glances with Rand and Lucy and wondered how many others at the table suspected that Meredith wasn't actually...Meredith.

If she was missed, it didn't dampen the festivities for long. There were toasts to the bride and groom, trips down memory lane, and a feeling of something so incredibly right. Again, Wyatt yearned for more than a professionally decorated and cleaned condo to come home to at night.

After the candles had burned low, some of the crowd retired, some headed for the hot tub, some for the pool tables and others for after-dinner drinks in the courtyard. Lucy and Rand walked with Wyatt to their neighboring suites and stepped inside Wyatt's room for a moment.

"What now?" Wyatt asked.

Rand patted the pocket that held the papers that Austin's courier had delivered that afternoon. "We need to get this information to Emily." Rand glanced at Lucy. "I'll be back in time for the wedding."

"You're leaving?" Wyatt asked.

"Have to. We can't leave Emily twisting in the wind. The more we keep her in the loop, the safer she'll be."

Frustrated by feelings of helplessness, Wyatt nodded. "Right. How did you figure out where she went?"

"Austin's P.I. found her a few hours ago." Rand paused and looked into his brother's eyes before he spoke. "She's in Keyhole."

Tiny hairs stood up on the back of Wyatt's neck and he

froze. Had he misunderstood? "*Keyhole?* Keyhole, Wyoming? You're kidding!"

"I thought that place might ring a bell for you." Rand narrowed his eyes, searching Wyatt's face.

"What rings a bell? Why?" Lucy's head swiveled back and forth between the two men as they talked over her head. "Why would some town named Keyhole ring a bell?"

"Emily's hiding out in Keyhole?" Wyatt asked, ignoring Lucy. "Why Keyhole?"

"Don't know. The P.I. didn't talk to her. Keyhole's not far from Nettle Creek, where Dad grew up, so I guess Emily maybe feels a little less homesick." His eyes narrowed. "Isn't Keyhole where Annie lives now?"

"Who's Annie?" Lucy wondered.

Wyatt gave his throat a noisy clearing in hopes that he didn't sound as screwed up as he felt. "Yeah. As far as I know."

Lucy sighed. "Hello? Guys? Remember me? Who is Annie?"

"How long has it been since you two saw each other?" Rand asked his brother.

"Not since college." Wyatt passed a hand over his forehead and rubbed at the familiar ache that settled in his brow every time he thought of the life Annie led without him. Just speaking about her marriage turned him into a melancholy mess. "She got married and had a couple of kids. Twin boys, I hear."

"I'm gathering somebody named Annie has twin boys. Don't feel like you owe me any explanation or anything. After all, I'm just *standing here,*" Lucy fumed.

"Wasn't her husband killed in an accident of some kind a few years back?" Rand asked.

"Yeah. I thought you told me that."

Rand shrugged. "Can't remember."

"Maybe it was Austin." Unfortunately, Wyatt hadn't learned of the accident that took her husband's life until long after the funeral, and by then, his condolences seemed untimely. Misplaced. At least that was the excuse he used to explain away his fears of contacting Annie. "Anyway, as far as I know she hasn't remarried."

With a moan, Lucy buried her face in her hands. "I'm invisible."

Rand laughed. "Lucy, honey, Annie was Wyatt's first—" he arched a brow at Wyatt "—and only love."

Lucy peeped between her fingers. "*You* were in *love* once?"

"You don't need to sound so shocked."

"Excuse me? Mr. I-Don't-Need-Nobody-Nohow-Never was once in love? Oh, baby. This is juicy." She hooted, then her eyes narrowed and she gently probed his cheekbones with her fingertips. "And, by the little flush in your cheeks, may I deduce that she still has your heart?"

Wyatt looked askance at Rand. "How do you put up with her meddling?"

Rand laughed. "With Lucy, it's an art form. Her talent at digging up dirt is one of the main reasons I fell in love with her."

"Aw, honey. You're so sweet." Lucy stepped into her husband's arms and met his mouth for a solid kiss. Soon, happy moans were rumbling from their throats.

Wyatt rolled his eyes. "Don't you two have a room of your own?" he groused. For crying in the night. Sometimes they could be so obnoxious. Not to mention thoughtless. It wasn't like he had anyone of his own to turn to when they skipped off to their room to do whatever came naturally to newlyweds.

"Honey," Lucy said as she nuzzled Rand's neck, "why

are *you* going to Keyhole? Don't you think we should make Wyatt go? After all, he has more reasons to go than you do, don't you think? Besides, I don't want you to go. Stay with me. I'll make it worth your while.''

"I can't think straight with you kissing my ear that way," Rand groaned.

"That's it. Get out of here," Wyatt ordered and, striding to the door, yanked it open.

With one smooth move, Rand lifted Lucy and carried her to the hall.

"Don't worry, Wyatt," Lucy called. "You can be back in time for Liza's wedding. Bring a date back with you!"

Their laughter echoed down the hall and into their suite. And then it was silent.

Wyatt kicked off an insanely expensive pair of Italian leather shoes and, wiggling his toes, allowed his gaze to travel leisurely around his suite. Never—not even in his wildest dreams—would he ever have believed that he'd build a decent life for himself on this old planet. But he had.

Thanks to the fact that Joe had been a foster child himself and remembered how it had felt to be taken in and loved when the people who'd brought him into this world had been unable. The fact that Wyatt hadn't been in Prosperino for nearly five years, then could sit down at the table and pick up where he left off as easily as if it had been five minutes, proved that family was about far more than blood. It was about shared history. About caring. Love.

As Wyatt leaned back into the pillows that were propped against the headboard, his thoughts moved to Annie.

Always to Annie.

Her family came from Keyhole. The same small town where his foster sister Emily had gone. Lord have mercy, what were the odds of that? Some astronomical number, he decided as he considered the bizarre coincidence.

Keyhole, Wyoming. The quaint little village came to life in his minds' eye. It had been years since he'd been there. To visit Annie. To meet the family. To mess up the best thing that had ever happened to him.

His mind, like a runaway locomotive, churned and screamed with thoughts of Annie. He'd learned a long time ago that once he started thinking about her, he couldn't stop. It made him miserable, left him sleepless. But there didn't seem to be any cure. It was almost as if, after their first kiss, she'd become entwined with the ladder of his very DNA. Even after all these years, memories of her made his mouth go dry as the Mojave desert and his face feel the burn of his changing blood pressure. With a tortured groan, Wyatt shifted his position and covered his head with a pillow.

Fool. Fool. Fool. The downy feathers couldn't seem to drown out the incessant refrain.

His eyes slid closed and he entertained a vision of Annie's delightfully expressive face. She could have been a poster child for the musical that bore her name. Curly and carrot red, Annie always said that her hair was the bane of her existence. She wouldn't believe that it had been one of the things that had first drawn Wyatt. That, and her clear ivory skin and fresh wholesome features. But the thing that he'd most loved were her amazing green eyes. Almond-shaped eyes that tilted slightly up and lent her otherwise all-American face an exotic look.

Eyes that could see through to his soul.

Wyatt pulled the pillow off his face and stared at the ceiling.

The very first time he'd met Annie, ten years ago, they'd been working together in the dish room at one of Prosperino State College's many cafeterias. A conveyor belt carried the dirty trays toward a giant dishwasher. Along the way, student workers would remove the silverware, the paper, and the glasses. Then the trays traveled to the garbage disposal where more student workers scraped the scraps and sprayed the dishes and loaded them into the mouth of the dishwasher. The machine would haul its load, in a never-ending car-wash style, to the other end where more workers would unload. It was a hot, dirty job, but it helped to pay the bills his scholarship wouldn't cover.

Wyatt's job had been to load the dishwasher.

Annie's had been to make sure all the silverware was taken off the trays before they reached Wyatt.

Her first day on the job she'd grown flustered as the trays came speeding by and, when a piece of silverware had jammed the garbage disposal for the third time, Wyatt had gotten mad. Turning off the belt, he'd marched down to the silverware station brandishing a mangled spoon.

"What the hell is the problem down here? Any idiot should be able to handle pulling three lousy pieces of silverware off a passing tray."

Eyes snapping with anger, Annie had tossed her wild coppery mane out of her face and fired a fistful of silverware at the soapy container at her side. "Hey, buddy, I'd like to see you get it all when the belt is going a hundred miles an hour."

Enjoying the break, their more experienced co-workers had settled in to watch the show. At the same time, students attempting to turn their trays in poked their head into the dish room to see why the belt was off and what the shouting was about.

"Nobody else seems to have a problem keeping up." Wyatt knew that wasn't exactly true, but he'd had a hell of a day and with midterms coming up, he was in no mood to deal with this rookie.

"Baloney. Nobody wants this stupid job. That's why I got it before the ink was dry on my application. This is my first day, so you can just *cut me some slack!*"

Wyatt stared at her. "This is your first day on the job and you're yelling at me?"

"Yes!" The little veins stood out on her neck and she fairly pulsed with frustration.

The humor of the situation suddenly struck him and Wyatt threw back his head and started to laugh. Soon, everyone but Annie was laughing. Then, lips twitching, she'd cracked and they'd all howled until the boss came in to see why trays had stacked up waist deep in the cafeteria, just outside the dish room.

The next time Wyatt had seen Annie was at the time clock a week later on Valentine's Day.

"Hi," he said as she punched out. He glanced at her time card. "Annie."

"Hi." She glanced at the card he held. "Wylie."

"Wyatt."

"Whatever."

She was a smart aleck. As casually as he could, Wyatt draped an arm over the time clock and winked. "So. It's the fourteenth. Where's my Valentine's kiss?"

She snorted. "Are you off your rocker? I barely know you."

"Aw, c'mon. We've already had our first fight. Surely it's time to move on to a kiss."

"Forget it." Her smiling green eyes belied the stern tone of her voice.

"Just a little one." He puckered up and waited.

She giggled. "Are you always so delusional?"

"You wound me." He thrust out his lower lip and pretended to pout.

Noisily, she exhaled. "Okay. One kiss. On the cheek."

He wasted no time in presenting his cheek. "I'll take what I can get."

As she stood on tiptoe to press her full lips to his cheek, Wyatt turned at the last instant and caught her lips with his own.

She'd recoiled and shrieked with laughter. "You cheater," she squealed, "I can't believe I fell for that old trick!"

In a flash, she spun on her heel and tore through the industrial kitchen, pushing stainless food carts in his way as he gave chase. Cat and mouse they ran and played, darting out of the kitchen and into the now nearly empty dining room.

"Come back," Wyatt yelled.

"Never," Annie yelled back.

He admired her spunk. She was fast for such a short little thing. As she plunged into the great outdoors and sped down the sidewalk toward the dorm across the street, Wyatt had shouted after her, causing passing students to stop and stare.

"Someday I'm gonna kiss you proper, Annie Summers, just wait and see."

And he had.

Two

One month after that first Valentine kiss, Wyatt lay on a blanket in the Memorial Union Quad, Annie curled at his side, her head resting on her backpack. She was close enough to set him on fire with desire, but not close enough to kiss. Oh, yeah. Wyatt released his frustration in a long, slow breath directed at the high clouds that scudded by.

That was Annie for you.

It was a beautiful spring day. Here in Prosperino, the college campus by the sea was a riot of color and the fragrant aroma of a landscape in bloom. A perfect day for lovers. For kissing. For ducking off into the bushes for a little "hot and bothered."

Wyatt stripped off his T-shirt to better work on his tan. He glanced at Annie. She was studying her biology.

For crying out loud, didn't she ever give it a rest? He had some biology he'd like to show her. He flexed a biceps and watched her from his peripheral vision to see if she noticed. She didn't. He flopped over onto his back.

Annie was a nice girl. The type of girl a guy brought home to mother. Even the kind of kooky, hormone-ravaged woman his foster mother, Meredith, had been lately.

Yep. Annie Summers was the kind of girl a guy married.

The renegade thought shocked him and he nearly choked on his gum. *Married?* Where had that come from?

The pink tip of her tongue protruded from her mouth as she scrunched her brow and highlighted endless paragraphs of proton/neutron-type information. He groaned, low in his throat. She was driving him batty.

Overhead, seagulls wheeled and cried, begging the students for leftover crumbs from lunch. Annie was such a sucker for the noisy critters. She called them "baby" and "honey" and enticed them with bits of her sandwich. She didn't even do that for him, he thought grumpily.

He called the stupid, noisy birds "air-rats" and shooed them off. They reminded them too much of himself as a boy he guessed. Always begging for food.

He fired a pebble at one now, and without looking, Annie reached up and smacked his hand. He chuckled. She was so cool.

They'd been dating for nearly a month now, and it had been the slowest, most torturous month of his life. Courting this woman took finesse. Savoir-faire. A patience born of wisdom and maturity.

A veritable sainthood.

Hell, he'd be a monk by the time she got done with him. So far, she'd given up three dinky little good-night kisses and some hand-holding at the midnight movie. He'd relived every moment of these whisper kisses a million times after each successful union of their lips. But always, she'd push him away, shyly claiming that she needed time.

Time? Time for what? he wanted to know.

Normally, he'd have moved on to greener pastures by now, but this was Annie.

Annie was different.

Annie was his soulmate. He'd known that from the moment his lips had touched hers back there on Valentine's Day and a clap of thunder had gone off in his head that left him deaf to any kind of rhyme or reason when it came to one flame-haired, fiery-tempered, good-humored, overly studious Annie Summers.

"Hey." He reached over and tugged a strand of her wild red mop away from her cheek.

"Mmm?" Her highlighter squeaked as she found a particularly interesting section in her text.

"Want to go to a party on my dorm floor tonight?"

"Sure."

"Really?" Annie wanted to party tonight? During dead week? Had a Frosty Freeze opened in hell?

"Yeah. I could use a study break."

Wisely, Wyatt bit back the sound of impatience he'd been on the verge of snorting.

Study break?

This would be no milk and cookies study break. This was to be a kegger of mass proportion. An out-and-out rock-n-roll, get-down-and-funky brawl. He couldn't wait. Right now his roommate and a couple other guys who were freshly twenty-one were out scoring the beer and other accoutrements. He could fairly hear the electric guitars tuning up from here. By ten o'clock that night, people would be swinging from the chandeliers. He just hoped Annie would loosen up for once and enjoy herself.

No such luck.

By ten that night, Annie was angrily shrugging into her slightly beer-stained jacket and marching out the door and back to her room. Wyatt, whipped puppy that he envisioned himself to be these days, followed, bellowing her name like a lovesick bull.

"Annie!"

"Shut up," she barked.

She jerked her arm out of his grasp when he finally did catch her out on the sidewalk. The moon was full—which no doubt accounted for at least some of the insanity up on his dorm floor—and he could clearly see the disgust etched into her flawless brow.

"But wait. I can explain. I had no idea, really, that it was going to be such a big, well, riot, actually—"

"Bull."

"No, really, I'm not lying. I knew it'd be wild, but not that bad. Especially that guy with the can of Crisco. He was kidding, I think. Anyway, I'm sorry. Forgive me?"

She slowed slightly. He was breathless. Man. When the woman was mad, she could move. They reached the end of the street that fronted his dorm and Annie turned down a main drag that led to the library.

No doubt she had some studying to do, he thought sourly. The street lamps shone through the trees and cast eerie patterns on the pavement. Now and then a Thursday night reveler or two would pass. Staggering, slurring, singing and generally firing Annie up even more. He grinned, imagining that her face was nearly as hot as her hair.

As her body.

Oh, man, she had to forgive him.

Out of energy reserves, he grabbed her arm, and when she tried to jerk away, he didn't let go.

"Annie." He was breathing heavy now, from the exertion or from the effect her anger had on his libido, he couldn't tell. "Annie, please, honey, I'm sorry."

Annie sighed. "I can't believe you like hanging out with

those…those…'' She groped for the perfect word, meant
to scathe. To blister. To singe.

''Animals?'' he supplied helpfully.

''Yes!'' she exploded, sending the word into the next zip
code. ''They were horrible!'' She gave her arms a frenetic
waving. ''All gropy and dopey and—''

''Freaky and geeky?'' He pulled her off the beaten trail
and into a small grove of trees at the side of the library.
''Goofy and doofy?'' Steering her against a tree, he leaned
across her body, balancing against a smooth trunk with his
palm. Looking into her eyes, he arched a brow and grinned.
''Dancy and fancy?''

''Don't make me laugh.''

''Why not?''

''I'm mad and I want to stay that way.''

''What if I don't want you to?''

''Tough noogies,'' she said petulantly.

He brought his lips to hers and rubbed them lightly
across. ''Don't be mad,'' he whispered into her mouth. Her
breath was sweet. Minty and warm and fresh and…Annie.

''I can't help it. I want you to respect me. Not treat me
like some kind of brain-dead, sex-crazed party animal.''

''I'm sorry,'' he murmured, raining kisses in a line along
her jaw until he reached that little place behind her ear
where she'd dabbed something musky. ''I'll never treat you
like a sex-crazed animal again,'' he murmured, reclaiming
her mouth and speaking against her lips, her nose, her chin.

''Promise?'' she breathed.

He noted that her lungs were laboring nearly as hard as
his now.

''Promise.''

''What?'' she murmured and wound her arms around his
neck. ''What did you promise? I—I forgot.''

''I promise to treat you like a sex-crazed party animal.''

"Good." She didn't seem to realize, or care about, his mistake.

Wyatt wasn't actually sure that it was a mistake, but he was too busy filling his hands with her silky red curls to analyze. Just the same, before she could protest, he closed his mouth over hers for their first real kiss. A deep, soul-searching kiss that he put everything he had into, knowing that—for this evening anyway—it was all he'd get from Annie.

He eased her flat up against the tree trunk and pressed his body into hers, absently noting how well her valleys fit his hills and vice versa. As he lay over her, he lowered his hands from where they'd been tangled in her hair and captured her wrists and pulled her arms up over her head.

She writhed beneath him, arching against him, returning his kiss with every bit of the passion he'd dreamed of from the moment he'd laid eyes on her. From deep in her throat, a whimper of sorts issued, and she melted against him, her head moving back and forth, seeking, searching for a better fit of her mouth under his.

He moved with her, accommodating, anticipating her every move, straining to become a single unit with her. He released her arms and she wound them at the back of his neck. His own hands settled at her jaw. Beneath his onslaught, Wyatt could feel her losing herself, becoming weightless, boneless, fearless. He knew because the same thing was happening to him.

It was a blissful feeling that he'd never experienced before. A feeling he never wanted to lose. A feeling of unity.

Of belonging.

This. This must be what love was all about, his muzzy mind reasoned, as he tore his mouth from hers just long enough to gasp for air and go back for more. No wonder so many people spent their lives searching for it. If this was at the end of the rainbow, count him in.

With his fingers, he traced the contours of her face, memorizing the feel of her cheeks, the union of their mouths, the way her fabulous hair tickled his cheeks, his neck. He breathed in the sea air, the scents of spring flowers, the velvety, cool darkness, the scent of Annie's perfume mixed with spilled beer and old leather. He listened to the serenading crickets, the distant music and laughter of a party in progress and the footfalls of the occasional passerby. He committed each of these things to memory, realizing this was an experience he never wanted to forget.

What Wyatt hadn't realized at the time was that this very kiss welded him to Annie Summers for the rest of his natural life.

Even after she married another guy and bore his sons.

Wyatt woke with a start, and for a moment, couldn't remember where he was. Slowly reality began to dawn and he realized that he'd fallen asleep in his clothes. Again. And dreamed of Annie. Again.

Blearily, he rolled on his side and checked the clock. Three in the morning. The Hacienda de Alegria was wrapped in the kind of cottony, deep silence that only happened at that particular hour. He sat up and pulled off his T-shirt and flung it on the floor.

He'd been sweating.

Must have been some dream.

Right now, he could only recall fragments, but as usual, Annie played a starring role in his bed. He unzipped his jeans, eased them over his hips and kicked them off. Then, reaching for the light on his nightstand, he clicked the room into a blackness the color of the hole in his heart. Even now, fully awake, he could feel Annie's body pressed against his.

How had he ever been stupid enough to let her go?

Back then, as a child of a broken home, he'd had something to prove, he guessed. Making it to the top was all-important.

When Annie had to leave school during her junior year and return home after her father had a debilitating stroke, their long-distance relationship had begun to suffer under the strain. She'd felt strongly about her family ties and decided that she was needed at home to help run the family business. It was a heartrending decision, but family had come first to Annie.

And at the time, being so young, he hadn't understood the deeply precious gift that family could be. But Annie had. To Annie, family was everything.

Always.

Still.

And now, seven years later, Wyatt lived in regret.

His Annie had married someone else. Borne his children and was now his widow. She would probably always love the father of her sons and carry his insurmountable memory in her heart till the day she died.

He could have been the father of those children. Her one and only love. If only he hadn't thrown it all away for a meaningless career that did not love him back at the end of the day.

Wyatt punched his pillow. He knew eating his heart out was fruitless, so he tried to envision Annie older now. Grayer. Life-ravaged. Age-spotted. Stoop-shouldered. Knock-kneed. Tongue-tied. Rotten-toothed.

Wyatt's chuckle was grim.

Seeing Annie face to face again would no doubt be the only way he'd ever be able to fully purge her from his soul.

To get on with his life. To realize that what they had was now dead. Over. Ancient history.

By now she was undoubtedly a battle-scarred old crone. The nagging, perpetually weary mother of two identical little demons. He was lucky to be footloose and fancy-free of that ugly scene.

And, if he repeated this mantra often enough, he might just start to believe it.

The next morning in the wee Saturday hours, after a quick discussion with Rand, Wyatt phoned the airline from his room and reserved the last seat on a flight leaving from San Francisco to Seattle. From Seattle he'd catch a commuter to Jackson Hole and be in Keyhole by early lunchtime. Then he called and arranged for a cab to meet him out front in fifteen minutes.

At least now he had a legitimate excuse for going to Keyhole without looking like the loser he feared Annie would see in him. He hoped she was still single. He guessed that she was probably was. He'd have called and asked before now, but until this deal with Emily came up, he hadn't been able to figure out a way to barge back into her life. A life that seemed to have gone on quite happily without him. He had to give her credit. That was something he'd been unable to do.

Maybe this trip would give him a chance to apologize and maybe work on a sense of closure, if nothing else.

For once, Wyatt was glad that Lucy was a terminal matchmaker.

He could barely believe that within a matter of hours, he'd be in the same town as Annie. His gut clenched and his heart picked up speed at the thought. He and Rand had agreed to keep this trip low-key with the family. No need to risk Emily's location by letting too many in on the secret.

Already, he'd repacked and made his excuses—an un-
expected business appointment in the Midwest—to Liza,
Nick and Joe, whom he'd found having coffee out by the
pool. They'd all been disappointed, but understanding. Especially since he'd promised Liza a pound of flesh if he
didn't make it back in time for her wedding.

Nobody had a hard time believing that Wyatt put business first. He always had.

They had no way of knowing that he was a changed man.
Or at the very least, an evolving man.

On his way out to await his cab, Wyatt breathed in all
the familiar morning scents of Joe Colton's "House of
Joe." Rich, aromatic coffee wafted in from the kitchen and
a warm breeze carried the fragrance of blooming roses in
from the courtyard where Nick and Liza were to be married
next week. The bakers were working overtime, and though
the fresh cinnamon rolls and coffee cakes smelled heavenly,
Wyatt couldn't eat. He was too keyed up over the thought
of seeing Annie again.

Before he stepped out the front door, Wyatt heard voices
coming from the parlor, just off the foyer. He paused to
poke his head inside and bid a quick goodbye to whoever
might be in there. As he cracked the door, the voices grew
heated, rising in both volume and intensity.

Uncle Graham and his son, Jackson, were at it again.

Grimacing, Wyatt backed away. Rather than chance
drawing their attention, he left the door ajar and moved as
far away from the parlor as possible, and still be in the
house and able to watch for his cab through the leaded glass
sidelights at the front doors. Unfortunately, as much as he
tried to block it out, it was impossible not to overhear the
content of the disturbing conversation.

Jackson's voice had an ominous, feral quality. "Okay,
Dad. One more time. The reason you've been making these

massive deposits into this mystery account is because you are being...blackmailed?''

"Keep your voice down," Graham growled.

"Why the hell should I keep my voice down? Blackmail is illegal! Whoever is doing this to you can be stopped. Get yourself a good lawyer. I'm available. If you don't want me, the family is loaded with them. Just ask Rand or Wyatt. I'm sure they can think of a way to bail you out of whatever mess you've gotten yourself into." Jackson's voice was filled with the parental censure usually reserved for father to son and not vice versa.

Wyatt could hear the soles of Jackson's shoes tattooing out an agitated beat that must have had him pacing in furious circles.

"That wouldn't be prudent."

"What, you don't like Rand? Wyatt?"

"Has nothing to do with them. Or you."

"Then what?"

"I'm being blackmailed by a member of the family."

The echo of pacing footsteps stopped.

At this, Wyatt felt a warning tension grip the muscles at the back of his neck and he abandoned his position behind the giant potted palm and as casually as he could—given the circumstances—moved to the parlor door to listen. This was far too interesting to ignore.

Jackson sounded incredulous. "Come again?"

"I'm being blackmailed by a member of this family."

"Who?"

"I find it difficult to say, as I don't want to tarnish your image of someone you hold to be nothing less than a saint." Graham sounded smug. Arrogant. A man who had not one whit of his brother, Joe's, grace and maturity.

"I find your childish games tiresome, Dad. Why don't you cut to the chase before I doze off?"

"Can't have that." The legs of a chair scraped against the floor. "Perhaps this will wake you up. I'm being black-mailed by Meredith."

Silence.

"Cat got your tongue?"

Jackson snorted. "Why would Aunt Meredith blackmail you?"

Graham seemed to take great pleasure in dropping this particular bomb. "Because I'm Teddy's father." The snick of a lighter sounded and a haze of pungent cigar smoke filtered out to the foyer. "Surprised?"

Silence.

"Son, you seem a little dismayed by the indelicate truth." Graham's harsh laughter rumbled. "Having a hard time believing that Joe's lily-pure wife could take pleasure in my bed? Or perhaps it's finding out that you have a little brother that's a bit off-putting."

A sound of pure disgust issued from Jackson's throat.

"Not so perfect after all, are they?" Graham sucked on his cigar for a moment. "Still have good old Uncle Joe and Aunt Meredith up on the damned pedestal?"

Wyatt's mind raced. More than ever, he was convinced that Meredith was not Meredith. Emily's situation seemed increasingly grave with every tick of the parlor clock. Clearly, Patsy Portman had a dangerous agenda. He couldn't get to Keyhole soon enough. A sense of urgency had his mouth dry as day-old toast and his heart roaring like a wounded lion in his ears. He'd have to call Rand and Lucy from Keyhole and tell them what he'd overheard.

Outside, a car horn sounded. His cab. As quietly as pos-sible, Wyatt retrieved his luggage and made good his es-cape. Fresh air filled his burning lungs as he opened the double doors that led out of the house. With a gentle pull, he closed the door behind him, then moved to the portico and handed the cabby his luggage.

"Airport," he instructed.

As he left the parlor and headed for the dining room, Jackson Colton fought the bile that rose in his throat. His father's confession disgusted him more than he could ever put into words. Although he couldn't say he was surprised. His father was no choirboy.

And Meredith. Meredith had changed.

As a child, he'd adored his Aunt Meredith. In fact, he'd looked upon her as a second mother. But in the past years— before the time of Teddy's birth, in fact—Jackson had noticed changes in Meredith that more than disturbed him. For so long, everyone had tried to pass these changes off as postpartum depression or the accident, but Teddy. was eight years old now and the accident happened a decade ago.

His sister, Liza, had once hinted that she believed something very amazing and unbelievable accounted for the changes in Aunt Meredith. At the time, Jackson had brushed off the wild notion. But now, as he reflected back on Liza's crazy theory, a chill raced down his spine and he feared there might just be more than a grain or two of truth there.

When he arrived in the dining room, he was dismayed to discover that he was not entirely alone.

Meredith was seated at the head of the table with a cup of coffee, a croissant and the society page. Languidly, she lifted her gaze from the print and trained it on Jackson. A small smile played at her lips, and she sat up a little straighter.

"Good morning, Jackson."

"Is it, Meredith?"

He could feel her watching him pick up a serrated knife and begin to saw his bagel in half.

"Something wrong, dear? You don't seem quite yourself."

Still holding the knife, Jackson turned to face her. "Funny, I could say the exact same thing about you."

Meredith's face hardened. "What is that supposed to mean?"

"Just this—If you don't stop extorting money from my father, I will go to the police."

Meredith laughed, playing it light, as if she thought he were joking. "Jackson, honey, what in heaven's name are you talking about?"

Jackson had to hand it to her. She was as cool as the other side of a pillow on a hot summer day. "I'm talking about the fact that my father is paying you hush money because he's afraid Joe will write him out of his will, *if*—" his voice grew steely "—Joe finds out that his rotten little brother is really the father of your son." He ran the blade of the knife across his fingertip, testing its sharpness. "So, since my father is too much of a spineless jellyfish to call your bluff, I guess the dubious pleasure is mine." Jackson stabbed his knife into the cutting board and turned to look her in the eye. "Back off. Do I make myself clear?"

Meredith blanched and clutched her cup till it rattled against the saucer. "Don't you dare threaten me, Jackson Colton."

"Or what?"

"Or you, my precious nephew, will be sorry."

"I'm already sorry."

Shaking with rage, Meredith watched Jackson stalk out of the room and frantically wondered exactly what he knew. He couldn't know that she was an impostor. No one knew that—with the exception of Emily—and soon, that would no longer be a problem.

Meredith reached into the pocket of her robe for her ever-present bottle of tranquilizers. After several botched attempts, she was finally able to shake two into her palm. She tossed them into her mouth and chased them down her throat with a gulp of coffee.

She took a deep, cleansing breath, and waited for the rage to subside and the little voices that shrieked in her head to quiet down.

Breathe in, breathe out.

In…out… In…visualize the peaceful place…out. She focused on the hands of the wall clock and watched a minute dissolve into ten.

Yes. There now. She was fine. She would be just fine.

Better than fine, actually.

A rough plan began to form in the back of her mind. She needed Jackson gone now too, but it would get a little messy if there were too many murder attempts all at once. No, there had to be an easier way to get rid of Jackson.

Too bad she couldn't send him to jail. That was a good place to go, if you were an annoyance. She ought to know. She'd certainly spent her share of time in jail. The tranquilizers began to kick in, giving her a relaxed and vaguely euphoric feeling. Jail. Hey, now. Maybe she should give this jail thing some thought. Maybe that wasn't beyond the realm of possibility.

But for what?

Unless…

Unless she could get him to go for the attempt on his uncle's life.

A light bulb flashed on in Patsy's mind.

That was it.

Her heart began to hammer. In fact, while she was going

to all the trouble, she'd set him up for *both* attempts on
Joe's life. A slow smile crept across her lips. *Oh, yes, Patsy,
honey,* she gave herself a mental pat on the back, *you are
good.*

Satisfied as a cat with a bowl of cream, Meredith went
back to the society section and her half-empty cup of coffee. After a little nap, she'd get started on her plan to get
Jackson out of the picture, and thereby solve a lot of nasty
problems.

Annie Summers, her mouth full of bobby pins, looked
into an antique, gilt-framed wall mirror with disgust. Her
hair. Her lousy, rotten, crinkly, goofy hair was having one
of its notorious bad days. The April sun streamed in from
a nearby window, creating a rusty halo that gave her a bit
of a fallen angel look. She curled an upper lip to enhance
the effect. It was hopeless. No amount of spray or gel or
relaxer or blow-drying or clippy doo-dads would whip it
into submission, either. They hadn't invented the product
that could handle her particular mop, and the day they did,
she was buying stock. She'd be a millionaire overnight.

"Moah? Amicks?" she muttered around the hairpins.

"Yeah?" Noah and Alex's muffled voices came from
the back of her shop.

"Mat are oo doing?"

"Playin'."

"Id oo tut 'er shoes on, yike I asked?" Annie removed
the pins from her mouth and crammed them into her make-
shift bun and hoped for the best.

"Uh…" Whispered laughter and some scrambling
reached her ears. "Yeah, we're putting our shoes on."

"Are you putting them on your feet?" She grinned at
their giggles. One didn't live with two five-year-olds and
not know when they were up to no good.

"Er, uh, okay," Alex, self-appointed spokesman for the two, answered.

"Are you putting them on now?"

"Uhh…yeah."

"Are you wearing socks?"

"Oh…well—"

With a sigh, Annie dropped her brush on a Louis XIV love seat and strode from the showroom of the antique store, Summer's Autumn Antiques, that she'd inherited from her father. Moving into the play area she kept next to her office for her boys, she stopped short and stared.

"What the—" Exasperated, Annie shook her head. "What are you guys doing in your—" she took in the bare chests and, in one case, bare bottom "—underwear? Alex, *where* is your underwear?"

"It was his idea," Alex said, pointing at Noah.

"Was not."

"Was too!"

"What idea?" Annie asked.

"We were going to put our clothes on the dog and surprise you."

As Alex explained, Chopper, the aging black Lab, came hobbling out from behind the toy box, his foot caught up in the arm of a sweater. He sported socks and shoes on three of his four feet. His tail, which he wagged pitifully, protruded from the fly of some small body's—obviously Alex's—underpants. Chopper looked absolutely miserable.

Try as she might, Annie could not hold back the giggles. Screaming with delight, the boys joined in, doing a little jig that had their skinny little bodies flailing and leaping.

"Why on earth did you think to put clothes on poor Chopper?"

"No shirts, no shoes, no service," Noah offered.

"What is that supposed to mean?" Annie looked back

and forth between the two faces, mirror images of hers, both earnest in their explanation.

"We wanted Chopper to come out to lunch with us—"

"—and he couldn't go if he was naked—"

"—cause Emma says the sign in the window says—"

Annie held up her hand. "Okay. I get it. But you guys need to know that they don't serve dogs at the Mi-T-Fine Café. Even well-dressed dogs, like Chopper, here."

Alex's face fell. "Never?"

"Never?" Noah echoed.

"Nope." She gestured to the dog. "And since they don't serve naked kids either, put this poor animal out of his misery and you two get dressed." She glanced at her watch. "I'll give you five minutes. If you're not ready, I'm going without you. And I'm ordering hot dogs."

"Hot dogs!" the boys shouted with glee and in record time were ready for lunch on the town—or at least at the restaurant next door—with Mom.

Over the glass entrance doors of the Mi-T-Fine Café in Keyhole, Wyoming, an electronic chime announced Wyatt's arrival. The restaurant was doing a healthy business and no one in particular looked up to see who'd come in. From inside the kitchen a wonderfully familiar female voice called, "Take a seat. I'll be with you in a minute."

It was Emily. She sounded safe and healthy, anyway. That was a good sign. Wyatt breathed a sigh of relief.

"Take your time. I'm in no hurry," he called and wandered to an empty booth in the front of the restaurant near a bank of windows that overlooked the quaint main street.

Keyhole was a Mecca for tourists on their way to or from Yellowstone National Park. Nestled in a lush valley, surrounded by spectacular, majestic mountains, the little town ingeniously mixed the new and the old to create a trendy, upbeat feel. Keyhole was known to antique hunters all over the country for its delightful painted lady Victorians, western facade buildings and the historic treasures they held within.

Skiers—both water and snow—hikers, climbers, windsurfers, hunters and fishermen enjoyed the sports offered by the great outdoors. All around the perimeter of town, hotels were popping up as Keyhole became a mini-Aspen. It wasn't unusual to see celebrities shopping or skiing in Keyhole anymore. Luckily, growth was relatively slow and Keyhole had managed to maintain its small-town flavor.

Wyatt could see why Annie loved this town. Like Prosperino, it was a bit of heaven on earth.

He plucked a menu from between the sugar container and the salt-and-pepper shakers and studied the special that was clipped to the cover.

At the other side of the café, Annie shushed her rowdy boys and, cocking her head, listened for the mellow baritone again, to no avail.

"No," she whispered. "Couldn't be." Craning her head, she searched the aisle and tried to peer over the high-backed booths and the partitions that blocked her view of the front of the room.

That voice.

Just the sound of it unleashed a plethora of emotion within her, both good and bad. Annie shrugged off the crazy notion as her boys distracted her, wrestling over crayons. Must be someone who sounded incredibly like him, she thought and rubbed the gooseflesh that had risen on her arms.

"Alex, eat the bun too."

"But I'm saving it for Chopper."

Annie threw her hands up. Where Chopper was concerned it was impossible to reason with her boys. "Fine. But don't put it in your shirt pocket. You're getting mustard everywhere."

"Okay." Alex removed the mustard-slathered bread and slapped it into her hand. "Here. Could you put this in your purse?"

Annie exhaled mightily and searched the ceiling for patience. Her crisp white blouse now sported yellow polkadots in various shapes and sizes. Dabbing at them with a napkin only made them worse.

From inside the kitchen, Emily recognized the familiar voice and openmouthed, flew to the pickup window and craned her neck to catch a glimpse. *Wyatt!* After seven solid months on the lam, to finally see a member of her family was overwhelming. She blinked back the tears of joy. Help had arrived at last and now, perhaps, someone might just take her seriously.

Reaching behind her, she untied her apron and waved at Roy who was busy over the sizzling grill. Helen was making coffee and Geraldine was out on the floor. They'd be fine without her for a few minutes. "I'm taking a break," she called and they nodded.

Emily rushed through the restaurant as old fashioned as its name implied. The walls were a rough plank and overhead, shelves were loaded with historic knickknacks and plants. In the background, some easy listening was piped in through speakers in the ceiling. The murmur of voices ebbed and flowed, and underscoring it all, silverware clanked and the grill sizzled.

Wyatt glanced up at the sound of her approach. "Emily!" He held out his hand and pulled her into the booth beside him and gave her temple a sound kissing. Eyes thirsty, he drank in the sight of her, checking her over until he was satisfied that she was all right. He reached up, touching her shock of chestnut-red hair and was once again reminded of his Annie.

Emily plucked a napkin from the chrome dispenser on the table and crushed it to her mouth. "How did you find me?"

"Rand and Austin tracked you down."

"I would have called, but it's not safe."

"I know."

"You do?" She pushed her napkin to her eyes and cast him a watery smile. "You believe me?"

"We all do."

"Oh," she blubbered. "Finally."

"Better late than never?"

"Oh, yeah." Smile tremulous, she turned her back to the aisle. Facing him, she leaned on her elbow to create some privacy. "I don't have much time. This is the middle of the Saturday lunch rush and it can get a little hairy here."

"That's fine," Wyatt said with a nod. "We can talk later. I plan on staying for several days—"

"Really?" Emily heaved a ragged sigh. "I've been starved for news of home."

"Well, I'm loaded with that, and more." He tapped the envelope that lay in front of him on the table, then slid it over to rest in front of her.

Emily stared. "What's this?"

"The news you've been waiting for. It'll make some interesting nighttime reading, that I can guarantee."

"It's about Mom?"

"And her identical twin sister. A woman named Patsy Portman."

"A twin. I knew it," she murmured.

"We're guessing that you were right all along about Patsy taking Meredith's place."

"It happened the day of the accident. I just know it. Remember when Mom went off the road and wrecked the car?"

"Emily, do you have any idea what may have happened to Meredith?"

"I can't remember," she whispered. "It happened so fast, and it's years ago now. I was crying and confused. My head hurt and Mom's head was bleeding so much. I think I passed out. What I do remember is seeing another woman there who looked exactly like Mom. Then, I don't remember anything until she brought me into the emergency room. I couldn't figure out why she wasn't bleeding anymore…"

Wyatt slowly nodded. "Meredith must have disappeared between the accident and the emergency room, while you were unconscious."

Snatching another napkin from the dispenser, Emily scrubbed at her nose. "Mmm. That's what I've always suspected. But no one believed me until now."

"We believe you, honey. We're on your side and we're here to help you."

"What about Mom?"

Wyatt slipped an arm around her shoulders and brought the top of her head to his neck. "We're working on that. Austin's on her trail, as we speak." He tried to inject a note of confidence into his voice. "What exactly happened the night you left?"

In a halting voice, Emily spoke. "Someone tried to kill me. And, he nearly succeeded."

Three

Wyatt drew a long, slow breath. Hearing the brutal truth had the bile rising into his throat. "I could use some fresh air. How about you?"

Emily peeked up at the counter. Geraldine and Helen were still busy with customers and no one new had come in since she'd sat down. "Yes. I think that would be okay. If we don't stay long." She tucked into her apron pocket the envelope that Wyatt had brought, then waved her hand at the counter. "Geraldine?"

"Yes, honey?" Geraldine took in the tear streaks on Emily's cheeks and frowned at Wyatt.

"I'm just gonna take a quick break. You guys okay without me?"

Geraldine glanced around, then returned her suspicious gaze to Wyatt. "For a few minutes, sure."

"I'll have her back pronto," Wyatt assured her. "Don't worry, she's in good hands."

Geraldine looked skeptical.

The doorbell chimed again as Wyatt held the door for Emily.

"Noah! Alex!" Annie strained to hear above the hubbub of her children's voices. "Pipe down for just a second, will you?"

"Why?" Alex asked.

"Because I'm trying to hear something," Annie snapped, flapping her hands and making lip-zipping motions.

Noah found her wild gesticulations most amusing and howled with laughter.

"Whater ya trying to hear?" Alex pressed.

Annie pressed her nose to the window and tried to see around front.

Noah tapped her arm. "Whatcha see?"

Her exasperated sigh fogged the pane of glass. "Nothing."

Wyatt took Emily's hand and led her to a bench on the wooden sidewalk just outside Summer's Autumn Antiques. He pulled her down beside him and once again, slipped an arm around her shoulders.

"Someone tried to kill you."

Emily's head bobbed beneath his chin.

Sick at heart, Wyatt pressed a kiss to the top of her head. "I know it's probably pretty hard to talk about, but the more you can tell me, the more we can help."

Emily glanced around. When she was satisfied that no one was listening, she continued. "I was on my way to bed when I noticed that my bedroom door was nearly closed. You remember how Dad would never let us kids close our doors until we were in bed? Even so, normally, I'd have just thought Inez made a mistake, but because of what had just happened at Dad's birthday party a few months earlier I was still a little wary.''

''Mmm.''

Wyatt knew all about the attempt on Joe's life. That night, Rand had called from the party, shaken. *''Dad made a speech. There was a lot of confusion,''* Rand had told him. *''Balloons, confetti, sixty white doves flying everywhere. Then, Dad lifted his glass, and there was a shot. His glass shattered…I was stunned. We all were. Then people started to scream. At first we thought…we thought he might be dead, but thank God, the bullet only grazed his cheek. Nobody else was hurt. Dad grabbed Mom's hand and pulled her to the ground for cover…''* That night, Rand's emotion-packed words had Wyatt's skin crawling. Just as it was now. It was ironic, Wyatt mused, how Joe may have saved the life of the very person who wanted him dead.

Emily's shaky voice brought him back to the present. ''I tiptoed in my room and before I saw him I knew I was not alone. Someone was there with me and I was scared, thinking that whoever it was had come back for Dad.''

From his hip pocket, Wyatt retrieved a handkerchief and, tipping her chin, dabbed at the tears that ran down her cheeks. Several passersby cast her a curious look.

''Wait until you're ready, sweetheart,'' Wyatt said. ''In fact, if this is too painful, you can tell me another time.''

''No!'' Emily gave her head a vehement shake. ''I've been waiting to talk about this for months now. I want to tell you. It's just…hard.''

''I know.''

''Anyway once my eyes adjusted, I could see a man—a stranger—hiding behind the drapes, near the bed. And, Wyatt, he had a knife.''

Emily looked up at Wyatt and he gave her shoulder a squeeze.

"I thought I was going to faint, but somehow I managed to stumble down the stairs and out the front door. He—" Emily swallowed "—he followed me." Wyatt closed his eyes. "What'd you do?"

"Kept running until I remembered the alcove where Liza and I would play when we were kids. The entrance is easy to miss if you don't know it's there."

Wyatt was filled with brotherly admiration. "Wow. Quick thinking saved your life."

"It was instinct. Oh, Wyatt, I've never been so scared in my life. I hid in the alcove until sun up. All I could think to do was hide. Somewhere. Anywhere.

"After a while, this really nice older trucker picked me up and told me he was headed to Wyoming. Wyatt, it seemed like a sign. Dad had been harbored here, back when he was a little boy and the McGraths fostered him. So, I climbed into his truck, and here I am."

Wyatt gestured down the street. "The McGrath farm where Dad grew up in Nettle Creek is only a few miles from here."

Emily's smile was wan. "I know."

"Are you okay now?"

"I still have all kinds of bad dreams. And I'm not using Blair as my last name anymore. Everyone here knows me as Emma Logan." She blinked up at Wyatt. "But I think I'm pretty safe here."

"Let's keep it that way, okay, Emily...Logan?"

"Okay," she whispered.

"I'd better get you back to work now. But listen. I'm staying across the street at that little hotel," he pointed to The Faded Rose, a quaint, pale yellow building with flower baskets adorning the porch. "Room 102. You call me if you need anything, okay?'' Standing, Wyatt pulled her to her feet.

"I will." She slipped an arm around his waist as they walked back to the grill. "Wyatt, I can't tell you how glad I am to have you here."

"I'm glad, too."

He held the door open for her and Geraldine, noting Emily's blotchy, tear-stained complexion and red-rimmed eyes, scowled.

"Geraldine, I'll be back on the floor in five."

"I'm here, honey. Don't you worry about a thing."

"I don't think Geraldine likes me," Wyatt murmured.

"She'll come around." Emily moved to the other side of the counter, poured him a cup of coffee and motioned for him to take one of the empty stools. "Can I get you something to eat?"

"Yeah, come to think of it, I'm starved. The special will be fine. And, Em, before you go, listen. I know it's going to be hard, but you are going to have to continue to lay low until Austin and Rand have enough solid evidence against Patsy to bring to the police."

"Poor thing. Something awful must have happened to make her this way."

Wyatt's admiration for his kid sister jumped up yet another notch. Trust Emily to have compassion for the woman who tried to end her life. Again, she reminded him of Annie. "Oh, and one last thing. I know Keyhole is a growing town, but I just wondered if you've ever met a woman named Annie Summers. I heard from Rand that she kept her maiden name when she married. Anyway, he says she owns an antique store in the area."

Emily nodded. "Of course I know Annie."

"You…do?" Wyatt felt his stomach clench.

"Sure. Keyhole's not that big. She owns Summer's Autumn Antiques, next door. I used to help out there on my days off. Annie and I are friends. In fact, that's her over there.'' Emily pointed to the other side of the restaurant. ''She comes in for lunch with her twin boys, Noah and Alex, pretty much every Saturday.''

Wyatt felt a bolt of lightning blast through him the likes of which he'd not experienced since that Valentine's kiss, so many years ago. Slowly, his gaze followed the direction Emily pointed and, for the first time in years, settled on the wonderful face of Annie Summers. Luckily, she was too busy to notice him and he took the time to look her over.

She hadn't changed a bit.

She was neither graying, nor age-spotted, nor knock-kneed, or even snaggle-toothed, the way he'd hoped. No, she was still the smooth-skinned, fiery-haired young woman that he'd fallen in love with back in college. In fact, if possible, she was even more attractive than before. Motherhood definitely seemed to agree with her. Even though she had two kids now, she was still as trim as ever. Her facial features had lost their girlishness and were now more angular and womanly, highlighting the enormity of her eyes and the fullness of her lips.

Unnoticed, he watched as she interacted with the two frolicking puppies that were so obviously her sons. Her kids had creased a permanent smile into the corners of her eyes and mouth and she looked content in her new life. More than content. Happy.

A cloud of self-doubt rolled in and settled over his heart. Surely, she wasn't pining away for him, the way he had been for her. Just by looking at her, he could guess that meeting up with the unresolved past and all the emotions that went with it was not on her agenda for today.

He watched as she dipped a napkin into her water glass and mopped the mustard from her boys' freckled faces.

They resisted her ministrations in a typical reaction for their age. One of them picked up a napkin and dabbed at something on her face, causing her laughter to ring out.

Wyatt closed his eyes and struggled to inhale. The sound of her laughter caused such an explosive reaction in his body, he could barely breathe. For him, nothing had changed. The past seven years evaporated like a puddle on a midsummer's day and he was vexed to discover that he was as fiercely in love with her this minute, as he'd been the day she said goodbye.

Clenching the countertop, he watched her gather her things and herd the boys to the cash register, only two dozen feet away, to pay her bill. Dressed more sophisticatedly than the simple jeans of their college days, she wore a pair of khaki slacks and a white blouse. Her wonderful hair was swept into a knot at the top of her head, but curly wisps escaped, still defying her attempts to tame them.

After she'd signed her credit receipt, she called her boys and with a *bing-bong,* was gone.

"Where is she going?" Wyatt wondered aloud.

"Back to work, right next door. The place we were sitting in front of, a minute ago. She works there till five on Saturdays."

Distracted, Wyatt scooted off his stool and stood. He bent to press his lips against Emily's temple.

"How do you know Annie?" Emily asked.

"You too," Wyatt answered and laid some cash on the counter.

"Me too, what?"

"You'll call me tonight, right?"

"Okay, sure, but—" Emily watched him go, a puzzled frown marring her brow. "Uh, wait a minute. Where are you going? What about your lunch?"

"Thanks, Em," he called and was gone.

* * *

What on earth was that all about? Emily leaned over the counter and watched Wyatt stride past the window after Annie Summers. She pulled her pencil from her bun and thoughtfully scratched her head with the eraser tip. He'd had the strangest look on his face when he'd looked at Annie. It was almost as if they'd known each other. But Wyatt had never lived in Wyoming, so that couldn't be it.

Her thoughts were distracted by the front door's bell.

Lean and lanky, Toby Atkins, Keyhole's resident law officer, pushed through the glass door, his gaze searching for, and immediately landing on, Emily. His boyishly handsome face lit up at the sight of her, and Emily returned his smile.

She moved behind the counter to pour him his usual cup of coffee. "Pie?" she asked, as he straddled a stool on the other side of the counter. "We've got your favorite. Lemon meringue."

"How can I say no?" Toby's fond gaze followed her as she cut his pie and found him a fork.

"So," Emily asked, as she set his plate before him, "what's new, Toby?"

"Nothing much. I did want to mention to you that there have been some reports of petty thievery in the Nettle Creek area. So, I thought I'd swing past your place several times each night on my nightly rounds for while. Thought it might be a good idea, all things considered, but I didn't want you to worry if you saw me."

"I don't worry when you're on the job, Toby," she said gently, and meant it.

His fair features flushed a charming shade of red.

Emily knew that Toby believed he was falling for her. It was evident in his smile, the way his gaze followed her as she worked, the interest he'd taken in her.

Even now, she could feel his deep blue gaze protectively

following her every move. Emily caught his eye and they exchanged an awkward, bashful moment. He was such a darling. And she was exceedingly relieved and grateful that he was taking such care with her safety.

But that was all. When it came to returning his feelings, Emily wished she could. Toby was a good man. One of the best. Her smile grew melancholy. Unfortunately, she was simply not in love with him.

Annie Summers felt the tips of her ears grow fiery hot and a tingle spread from the base of her spine throughout her entire body. Light-headed, she took several steps backward until she bumped into the ornately carved arm of a settee, which she grabbed onto to keep from slumping to the ground.

The man who stood silhouetted in the door looked exactly like Wyatt Russell, but the shadows that fell across his familiar face made it impossible to tell for sure.

No, she assured herself. It couldn't be. Wyatt here in Keyhole? Impossible. He was in Washington D.C., making a name for himself as a hotshot lawyer. He had no business here in Wyoming. It had to be her imagination playing tricks on her. She simply had Wyatt on the brain because she thought she'd heard his voice in the restaurant.

Marshaling her powers of concentration, she donned her most professional smile, smoothed her wacky hairdo and forced herself to move to the front door.

"Hi. May I help you?"

"Annie?"

Her breath caught in her throat. Okay, this was just too weird. This guy not only sounded exactly like Wyatt, he knew her name. "Yes?" More rattled than ever, she squinted into the sunlight, slowly sidestepping, looking for a spot in the shade to better help her see.

"It's good to see you."

She wished she could say the same. "I—uh—"

"It's me."

"Oh." *It was Wyatt.* The scar upon her heart tore open again, making her defensive. Vulnerable. Disoriented. "Hello."

"Hello."

He took a step toward her into the shadows and she could suddenly see that the person in question was indeed the Wyatt of old. And, except for a few lines at the corners of his eyes and mouth, he looked exactly the same as he had the day they'd said goodbye. His still-steely arms were crossed over his still-steely chest, and he leaned against an armoire in that still nearly cocky manner she knew so well.

However, under his confident pose lurked the same uncertainty she was feeling and this emboldened her even as myriad emotions warred within her mind. Extreme joy and, at the same time, extreme agitation. Agitation bordering on fury.

How dare he come waltzing in here after she'd taken so many years to purge him from her heart?

And without calling first?

Her hands traveled to her hair, tucking, fussing, smoothing. The unmitigated audacity. Showing up, out of the blue and still irresistible.

Well, she could resist him now. She'd had plenty of time to fortify her defenses over the years. She wished she would have freshened her lipstick, and changed her mustard-stained blouse, after she ate. For heaven's sake, she must look a sight. She wanted to run and hide under the little tent in the playroom with her boys. From here, their voices rang out, giggling, bickering, bossing.

Save for the two of them and the boys, the store was

empty. Silent. Annie was sure he could hear her heart knocking against her ribs.

"What are you doing here?" she ventured when she finally found her voice.

"Had some business in the area and thought I'd stop in and say hi."

He had business in the area? Business in *Keyhole?* "Hi?"

"And to see how you were doing."

"I'm…uh, fine." At least she was a minute ago.

"So." His arm swept the showroom floor of her store. "This is where you work."

She could only guess that the soft tone in his voice indicated pity. He'd moved on to the big time, and she'd never left Keyhole. Instead of taking the New York art galleries by storm, her paintings hung on the walls of her family's shop, alongside the work of other amateur artists.

"Yes. I run the store and refinish furniture. And, in my spare time, I still like to paint."

"You were always good, Annie. Very good."

"I…thank you." But not good enough to make it out of Keyhole, he was probably thinking. She licked her lips and squaring her shoulders, tried to appear a little taller. More confident. Put together. Lord only knew how she compared to the sleek, well-dressed career women in Washington D.C.

Wyatt pushed off the armoire and began to wander a bit, looking here and there, pausing to pick up an object and then set it back down. She wondered what he thought of her little shop. Following his movements with her gaze, she tried to see what it might look like through his eyes.

Quaint, to be sure. Smallish. Homey. Creatively decorated. Inviting. Cheerful. Cluttered. Almost too cluttered. Rather messy, actually. For the first time, she noticed that the boys had left toys strewn about, and that Chopper was shedding black Lab hair in fluffy tufts in the aisles where he liked to doze when the kids would let him.

In a shaft of sunlight, the cobwebs that she hadn't seen before this very minute were quite visible, as was the slight layer of dust that coated...everything. All mirrors from the level of four feet on down sported streaks and fingerprints. Have mercy, didn't she ever clean this place? She allowed her eyes to slide closed in order to hide her disgust.

Summer's Autumn Antiques was a pit. A glorified junk shop. Nothing like the places she was sure Wyatt must frequent in D.C.

Once again, Annie wished she'd had time to check her appearance in the mirror. Heaven only knew if there was a chive or something stuck in her tooth.

"You get a lot of business on Saturdays?" he asked conversationally as he turned to face her.

Oh, my. Annie's heart did a little flip. She'd have thought that by now she'd become impervious to that curl in his upper lip. "Some. It's late in the winter season and early in the summer season, so we're kind of...between seasons."

He wasn't listening. She could tell. He was staring. Taking in every detail. No doubt noting the mustard splotches and the bad-hair-day thing.

She swallowed and the ticking of several grandfather clocks seemed inordinately loud all of a sudden. But still, they stood. After a moment, some customers came in and moved through the store, murmuring to each other over various objects of interest.

"You were in the café for lunch?" She tried to fill the yawning chasm in their conversation with idle chat.

"Yes. You knew? You should have come up and said hello."

"I didn't see you. I heard you. Sort of. I thought. There was a lot of noise."

From the back room, there was an explosion of five-year-old laughter and Chopper's loud barkings. In an abstract way she wondered what they were up to now. But, rooted as she was to her spot, there was no way to tell.

"You have children," Wyatt said, seeming to refocus from the past to the present.

"Yes. Two. You?"

"No. Never married."

Again, Annie's heart stalled. "No?"

"Never felt the need. Never found the time. Never—" he shrugged "—fell in love."

"Oh." She echoed his shrug with a small lift of her own shoulders. "There is still time."

"There is always time."

At a complete loss, Annie stood, her gaze darting about, her tongue searching her teeth for a piece of spinach she just knew was there. It seemed that no matter how they tried, their conversation was awkward and feeling the strain of the years and a messy break-up.

Just when she felt she couldn't take another minute of the emotional stress, her sons, shrieking with laughter, burst from the playroom, leading poor Chopper by—she stopped and stared in mortification—a bra strap.

"Look, Mom! Chopper's got a hat!" Alex pointed to the bra cup that they'd pinned over the dog's head. Poor Chopper, looking quaintly Amish and decidedly miserable, cast a baleful look upon Annie for a rescue. The second cup was strapped under the dog's chin and, in the style of a good mountain rescue St. Bernard, they'd tucked in a plastic juice bottle.

"It was his idea," Noah shouted, pointing at his brother.

"It was not. It was your idea!"

"Naa-uh!"

"Uh-huh!"

Noting their mother's flaming cheeks, they squealed and danced with glee.

Wyatt looked from the dog, to the boys, to Annie, and just like the day they'd met, threw back his head and roared with laughter. At first, Annie did not see the humor in the situation at all, but the harder they all laughed, the funnier it all became, and soon she too was joining in.

"You boys take the dog into the back room and get that thing off him and put it back in my gym bag, where you found it. And," she directed as they reluctantly capitulated, "straighten up back there, will you?"

Moaning and groaning all the way, they disappeared into the playroom.

Wyatt was still smiling. "They're cute. They remind me of you."

"I was much better behaved than they are."

"I doubt that. You must remember, I know you."

"Yes, I guess you do." Annie smiled, the comfort of their old union slipping around her like a favored robe. "Wyatt, why are you really here?"

"I really do have some business here in town. But, at the same time, I have a few things I need to—"

A customer left and Annie called after her, "Thank you. Please come again."

"—I need to say to you."

"To me?"

"Ma'am?" Another customer stepped between them. "Do you have old salt-and-pepper shakers?"

"Over there in that glass case." Annie pointed.

"I saw those. Do you have any more? I'm a collector. I have a set just like those little hens you have there and I paid half of what you're asking."

Wyatt's heavy sigh signaled his impatience. Annie bit back a grin. Just like the old days.

"I have a few in the glass case under the register, but they're rare and even more expensive."

"I'll look." The collector sniffed.

"I'm sorry." Annie turned to Wyatt. "What were you saying?"

"Oh. Well, I was just trying to say that…" He ran his fingers over his jaw. "I thought maybe we could talk. Recently, it's occurred to me that I should apologize for being such an idiot back when—"

"Are these the rare shakers?" the collector called, pointing to a wooden case opposite the register that housed tea sets.

"No. Under the register. Glass case." She waved a distracted hand, still staring at Wyatt. "I'm sorry."

"It's okay. I was just saying that it might be a good idea for us to discuss the past. You know. Might help us get on with our lives."

"On with our lives?" Annie peered at him. What was he talking about?

"This case?" the collector called out.

"Yes!" Annie called back, then lowered her voice. "Wyatt—" She shook her head. "I'm not so sure that's such a good idea. I think we've said everything we have to say—"

"These two little crystal and silver shakers? Ah, yes. Okay. I'd like to see them."

"One moment." She gave the customer a pseudo smile, then whipped her head back to Wyatt. "It took me a while, but I've come to terms with what happened—"

"But," Wyatt interrupted, pleading his case, "I was wrong. I know that now. I want— No, I need to tell you. To wipe the slate clean."

The collector was becoming impatient. "I'm supposed to meet some friends for drinks soon—"

"One damn moment!" Wyatt snapped.

The customer's jaw dropped.

Annie let her eyes slide shut. This much she knew about Wyatt: he'd never leave her alone until she heard him out. And by then, she'd have no more customers left. "Okay," she whispered. "When?"

"Tonight? Over dinner?"

"Fine. What time?"

"Seven. I'll pick you up…here?"

"I'll be at home at seven." She strode to the counter where the collector was fidgeting and fuming. Snagging one of her business cards from a silver tray, she scribbled her home address on the back. "I'm just down the block from Mom's place. You'll find it."

That afternoon Patsy put on her most "Meredith" dress and fashioned her hair in her most "Meredith" style, and upon adding some jewelry and a dash of pale lipstick, couldn't have looked more like Meredith than Meredith herself. If Meredith were around, she'd be proud, Patsy thought with a harsh little laugh.

After one last glance at herself and then, into her satchel full of props, she snapped it shut and deemed herself ready to hit the road.

Patsy's sporty black BMW purred down the freeway, making the trip between Prosperino and L.A. a pleasure. In an effort to keep her courage up, she put on some of her favorite hard rock tapes and screamed along with the lead singers. When lunchtime rolled around, she poured herself a glass of fine champagne and lit an expensive gold-tipped cigarette. After all, she was watching her weight and a little liquid lunch was all she really craved.

When Patsy got to L.A., she knew exactly where she was going. She'd been in this neighborhood before to hire that idiot Snake Eyes Pike. The one who was *supposed* to have put Emily away for good. Patsy tucked the cork back into her bottle and exhaled. "Ah, well, can't win 'em all," she muttered. Besides, Snake Eyes was still on the job, so there was hope.

Consulting her map, she slowed, navigated several tricky lane changes and turns, not easy considering the champagne bottle and crystal stemware in the passenger seat. Ah, yes. There it was. Patsy tapped on the brakes and read the huge sign that loomed over the top of the broken-down warehouse.

The Look-Alike Agency
Celebrity look-alikes for movie doubles
Private parties, birthday messages and so much more!

Yes, this was exactly what she needed. She parked in the secluded lot in this seedy, industrial section of town and entered the warehouse through the front door. The musty smell of old clothing and mothballs instantly assailed her. Behind the counter, an older woman worked sewing buttons onto a jacket.

"Hello," Patsy said in that smooth, well-monitored tone that made people know they were dealing with someone special.

"What can I do for ya?" The woman did not pause in her stitching to spare her a glance.

"I need a double to pose as a friend of mine, for a practical joke we're doing for his…his birthday."

"Okay. What type you need?"

Patsy dug a picture of Jackson out of her satchel. "I need

someone who can look like him with the right hair and makeup.''

The woman stopped sewing and took the photo. ''Stu. You need Stu. He can look like anybody and you can't tell him apart from the real guy, really. Stu!'' she bellowed. ''Stu! Get your butt out here.''

''This Stu is really good, huh?''

''Or your money back. Used to work on Broadway till he ran into a little trouble with the law. Stu!''

Patsy arched a brow. ''Could happen to anyone, I guess. How much?''

Stu, an everyman kind of guy, wandered out from the back room. Patsy immediately noticed that he was not the right coloring, but that could be easily fixed. His height and build were perfect.

The woman behind the counter held up the picture Patsy had provided. ''How much to dress like this guy and run a few 'errands' for this lady?''

Stu studied the picture. ''Two hundred a day, plus expenses.''

''Oh. Okay.'' Patsy gestured for Stu to join her away from the desk area. Digging through her wallet, she extracted four crisp fifty-dollar bills. ''You get this now, and two hundred more when the job is done.''

''How will I find you?''

''I'll find you.'' Patsy extracted a file from her satchel. ''This is what you need to do.''

Stu flipped it open and scanned the contents. ''You need me to go to this insurance agency, Grimbles of L.A., and take out an insurance policy on some guy named Joe Colton for a million bucks?''

''Yes. And when you sign the policy, you need to make it look like this.'' She held up a sample of Jackson's signature. ''The policy is small enough that this company won't do any checking at all.'' She cackled. "After all, if they're willing to insure Jennifer Lopez's tush for ten million, I can't imagine that this is going to be a problem.''

"Not for me.'' Stu stuffed the two hundred dollars in his pants pocket and took the file from Patsy. Digging into his shirt pocket, he withdrew a business card. "My cell phone. I should be done by tomorrow afternoon. Call me and we'll make arrangements to meet. I'll give you the paperwork, you give me the cash. Deal?''

Patsy slipped on her dark glasses and prepared to leave. "Deal.''

Four

"Mama?"

"Hmm?"

"How did you know when you had forever love for Daddy?"

MaryPat Summers looked up from the magazine she was browsing through and regarded her daughter curiously. "Forever love?"

"You know." Annie gave her hand an impatient flapping. "More than just plain-old-love love. I'm talking about the kind of love that you have when you know, deep in your heart, that that person is your soul mate and that you will love him forever. And you couldn't live without him, and…you know."

"Hmm. Well," MaryPat placed the magazine on her stomach and folded her hands over the top. "I can only speak for myself, of course, but when it came to your father, the way I knew that I was in love with him was—"

she paused to chuckle ''—whenever he was in the room, I couldn't breathe.''

Annie turned from the hallway mirror, where she'd been studying her reflection and stared at her mother. ''You couldn't breathe? Mama, that sounds deadly.''

''No, no. I don't mean I couldn't breathe at all, I just mean it was hard to breathe. Don't know why. Just happened. Even after we were married, once in a while I'd look at your sweet daddy and...well, he always cut such a handsome figure of a man, don't you know, with all that wild red curly hair and that ruddy complexion and rugged body and that deep, deep voice.'' She sighed. ''Ah, me. I still have a bit of a problem catching my breath, just thinking about him.''

''So that's all the logic you needed to determine that he was the one?''

''It's all I needed, sweetheart. Some things simply cannot be based on logic, but must instead be based on how well one is able to breathe.''

Annie quirked a brow and went back to fussing over her appearance.

MaryPat pursed her lips. ''Your interest in forever love wouldn't have anything to do with Wyatt Russell's sudden appearance, would it?''

''Mama, don't be ridiculous.''

MaryPat harrumphed.

Outside on her quiet lane, the sound of an engine approached and then slowed and idled, directly in front of her house. MaryPat twisted around on the couch and after a brief wrestling match with the drapes, peered out the living room window and watched as Wyatt parked his rental car at the curb.

''He's here.''

''Mama! Stop spying,'' Annie chided. Nervously, she

fastened the clasp to her necklace and glanced in the hall mirror one last time at her hateful hair.

"I can't help it. I just wonder what he's up to." MaryPat let the blinds snap shut as she turned to her daughter. "After all these years, here he is again, out of the blue and after what he did to you I don't like it. Not one bit. I just don't trust him."

Scrunching, smashing, tugging, Annie fiddled with her bun. It was lopsided. How perfect. "Mama, I'm already wiggy enough, without you jumping on the bandwagon. Let's just give him the benefit of the doubt, okay?"

"Hmfp."

The doorbell rang and the two women froze in a tableau of nerves.

"It's him." The neighbors next door could no doubt hear MaryPat's stage whisper.

"I know."

"Do you want me to get it?"

"Yes. No. I don't know."

"Well, we can't leave him standing out there all night. Or can we? That might be funny." MaryPat's turkey gobble of a giggle warbled into the room.

Annie sighed. "No. We can't leave him standing there. I'll get it." She stood frozen. "How do I look?"

"Beautiful. Prettier than that girl on *Will and Grace*."

"Mama, please."

"Well, you do!"

Annie smoothed her hands over her khaki skirt and fussed with her stretchy top. "Is this thing okay? This style is kind of tight. I don't know. I certainly don't want to give him the wrong idea."

"What idea?" MaryPat's brow knit.

"That I'm, you know, trying to look sexy or something

stupid like that. On the other hand, I don't want to look frumpy... Ohhhh. I hate my hair.''

"Honey, you look fine. If I had your skinny little waistline I'd wear that outfit myself. And your hair? Why, it's glorious! People would kill for such body and color, such—''

"Okay, Mama. Thanks.'' Annie blew a kiss at her mother, then moved to the door and, upon opening it, was once more swept into the past by Wyatt's smile.

"Hi.''

"Hi.'' She leaned on the door frame, steadying herself and trying to reconcile this time warp. At least she was still breathing. That much was comforting.

He cleared his throat. "Can I, uh, come in?''

She started. "Oh! Sure.''

Embarrassed, she stepped back and admitted him into her small 1930s Arts-and-Crafts cottage. Again, her mind bent to fit his perceptions of her way of life, and again, she felt defensive. A failure, compared to his fast-track-to-success lifestyle.

Her furniture was what she liked to call "shabby chic,'' but was really just hand-me-downs, cleverly slipcovered. The paintings on the wall were a series of watercolors she'd done when she was pregnant with the boys, all floral pastels. Scattered pillows, books, candles and toys gave the place a homey, cluttered feel, and again, the missed cobwebs and fingerprints seemed to jump out and mock. Her life was neither polished nor organized. And, until now, that was the way she'd liked it.

"Please. Come on in,'' she urged and forced the fear and reluctance from her smile. "Wyatt, you remember my mother, MaryPat Summers.''

"Yes, of course. Wonderful to see you again.'' The deep

timbre of Wyatt's voice filled the living room as he came in and reached for MaryPat's hand.

MaryPat twittered. "Good to see you again, too, Wyatt."

Annie turned her head and rolled her eyes. Try as she might to be a tough old bird, MaryPat was a pushover for a handsome face.

The pitter-patter of growing feet pounded down the stairs. Ever curious, Noah and Alex had come to investigate. "Mom?"

"Who's here, Mom?"

Immediately, they recognized Wyatt as the man from her store. As only five-year-olds can, they came boldly up to Wyatt.

"Hey. We know you," Alex accused, his face puckered in thought.

Annie reached for her sons and drew them to her. "Boys, this is Wyatt Russell. We used to go to school together."

"Whater you doin' here?" Noah wondered assertively.

They were suspicious. Protective. How utterly adorable. Her heart filled with fierce maternal love and pride. She may not lead a life of privilege and glamor, but she was mad about her little men. She took an instinctive step between her boys and Wyatt, shielding them from heaven only knew what.

"You here to take our mom out on a date and *kiss* her and junk?" Alex demanded from out in left field.

Annie gasped. Then again, it might be Wyatt who needed protection. The palms of her hands began to sweat. MaryPat's nervous laughter trilled. Brows raised, lips twitching, Wyatt turned his gaze upon her and she felt the tips of her ears catch fire.

"Boys," she chided, "it's not polite to grill our guest."

"I'm not grillin' him." Alex snorted.

Noah guffawed. "He's not a hot dog."

"Although some might disagree." Though Wyatt's tone was serious, Annie could tell he was teasing.

"Are you guys gonna get married?" Alex folded his arms over his skinny chest.

"Married?" Breathless, Annie felt as if she'd plunged into an ice-cold pool. Above the buzzing in her head, she heard MaryPat's mortified hoot fill the air.

"Sean Mercury's mom just got married to this guy that came to their house to take her out to dinner one time," Alex explained.

"And then, they were always kissin' and junk," Noah continued.

"Are you gonna do that?"

His amused gaze still boring into hers, Wyatt educated Annie's sons. "Your mama and I used to be friends, a long time ago. Before you guys were born. So, since I just happened to be in your neighborhood, I thought I'd drop by and take her to dinner. Then, we will either go see a movie or go get married. I'll let her pick."

"Wyatt! Don't put any more ideas like that in their heads!"

In that infuriating way she remembered so well, Wyatt ignored her. "But our reservations aren't for another hour so there's plenty of time for her to make up her mind."

"You're joshin' us." Alex relaxed, warming to Wyatt's humor.

Wyatt winked. "A little, yeah."

"Do you have time to play?"

"Sure."

Delighted smiles creased the boy's noses, melding freckles one into the other.

"What do you want to play?" Noah looked first at Alex, then to Wyatt.

"What do you guys want to play?"

"We want to play—" Alex grabbed his brother and began to back away "—space monster!" Their giggling shrieks echoed off the ceiling as they pounded back up the stairs.

Wyatt cast a questioning glance at Annie.

She shrugged. "Don't ask me." Being twins, they had their own play world. She was generally at a loss when dragged into one of their active games.

Complete and total chaos ensued as Wyatt set off after the boys. Growling deep in his throat, he chased them up the stairs, down the hall and into what sounded like their bedroom.

"Is this safe?" MaryPat wrung her hands and Annie knew that her mother was concerned about leaving her precious grandchildren in the hands of the man who'd broken her daughter's heart.

"I don't know, Mama. But I'm betting that with his successful career, he's got great health insurance."

Mission accomplished. Time to celebrate. Patsy put the Beamer on cruise control and poured herself a drink. The best part of being ex-Senator Joe Colton's wife was the feeling that she was above the law. She lit a cigarette and issued a mirthless chuckle. Way, way above the law. Not that she knew all that much about the law, but there were plenty of people in this blasted family who did.

Take Jackson for instance.

Patsy focused on the white lines as they zipped under her car and thought about a case Jackson had once handled.

Seemed old Jackson had a roommate in college who needed Jackson to get his drug-dependent CEO father declared incompetent so that sonny-boy could take over the corporate reins. Over the years, this roommate had visited the Colton ranch a number of times, and Patsy had made it a point to stay near enough to overhear their conversation. Apparently, there was no wrongdoing on anyone's part during the lawsuit. But still, even though Patsy wasn't sure exactly how, she knew this knowledge was going to come in handy some day. Some rainy day. Sooner than later.

With a smile, she flicked a longish ash out the car window. Yep, yep, yep. Jackson knew how to take over Colton Enterprises just in case his father, Graham, should inherit in the tragic event of his poor brother Joe's untimely death.

Yeah. Old Jackson was going to come in handy on several counts. Patsy's reedy laughter echoed in the BMW's plush interior.

"Do you think we should check on them?" MaryPat never could take suspense.

"No." As she took the extra time to battle her bun with a can of hair spray and fistful of bobby pins in front of the entry hall mirror, Annie listened to the boys and a begrudging smile nudged her lips into an amused curve. "So far a whole fifteen minutes have passed and no one has cried. This is a very good sign. Let them get to know each other."

"Why?"

"Because a little male influence isn't going to kill them." Upstairs, the sounds of something crashing to the floor was followed by guilty silence. Annie sighed. "But I might." She tore the pins from her hair, intending to start over on her blasted bun. With this copper, pot-scrubber hair of hers, sophistication would be forever elusive.

Moments later, Wyatt appeared on the landing, holding a broken lamp. The boys hovered behind him. "Uh, Mom?" Tone sheepish, Wyatt spoke for them all.

Giving up on her hair, Annie came to the bottom of the stairs and reached for the railing. "Yes?"

"We, uh, got a little carried away and broke this."

"So I see."

Alex, wearing the lamp's crumpled shade, peered through the railing from the stairs behind Wyatt. "We didn't mean to, Mom."

"It was a accident," Noah explained.

Wyatt awkwardly cradled the bent lamp base. "I'm really sorry. We're really sorry, aren't we, guys?" The boys nodded. "I'll buy you a new one, I promise."

The cool wood of a turned balustrade bit into the palm of her hand as she tightened her grip. "I can afford a new lamp," she informed him, words clipped. Then, embarrassed by her defensive tone, Annie looked away and searched for something to say that might lighten the mood.

The sudden silence was deafening. Noah and Alex looked back and forth between the adults, their expressions a mix of curiosity and concern.

For once, Annie was grateful for her mother's interference.

The older woman cleared her throat. "Boys, go wash your hands. Your dinner is nearly ready." Seemingly grateful for an escape from the tension that shimmered between her daughter and Wyatt, MaryPat turned and headed to the kitchen.

"And go change your shirts," Annie added, noting the smudges and dust that told her the space monsters had been chased under the bed.

"Here." Wyatt held the lamp out to Alex. "Put this back and we'll deal with it later."

"No!" Giggling, Alex slipped his hands through Wyatt's belt and going limp, dangled. "I don't want you to go."

Taking a cue from his brother, Noah wrapped his arms around Wyatt's leg and head flopping back, laughed. "Stay!" he shouted. "Please?"

"Please, please, please?"

Clearly flattered and tempted to stay, Wyatt looked askance at Annie, his grin in full bloom. Laugh lines, deeper now than a decade ago, forked at his eyes. Eyes that were still the tempting, guileless blue of old, and mahogany hair that showed no signs of thinning. Crumb. She'd somehow managed to forget, or block out, how very handsome he was. No doubt he had a female client list as long as his arm.

"Mom, make him stay," Noah whined.

Annie sagged against the banister and rubbed her brow. It appeared that her sons were no more immune to Wyatt's allure than she was. Even though she'd rather laugh at the sight of them swinging from Wyatt's appendages, she affected a stern front. "Boys, please leave poor Wyatt alone and go wash up. Your dinner is ready."

"Do as she says," Wyatt urged when they didn't move.

Grumbling, Alex took the lamp from Wyatt and turned to slog to his bedroom to clean up for dinner. Noah, equally dismayed, relinquished Wyatt's leg and followed his brother.

"You ready?" Wyatt grasped the railing and in a few lanky steps was standing before her, reminding her too vividly of the way she used to melt when he stood this close.

Mentally bracing herself against the age-old pull between them, Annie touched her horrid hair. "I guess."

As Wyatt held Annie's chair, then helped her settle at the table, he simply could not get over how she hadn't changed. She was twenty-nine now, but still looked the waifishly thin nineteen-year-old. There was not a line on her face. Not one. And, except for a smattering of endearing freckles, her skin was the stuff of an Ivory soap commercial.

He was glad she'd taken her hair down from that knot she liked to stuff it into and let it flow freely to her shoulders. She had such a wonderful, eye-catching head of hair, tying it up like that seemed a shame. He loved the way it spiraled so flatteringly around her face and longed to reach up and tug one of these corkscrew curls and let it *boing* back, the way he used to.

"Thank you," she murmured in the voice that had haunted his soul in all the years since he'd seen her last. She scooted into a comfortable position and reached for her linen napkin.

Reluctance coloring his smile, he stepped away from the back of her chair and moved into his seat across the table. He'd chosen a restaurant that clung to the edge of a raging river, nestled in a valley halfway between Keyhole and Nettle Creek. It was a charming old building, all rough-hewn logs and plate-glass windows and best known for its prize-winning chicken and dumplings. It seemed neutral territory, what with the bright lights, squawking babies and simple fare. Hopefully, she wouldn't think he was trying to seduce her in these surroundings.

After the waitress had taken their drink order, they were once again left to deal with the uncomfortable silence that comes from years spent apart. Finally, Annie spoke.

"My boys seemed taken with you."

"They're great kids. Cute. Like their mama."

Annie glanced at the light fixture overhead, seemingly to dismiss the compliment. "They can be a handful."

"You've done well with them."

"My family helps out a lot."

Wyatt drew a finger over the condensation on his water glass. Family. It was the reason Annie had left college. He glanced up at her and could see that she was following his train of thought. Might as well get it over with.

"I—" He swallowed and could feel his Adam's apple straining against the collar of his polo shirt and unbuttoned the top button. "I asked you to have dinner with me tonight because I need to explain…to tell you that I'm sorry about what happened between us."

Annie held up a placating hand. "It's—"

"No. Annie, hear me out. This needs to be said and I've been waiting a long time to do it."

She lifted a shoulder in capitulation.

"I just want to tell you that I now understand why you had to come home. Back then, I was selfish and didn't really understand the importance of family."

"You had a bum deal as a kid."

Wyatt dipped his head in agreement and mulled over the miserable life he led before Joe rescued him. He didn't much like to think about the time when he'd been a frightened little boy whose pitiful existence before Joe consisted of a broken home, a drunken, abusive, sorry excuse for a father and an altogether absent mother. They were dead and gone now and he was a Colton in every way but name.

"That's true, but only until Joe rescued me. Because he cared for me, and—" Wyatt paused, as his throat grew tight whenever he talked about Joe "—loved me, I should have understood the way you felt about your own dad. About a year ago I almost lost Joe, which—" jaw jutting, he shifted his gaze to the far wall "—really served to drive the point home."

"Oh dear. I'm so sorry," Annie murmured.

"Thank you. Luckily, he's fine now, but I can't begin to describe the fear." Wyatt took her hand and laced his fingers with hers and in doing so, felt the familiar currents vibrate between them. "Annie, when your dad had his stroke, I didn't understand the gravity of the situation. I thought you were choosing him over me and that scared me.''

"I was," she whispered.

"I know." Urgency drove Wyatt forward in his seat. "And that's good and fine and I should have understood and I should have been there for you. When he was sick, and then again when he died."

"But how could you have understood? Your father had never been a father." Eyes bright, smile tremulous, Annie gave his hand a gentle squeeze. "You did the best you knew how. I've come to terms with that. Just as I have come to terms with the fact that Daddy needed me to quit school and help my mother and sisters run the business."

"You were mature beyond your years back then. I always admired that, even if I didn't say so." Wyatt studied her familiar hand as it lay in his. "Until recently, I never really got—or more importantly, trusted—the family unit. I chose career. It's the one thing I figured I could always count on when the chips were down." His laughter was mirthless. "And I wanted to get as far away from the stink of poverty I was born into as I could get."

He looked up from her hand and could see that he need not continue. She knew why he'd made his decision as clearly as if she could read his mind. They'd always been that way, finishing each other's sentences, thinking about obscure topics at the exact same time, knowing instinctively how the other felt. And he'd let it all go. What an idiot.

"Back then I always figured we'd get married," he said.

"Me too."

"I wish we had."

"I— What's done is done." She sounded so resigned. So final.

"We would have been great together."

She paused, flustered. Clearly, she didn't think so. "I wouldn't have my boys."

Right. Her boys. Or her husband, the sainted father of those boys. Wyatt swallowed back the jealousy that he'd battled since he'd learned of Annie's plans to marry, so very long ago. "I wanted children. Eventually."

"Someday, you will no doubt have some." She didn't seem to notice the defensive note in his voice and her smile was meant to encourage, not wound. But wound, it did. "I can tell you'll make a great father."

Someday. When you find a nice girl and settle down, her words seemed to imply. A nice girl who is not Annie Summers.

"You must miss the boys' father." He paused to figure out how to best proceed on this topic that frequented his thoughts more than he would ever care to admit. "I heard about his passing, and I'm...I'm sorry."

"Thank you."

Did you love him more than me? he wanted to ask. Was he the man of your dreams? Is he still? Did you ever wonder about me, the way I've obsessed over you?

Wyatt was burning with unasked questions. Questions that would no doubt never have an answer. "I wanted to call when I finally heard. Really. I just...I didn't know what to say. You were grieving and I didn't want to overstep my bounds."

She sighed. "I know."

"Okay." She knew. Annie always knew what he felt. No doubt she knew exactly what he was feeling at this very instant. Wyatt leaned back in his chair, slowly running his thumb over her knuckles.

He'd thought that purging his soul to Annie this way would help cauterize the wound in his heart. Instead, it seemed to be having the opposite effect. He mourned the fact that those boys were not his. That this simple life and caring community were not his. That she was not, and never would be, his because another man had beaten him to the vows. Vows to love and honor and cherish until death.

How the hell could he ever compete with that?

For sanity's sake, he changed the subject. "Your mom looks good."

"She is good. I think she should sell her place and move in with me, but she's a stubborn old bird. Says Daddy built that little sunroom just for her and it would be a sin to let someone else sit there and read the Sunday paper."

Wyatt chuckled. He'd always liked MaryPat. "How are your sisters?"

"They're fine. Uh, let's see. Judith is living on a small farm in Iowa. I haven't seen her in nearly two years. She's still happily married and is home-schooling her kids."

"Wow, that's a lot of work."

"True, but she's up to the task. The kids are in high school now, and pretty much take care of themselves. Rick is playing baseball, football, basketball, soccer and uh—" her brow furrowed "—I forget, but Judith says he's always sweaty and eating. He plays for the public high school and hopes to pick up a college scholarship. Lynn is an accomplished musician, artist, dancer, professional giggler and I hear she has a phone growing out of her head."

Wyatt laughed. "They sound like us, when we first met."

Annie's smile was wistful. "They do, don't they?"

"How's your little sister doing?"

"Brynn?" With her free hand, Annie pushed her hair out of her face and smiled. "She's still here in Keyhole. She's in real estate now and doing well. Property is really starting to pick up around here. She's still single and sassy as ever.''

"Sounds like you are all still really close.''

"We are. We miss Judith, but we talk all the time.''

"Nothing like family.''

"No. Nothing.''

Annie sighed and regarded him with her sweet, ingenuous expression, and suddenly all rational thought left his mind. He could sit here for the rest of his days, reminiscing, catching up, simply listening to her sexy alto.

A half carafe of wine was delivered and Wyatt filled their glasses. Touching his rim to hers, he toasted family and old friends and was warmed by the verdant light in her eyes. Dinner—chicken and dumplings for them both—lived up to its reputation, and not once did the conversational ball ever drop, as he'd feared it might.

In fact, so smitten was Wyatt by their animated discussion of everything that had transpired since college, that he did not notice the passage of time, the uneaten dessert, the lukewarm coffee, the dwindling crowd, or the entrance of a stranger who slipped into the bar and took a table in a darkened corner.

Silas—his christened name was rarely used save by his mother and his parole officer—"Snake Eyes" Pike settled himself into his chair, lit a cigarette and drummed his fingers on the table while he waited for the gum-snapping waitress with the hot set of gams to come back in the bar and notice his arrival.

Damn, his dogs were barkin'. His chair teetered on the two back legs as he wound his feet around the front two and debated taking off his boots. But, for several reasons, he thought better of it. No shirt, no shoes, bladdy blah, and he needed a drink. Smoke curled out of his nostrils and then coiled around his head in a bluish haze as he absently watched the tremor in his hand. Man. Where was that lazy waitress? With bloodshot eyes, he searched the dimly lit bar area. He needed a drink. Now.

All day he'd scoured this godforsaken countryside, and for what? If he didn't find the little brat soon, he was going to need more money. A lot more. Though he didn't relish asking for it. The woman who hired him could be a pain in the butt to deal with.

Wyoming.

He snorted. What did Emily get out of moving here? But he was on her trail now. For seven months he'd been thinking of revenge. Rocking to and fro in his chair, he closed his eyes and gripped the salt shaker, envisioning his fingers closing around her smooth little throat.

Then again, maybe he'd save that particular pleasure until after he had his way with her. Yeah. That was a good idea. For a moment, he imagined her fear as he overpowered her and his eyes narrowed even as he smiled. This time she wouldn't get away from him.

Nobody made a fool of Snake Eyes Pike.

Buoyed by the thought, he leaned even farther back in his chair, which was a big mistake, considering the hardwood floor had just been polished the night before.

With a *kawhomp,* he suddenly found himself prostrate, his table upended and his ashtray rolling away like an escaped hubcap from a traffic accident.

Curses, so violent the wallpaper on the walls certainly began to curl, fractured the restaurant's family-style serenity. Hissing and spitting, Snake Eyes rolled about, grappling with his chair—a heavy, curve-armed, mahogany affair—but it was useless. The chair's arms held down his arms and the chair's front legs had somehow jammed deeply into the backs of his boots. Had he not been aware that he now commanded the attention of every eye in the place, he'd have drawn his gun and shot his way loose.

"Hey, buddy, you look like you could use a hand." Some preppy-looking jerk and his flame-haired wife who'd been sitting out in the restaurant proper, came running, looking down on him, with big old concern etched into their pusses.

"No!" Snake Eyes stretched his lips into a pseudo smile, wanting to downplay the entire incident and remain incognito. He regretted the shouted curses, but that was habit for you. "Thank you, anyway," he demurred, stretching, attempting to look the lounging lounge lizard.

The man took the woman's hand and stepped back. "You sure?" he asked. "You don't look too comfortable down there." His voice held a note of pity.

Snake Eyes hated pity. Made his trigger finger twitch. "I'm plenty comfortable. I've had a long day, so, I just figure since I'm down here already, I'll rest up. That okay with you?"

"Sure." The preppy guy shrugged and led the curly-haired broad back to their table. Snake Eyes knew that they, along with everyone else in the restaurant, were staring. And talking about him. Damn.

If he could just get his boots off, he could turn the chair over and get up.

What the hell was keeping that stupid waitress?

Although, he thought, allowing his eyes to slide shut, lying down like this wasn't so bad. Beat standing all to hell. He stubbed his cigarette out on the beautiful hardwood floor and, reaching into his jacket pocket, shook a new one from his pack. He lit it and lay there for a moment, smoking and trying to remain as unobtrusive as possible.

The waitress finally emerged from the back room and, upon spotting him, rushed to his side.

"Oh, no! Oh, my! Uh, hi there." Flustered, she knelt beside him. "Are you all right?"

"Just ducky."

"Can I help you?"

"Yeah. Bring me a shot of whiskey and a beer chase."

"No, I meant—"

"I know what you meant. Just bring me a drink."

"I...uh, okay." She pulled a pad and pencil from the back pocket of her tight little jeans skirt and scribbled some notes. "Anything else?"

Yeah, Snake Eyes wanted to say, since I'm already here on the floor, how about you and me and a quick tussle? But he didn't. Snake Eyes was nothing if not professional when on a job. Speaking of which... He reached into his wallet and took out a photo of Emily.

"There is one thing. You ever seen this girl?"

Knees popping, the waitress hunkered down and peered at the photo. Snake Eyes peered down her blouse.

She nodded. "Um-hum."

Snake Eyes's blood pressure spiked, and suddenly he wasn't so tired. He flailed his way out of his boots, kicked the chair away and sat up. "Where?"

She squinted at him, debating. "Who wants to know?"

Luckily, Snake Eyes was a thinking man and had already come up with a story. He stroked his whiskered chin, hoping he affected an educated demeanor. "I'm on the high school class reunion committee."

"You?" She wasn't buying.

That ticked him off. Did he have *illustrated* tattooed on his forehead or something? He could read. "Yes. Me. Gonna be a big shindig and we want everybody there."

"You look too old to be in her class."

"I was a teacher." He returned her cool stare. "She was one of my best students."

Mulling, the waitress tapped her order tablet with her pencil.

"She was so smart. I bet she's rakin' in the big bucks by now," he tossed out, to get her spilling what she knew.

"Nah. She's just a waitress like me. Tips are okay, but I wouldn't call 'em big bucks." She dropped from her knees to her hip to more easily converse and leaned back against the fallen table top. "I used to work with Emma over in Keyhole before I got fired."

"Who'd fire you?" Snake Eyes allowed his gaze to rove her legs as she crossed them and settled in for a visit.

She guffawed. "Some loser named Roy. Runs the Mi-Ti-Fine Café."

Snake Eyes winked. This dumb bimbo had just given him everything he needed to supply little Emily with her halo. And, when he was done with Emily, he'd come back for— "What's your name, sweetheart?" He pushed himself to his feet and offered her a hand. As she stood, she fell against him and giggled.

"Roz." She cocked her head and shot him a sassy smile. "You got a card? I could give it to Emma for you."

"No, but if you give me your phone number, I'll stay in touch."

Five

Over her shoulder, Annie could see her mother furtively peeking through the blinds as she and Wyatt sat parked at the curb in his rental car. The untrained eye might not have noticed the subtle movement, but Annie was an expert when it came to MaryPat's curiosity.

They'd been chatting there for nearly an hour now, neither wanting the evening to end. But, as all good things do, this evening was reaching its natural conclusion. And not a moment too soon, if the fog that poured from MaryPat's nostrils was any indication.

Still, Annie was reluctant to leave. Comfortable and warm, she basked in Wyatt's undivided attention and hungrily devoured his tales of life in Washington D.C. For years she'd wondered what he was doing, whom he was with, how he was faring. And now she was beginning to know. And with this knowledge came pain. He'd made a good life for himself. Without her.

She steeled herself against the pangs in her heart.

It was a wonder that some sweet young thing hadn't snapped him up. Lord knew she'd agonized over that question, even after her own wedding to Carl.

"And so," she was embarrassed to find herself wondering aloud, "you never married."

Wyatt didn't seem to find her curiosity unusual. "No. Came close one time, but we were wrong for each other. She wasn't—" He lifted and dropped a shoulder. "She just wasn't right for me."

"Oh." Strangely jealous, Annie tried to arrange her face into a picture of mature serenity. Wyatt's private life was none of her business. "Well, it's good you found out sooner than later."

"Amen." He blew out a long sigh. "At least one of us made a good match, right?"

Much to Annie's relief, MaryPat snapped on the porch light, and dragged the miniblinds open, distracting Wyatt from further questioning.

"Uh-oh," Annie murmured.

"Suddenly I'm nineteen again." Wyatt's chuckle was soft. Sexy. Filled with the intimacy of old.

"She has to get home. It's way past her bedtime."

Seeming to realize that time was suddenly short, Wyatt leaned forward and took her hand. His words, though quiet, held an underlying urgency. "I want to see you again."

"Wyatt, I don't know if that's such a good—"

"I'm only going to be here for a few days. Indulge me."

"A few days?" Could her heart take even a few more minutes of being so near to Wyatt? It was torture, this being so close to something she shouldn't and, more importantly, couldn't have. She had to get her mind back under control, before it carried her straight into her painful past. Even as she inhaled the manly, spicy, warm scent that was etched

into her memory bank, she knew that before he left, there
would be pain. How much pain would depend upon how
many of the next few days she allowed him to upend in
her perfectly insulated world.

"You know, you still haven't told me your real reason
for being here. I can't believe that you'd come all this way
simply to apologize to me."

"I should have long before now." His smile was rueful.
"But I didn't and I'm sorry."

"Stop saying that."

"Sorry."

They laughed.

Wyatt coiled a strand of her hair around his little finger.
"The truth of the matter is, I do have another reason for
being here. One of my foster sisters has moved to Keyhole.
The family wanted me to come check on her, and so, here
I am. Thought while I was here, I'd do some apologizing."

Annie huffed noisily. "I told you, you don't owe me an
apology."

"I do. Let's have dinner tomorrow. There is so much
more I want to say. It'll help me sleep better in the future."

With his free hand, Wyatt cupped her jaw in his palm.
There was a vulnerability in his expression that Annie had
never seen in him before. Her mind swam. This was not
smart. It had taken her a good two years to get over this
man. Even so, she could feel her stoic resolve melting beneath his touch. Gently, he stroked her cheek with his
thumb and she leaned into his hand. Memories overrode
common sense and she felt herself nod in acquiescence.

"All right," she whispered, against her better judgment.
Against all of the rational reasons she'd used to purge him
from her heart years ago. "Dinner tomorrow night." Before
she could second-guess herself, she changed the subject.
"So. You have a foster sister here in Keyhole?"

He nodded. "Em—uh, Emma. She works at the Mi-Ti-Fine Café."

"*That* Emma? Emma Logan? Oh, my gosh. I've known her all these months and had no idea that you two were related. I mean that is such a strange coincidence."

Wyatt nodded. "A sign, I'd call it."

Annie's mouth went dry as his blue-black gaze penetrated her own. "A sign, huh? Of what?"

He didn't answer.

In this light, his eyes were the color of midnight, reflecting the lone porch bulb and the moon's soft glow. Hadn't it been only yesterday that she'd fallen under this very spell? And, as if not a moment had passed, Wyatt drew her to him and brought their noses together.

"I've missed you." Softly, he spoke these words, and she could feel his lips brush against hers.

She couldn't respond. Admitting that she'd missed him, too, would pull the plug on the emotional dam and the ensuing flood would mean another two years in therapy. Very slowly, he lowered his mouth and pressed his lips to hers in a kiss so gossamer she was tempted to wonder if she'd imagined it.

He pulled back and shifted his gaze over her shoulder. "Your mother is watching us."

Annie could see his grin bloom in the shadows. Her own lips curved. "She doesn't trust you."

"Do you?"

Annie sighed. "I don't know. I don't know if I trust my own judgment."

"I want you to trust me."

"What difference does it make? We live in different worlds."

"It matters because we share a history. Like it or not."

"Mama thinks I need to watch out for you."

"Speaking of the devil—"

"What?"

"She's coming down the walk."

"You're kidding."

"Nope."

There was a tap at the passenger side window. "Annie?" MaryPat's throbbing falsetto rent the romantic mood.

Wyatt's whisper was hot in her ear as he reached across her and unlocked the door. "I'll meet you at the store. Tomorrow. Right after you close."

MaryPat pulled Annie's door open and leaned inside. "Kids, it's getting late, and, Wyatt, I was hoping that you could give me a ride home."

"It would be my honor," Wyatt told her and squeezed Annie's hand one last time before she slipped out of the car and switched places with her mother.

Though MaryPat lived only a little over a block down the street, the drive seemed interminable to Wyatt. The silence was strained and he could only guess what was going through her salt-and-pepper-colored head. He pulled up into the driveway of her familiar residence and cut the engine. As he unfastened his safety belt and prepared to get out and assist MaryPat to her door, she placed a hand on his arm.

"Wyatt, dear, don't bother seeing me to the door."

"I don't mind."

"I know, but the porch light is on and I'm not that old. Nor—" she turned and eyed him in the dim glow of the panel lights "—am I too feeble to kick your butt if you do anything to hurt my daughter again."

Wyatt took in the pursed lips and squinty-eyed gaze and knew it would be best to remain silent and let MaryPat say her piece.

MaryPat took a deep breath, causing the voluminous purse that rested on her stomach to rise up. "Getting over you was a long time coming, but she did it, praise God, and she got on with her life. Married a local boy, had two great kids. She's been through a lot."

MaryPat shifted in her seat and, holding up her hand, she grabbed her index finger and began to tick off her list. "First, she lost you. Then, she lost her Daddy. Then, she lost Carl. Are you beginning to see a theme here?"

Mind churning, Wyatt slowly nodded.

"This girl can't stand any more loss. So, if I may impart a bit of wisdom, since—heaven only knows why—I have a soft spot in my heart for you, get the hell out of here and leave her alone."

If this was MaryPat's soft spot, he'd hate to run into her when she was in a bad mood.

Then she poked him in the chest and her fierce expression softened just a bit. "Unless, of course, you mean business."

Wyatt met her unwavering gaze with his own. Long moments passed as they stared each other down. Finally, the smile that Wyatt had been fighting stole into the corners of his mouth. "MaryPat, has anyone ever told you that you are a really classy dame?"

"Well...yes." Taken back, MaryPat giggled. "Annie's daddy used to say that. So." She slapped her purse. "Will I be seeing you around or is this it?"

Wyatt leaned forward and kissed her peachy soft cheek. "MaryPat, I do mean business. I have a lot to apologize about to your daughter. Right now all I can hope for is that she'll listen and forgive me. Hopefully I can make her see that I've done a lot of growing up. Someday," he hesitated, fearing that if he spoke the words out loud he could somehow jinx his chances, "maybe we'll have a future together. I just don't know."

MaryPat harrumphed. "I wouldn't count on it. She's pretty much sworn off men." She shoved open her door and flung her purse to the ground like an anchor off a dinghy. "But I'll put in a good word for you. That girl of mine could use a little happiness."

As he pulled out of MaryPat's driveway, Wyatt retrieved his cell phone from the glove box and with his thumb, pushed Emily's number into the illuminated panel. She picked up on the second ring.

"Emily?"

"Wyatt?"

"Yep. Just called to see how you're doing."

"I'm ducky now, big brother." Emily laughed. "I just can't believe you're here in town. I just hate being away from my family. Having you here is just so…cool!"

Wyatt grinned. Sometimes Em was still such a kid. "I hate being away from family, too. I think that's only just now beginning to sink in with me."

"Good! Then I'll count on seeing you much more often in the future. You can start by coming to the diner tomorrow. Show up around lunchtime. Burger baskets are on special all week."

"Mmm. Sounds great. I'll be there. Hey. You want me to come do a perimeter check at your place tonight? Make sure everything's buttoned up?"

"Oh, thank you, but no. Toby's gonna swing by on his rounds tonight."

"Toby your boyfriend?" Wyatt had always loved to tease her and was rewarded with a satisfactory squeal.

"No!" she cried. "He's just a friend, for heaven's sake."

"Oooo. Methinks she doth protest too much."

"He's the sheriff, so shut up."

"Okay. I'll leave your safety to the man in blue. Lock your doors," he commanded.

"Roger."

"And windows."

"Gotcha."

"Leave your porch lights on."

"Okay, already," she huffed, exasperated.

"Good night, Em."

"Night, Wyatt."

On autopilot, Wyatt tossed his phone back into the glove box and wove through MaryPat's older, yet well-maintained, neighborhood toward the downtown area. When he reached Main Street and Summer's Autumn Antiques, he tapped the brakes and perused the building's welcoming facade for a moment. Tiny white twinkly lights rimmed the windows and outlined the building. The window display was a page out of yesteryear: warm and colorful antiques mixed with whimsical arts and crafts made by the locals. On the boardwalk, twin benches flanked the front door and a sign over one read Husbands' Waiting Area.

Annie really had done well for herself. Built a good life. Far better than his, on an emotional level.

As he continued slowly down the street in search of a parking spot somewhere near The Faded Rose Inn, thoughts of Annie filled his mind, his senses. Impossibly, their light good-night kiss had left him wanting her far more than he already had. He groaned deep in his throat. Ah, man, he was so screwed up.

What the hell had he been thinking, promising MaryPat that he wouldn't bother Annie unless he was serious? How could he be serious about her? He was a big-city boy. She was a small-town girl. And now her world included two redheaded moppets and the ghost of that nice local boy she'd married.

But still, he loved Annie. That much he knew. And until things were set straight between them, he would never find contentment. Damn. Between Annie and Emily, he wasn't going to sleep a wink tonight. Frustrated and tired, Wyatt found a spot, parked his car, locked it and walked down the empty street toward the hotel.

So deep in thought was he that, as he mounted the lobby steps, he didn't see the flicker of a lighter flaring in a phone booth just outside the hotel. Neither did he notice the pungent aroma of cigarette smoke as it caught the evening breeze, nor did he hear the muttered curses as Snake Eyes Pike fumbled his way through a call to Prosperino, California.

Removing a solid gold earring as she went, Patsy locked the door to her bedroom suite and rushed to answer the incessant ring of her cell phone. Luckily for her, there was yet another pre-wedding party in full swing out in the courtyard. There were so many blasted relatives and shirttail foster people out there, nobody would even notice that she'd opted not to attend.

Patsy snatched up the phone and tucked it between her shoulder and ear.

"Yes?" she barked. She'd given this number only to Snake Eyes so she knew who it was.

Patsy wrinkled her delicate nose. She could fairly smell his fetid breath through the line. Sinking to the edge of her bed, she braced herself for more bad news. Trust her rotten luck to pick the only thug in L.A. known as Mr. Screw-up among his dubious peers. "You'd better not be calling me with some limp excu—"

"I found the brat."

Patsy froze. She touched her tongue to her lips. "You found Emily?"

"Yup. I was right about her heading for Wyoming. Finding her trail was a pain in the—"

"You found her. That's all that matters." Patsy glanced over her shoulder, feeling paranoid. Joe had a way of popping in at the least opportune times these days.

"Yeah, I found her, but I'm gonna need some more cash."

"You'll get what you deserve and not a penny more when the job is complete," Patsy hissed. "When are you going to do it?"

"Soon. I gotta follow her home from work tomorrow and figure out where she lives."

A slow smile of satisfaction crept across Patsy's lips. Soon, at least half of her worries would be over. "Where is she?"

"Wire me some money and I'll tell you."

Patsy's eyes narrowed. "I don't like to be jacked around, Mr. Pike."

"Neither do I. I have business expenses. You want the job done? Pay up."

As if it were Snake Eyes's hairy throat, Patsy clutched the phone until her knuckles glowed white. "Where?"

"Some little backwater called Keyhole. There's a Wyoming Federal Savings and Loan on Main Street. I opened an account in Cheyenne last month."

Without the usual pleasantries, Patsy ended the call. She hated blackmail. Unless, that is, she was the one doing it. No matter. Her luck was changing.

The police seemed to have stopped looking at her as a suspect in Joe's murder attempt and Graham had been making regular deposits into her Swiss bank account.

And soon Emily would be dead.

The following evening, as she was flipping over the Closed sign in her window, Annie spotted Wyatt coming down the street. Just as he'd promised. Just as she'd known he would.

Her stomach jumped as violently as it had when she was first pregnant with the boys. She pressed her hand to her breastbone in a feeble attempt to still her furious heartbeat. Behind her was the cashier's counter and she clutched it for balance, feeling light headed, faint. Emotions warred within as she was at the same time anticipating and dreading his arrival. For as much as Annie longed to toss caution to the wind and throw herself into the past, she couldn't.

Last night, after much soul-searching, she'd decided to beg off of her dinner with Wyatt tonight. Spending time with him this way simply wasn't healthy. If one little dinner and a tiny good-night peck could have her heart in such an uproar, what would another day do to her? She couldn't take that risk. She was far too vulnerable. Especially where he was concerned. Besides, there were her boys to consider now.

As she stood hyperventilating and panicking over exactly what to say, the door to her store swung open. There stood Wyatt, just as confident and sexy as ever. Her fierce resolve to send him packing took a hit.

"Hi," she breathed, assaulted by the physical attraction to him that had never truly gone away. She hadn't slept a moment last night, for reliving that ephemeral kiss.

"Hi."

His grin, reminding her of the audacious teenager she once fancied she'd spend her life with, bloomed. A part of her longed to rush to him and throw her arms around his neck for a kiss. The way she used to.

No!

With a slight shake of her head, Annie took a deep breath, then pushed off the counter to stand on her own two feet.

No, no, no. This was ridiculous. She could not let ancient history interfere with her well laid plans for the future. She could resist him. She'd done it before. She'd do it now.

From the back room, Alex and Noah could be heard laughing and arguing over the electronic sounds of a video game. Chopper barked.

Wyatt's eyes shifted to the rear of the store, then back to her face. "Shall we drop the kids off at your mother's before we go?"

"Go?"

"We're going out to dinner, remember? I won't keep you out late, if that's a problem."

"Oh, no. It's not that. It's just that I…" *Can't be in the same room with you and remember my own name, let alone why we shouldn't be spending time together.* She swallowed, her mind racing, searching for the wording to the careful speech she'd rehearsed all day. "I, uh, I have some work to do." That was not it. Annie frowned. That was not the speech. The speech was something about their diverse futures and lifestyle choices and…

"Work?" Brow knit, he glanced around.

"I, well, I have some, er, stuff to do."

"What stuff?"

"Oh, a whole bunch of…you know, stuff. Some book work and uh, some furniture rearranging, and, um—"

"You're going to move furniture? By yourself?"

Bristling, Annie planted her hands on her hips. "I always do. I'm a lot tougher than I look." This was partly true. She'd been known to slide a piece here and tug a piece there. But she also had a crew of movers that came in once a week to unpack new arrivals and carton up the pieces that had sold.

His eyes held a spark of humor. "That you are a tough cookie, I don't doubt in the least. But still, you shouldn't be dragging this stuff around by yourself. It's a good way to end up in the hospital." As he spoke, Wyatt unbuttoned the cuff of a sleeve and began to roll it to the bulge of his biceps. An impressive muscle. Did he still spend his mornings in the gym? "I'll give you a hand. What needs moving?"

"I, uh—" Annie dragged her gaze back up to his face. "You don't have to do that! Honestly, I am perfectly capable of doing it myself. Really. Go." Go! Please! Go, go go. She wanted to jump up and down and scream. He had to go. She couldn't deal with the havoc his presence created in her heart. She waved him toward the door. "Have dinner. Eat. You must be starving."

He lifted one lazy brow and stared right through to her soul. "No more so than you."

"Oh. Well, no, I ate a late lunch…" Annie's voice dwindled. She knew him well enough to know that he wasn't talking food here. The rakish look and the sinful curl to his lip told her that much.

"C'mon, Annie. I couldn't eat a bite knowing you were here, most likely lying under some armoire or another. Go ahead. Put me to work."

Annie exhaled heavily, knowing her plan had backfired big time. He stood there like Excalibur wedged in the stone, immovable, stubborn, waiting for direction. Now she had to trump up some phony work for them to do.

Although…as she glanced around her cluttered store, she realized that she had been meaning to do a bit of rearranging for quite some time, but had just never got around to it. The aisles were far too crowded and virtually impossible for a wheelchair to maneuver. And some of the pieces against the far wall hadn't seen a dust cloth in months.

"Okay. I guess we can move some of the bigger—"

From the back room, the sound of Alex's precocious voice rent the silence. "Hey! Noah! The space bogey man is here!" His gleeful shriek drew his brother and soon Wyatt was fending off two copper-topped whirlwinds. A happily bobbing boy tucked under each arm, Wyatt loped around the lobby and then trotted up and down the wider aisles.

"Space monster need food!" he growled. "Have little boys for dinner!"

Tail wagging, Chopper jumped into the fray, barking and frolicking with the boys.

The twins' hysterical giggles created a bubbly smile that started in her stomach and rose to settle upon her lips. Her boys so needed a man's influence. A man's attention. His play. His rough-and-tumble touch and teasing. They seemed to revel in his presence.

The way she did.

She twisted a ringlet around her finger and watched them enter a male world to which she was not privy. And, as much as she tried to be there for her boys, to make up games and wrestle with them, it obviously wasn't the same. They needed a father figure.

Even knowing this—and try as she might—she still could not grieve for Carl.

"Hey, you monster types!" Annie shouted above the hubbub. "I'm going next door to order some takeout."

They did not pause in their hilarity to respond. Wyatt had Noah sprawled out on a couch and was tickling him, while fending off an attack from Alex on his back. "Arrrrgg!" he hollered, flipping Alex over and onto the couch next to his brother. Undaunted, they sprang up and were crawling over him within moments.

"Auggh!" Alex howled. "You have really big teeth, bogey man!"

"The better to gobble you up with!" Wyatt peeled the giggling boys off his torso and tossed them back against the springy cushions of the old couch.

Noah laughed so hard, Annie feared he might be sick. "No!" he panted, "you're not gonna get me!"

Annie squeezed her eyes closed and solemnly echoed this vow as she backed toward the shop's front door.

Six

The wrappings from their dinner of roast beef sandwiches, chips and giant dill pickles were crumpled and strewn about the top of a turn-of-the-century, drop-leaf table. Around the room, furniture had been dusted, polished, vacuumed and stacked and pushed into a much more user-friendly arrangement, pleasing to the eye as well as more easily accessible.

Noah and Alex were sawing logs on the couch, exhausted from chasing Wyatt around the store. Bellies full, they sprawled like lanky puppies around Chopper dreaming of nails and snails and space monster tales.

Wyatt stood in the middle of the store, hands on his lower back, arching and stretching and regarding Annie with a leery eye. "What now?"

"Well, uh, actually, that china cabinet should be over here, with the matching table and chairs."

She ignored his grimace. Afraid of being alone with him, Annie kept Wyatt moving furniture more as a reason to keep him busy, than any real need to continue organizing. When they were alone, she lost her ability to reason.

"That china cabinet? The huge one?" He plunged his hands through his hair. "The one loaded with all those little breakable frou-frou knickknacks?"

"Those 'knickknacks' are very valuable. I'll get you a box so that you can pack them up."

"Oh, wow, thanks." His sarcasm lacked bite. Opening his mouth wide, Wyatt yawned and ran a hand over his face.

"Am I keeping you up?"

"Actually, I could use a little kiss as incentive." He pointed to his cheek. "Right about here."

Annie laughed. "I fell for that old trick once. But I'm older and wiser now."

"And cuter." His brow see-sawed dramatically. "And more voluptuous…"

"Get back to work." She laughed and backed away, knowing that she had to keep her distance or live to regret it.

"Still just as bossy," he grumped as she skipped out of the room.

Annie found an empty box and some packing material in the back room and brought it to Wyatt. Immediately, he reached for the bubble wrap and began popping the air pockets.

"I love this stuff! This is what I want for Christmas, if you're taking notes on these things."

"You're still such a child. Give me that, before you wake the kids up." She reached for the bubble wrap, but he held it over his head, snap-crackle-popping, a Zen-like grin gracing his lips.

"No way. I haven't had this much fun in ages." *Pop. Snap. Crack.* "Besides, I bet the boys would like it too."

"They do! That's why this piece is all I have left." She jumped up, but again, he snatched it away. Much to her chagrin, she found herself laughing. "You're mashing it all up! It doesn't work when it's flat. Wyatt Russell, give me that stuff. Now!"

"Make me." *Pop. Crack.* His grin broadened.

"Wyatt!"

"Wha-aat?" he sang and jogged backward a few steps.

Annie crossed her arms over her chest. "Get over here now, buddy!"

"Ooo, I love it when you're masterful." *Snap. Pop.*

Giddy mirth rose in her throat as he turned and bolted. "Wyatt, we don't have time for this. We have work to do."

He darted around a corner and headed down the armoire aisle. *Pop. Pop, pop.* Unable to resist, she headed after him. They dodged and weaved, laughing and grunting and leaping over settees and other small antiques. Annie puffed, trying to keep up with his lanky stride. Wyatt ducked around a corner and then stopped and hid. When Annie came shooting after him, he leaped out and grabbed her. She squealed and he covered her mouth with his hand.

"Shhh!" Chest heaving, he pulled her into his arms. His laughter was hot in her ears. "You're going to wake the kids."

"Oh, yeah. Like I'm the one making all the noise!" She reached around his back and snatched the bubble wrap from his hand.

"Give me that!"

"No! Never!" She wriggled, struggling to free herself from his embrace.

"Never?" He tightened his hold.

She giggled, feeling limp. Lazy. Giddy. Happy. Sexy. All for the first time in far too many years. "Never!"

"Even if I threaten to kiss you?"

"Even then!"

"Is that an invitation to kiss you?"

"You are still such an egomaniac!"

"But I'm cute, right?"

He buried his nose in the hollow where her shoulder joined her neck and delightful gooseflesh darted like lightning down one side of her body.

"Yes," she gasped. "You're still cute. Even in middle age."

"What?" He reared back and growled. "I'll show you middle age." Gathering her to him, he attacked her neck, nipping and biting and kissing, his tongue burning a warm, wet path to her jaw. Her head dropped back and she could fairly hear the electricity snapping between them.

Or was that the bubble wrap she was clutching for dear life?

"I see you two are hard at work."

Annie and Wyatt leapt apart, their heads jerking toward the sound. Neither of them had heard Emily come in. Annie knew that Wyatt's sheepish smile mirrored her own.

Brow arched in curiosity, Emily closed the door behind her and moved into the store.

"Hope I'm not interrupting anything."

"No!" Annie flushed. "Not at all. We were just...well, we were—"

"Making sure the bubble wrap wasn't flat after all this time," Wyatt offered, a rakish note in his voice. "Luckily, even after a lot of fondling, it's not a bit flat."

"Would you just shut up," Annie muttered and jabbed him in the side with her elbow.

"Well, good." Emily smiled and held up the Thermos she'd carried over from the restaurant. "I brought coffee. Figured you could use a...er—" they all stared at each other for an uncomfortable moment ''—break.'' She twittered.

They all laughed and the tension left.

''A break sounds heavenly. This woman has been working me like a slave.''

Emily snorted. ''Yeah. I see that.''

''Hey. Keeping her in line is hard work.'' Wyatt made a face at Annie.

''Me? Don't you have a china cabinet to move?''

''See what I mean?'' He didn't budge.

''So,'' Emily chirped as she set about finding cups and coffee accoutrements. ''Wyatt tells me that you two knew each other in college.''

Annie lifted her hands in a noncommittal gesture. ''We were acquainted, yes.''

Wyatt shot her a droll look. ''Yeah. We worked together.'' His smirk said there was more to it than that.

''Wow.'' Emily poured them each a mug of steamy, fresh java. ''What a small world. All this time I know you Annie, and I had no idea that you went to school with dingbat.''

''Watch it, runt.'' Wyatt ruffled her hair in the easygoing way that siblings do, and then, with a last wink at Annie, took his mug over to the china cabinet and set to packing her small glass pieces.

''I couldn't believe it either, when Wyatt told me you two were related. Keyhole is a far cry from Prosperino, no?''

''I love it. It's...home.''

''I think so, too.''

Wyatt glanced up at her, wearing an enigmatic expression that unsettled her. Why did she suddenly feel guilty? She shrugged off the feeling and pointed out what she and Wyatt had accomplished that evening.

As Annie wandered with Emily around the store, Emily complimented her on the new furniture placement and, as unobtrusively as possible, fished for information regarding her relationship with Wyatt.

Back turned to Wyatt, voice low, Emily probed without compunction. "Are you two an...item? Because, if you are, I need to know. I have to pay him back for years of teasing, no, no, no, *persecuting* me about every guy whose name I happen to mention in passing. It's so annoying. You'd understand, of course, knowing Wyatt as you do."

Hand to jaw, Annie glanced over at Wyatt. Though he'd been pretending to mind his own business while muscling the china cabinet into place, he was clearly eavesdropping.

"I understand." Amused, she bit her lower lip. "Actually, we're just old friends. Wyatt simply dropped by to say hello for old time's sake."

At her hushed proclamation, Wyatt looked up, his lazy grin and seductive gaze challenging her words. She presented him with her back, for as much as Annie wanted to confide in Wyatt's sister, to bounce her theories about what he was up to off her, she was reticent to talk about it. With anyone. For by talking about it, the problem became real and Annie preferred to hide behind the safety of her denial.

So what if Wyatt was in Keyhole for a few days? The long-run ramifications were pretty much nil. When he blew back out of town, her boys would soon forget him and life would get back to normal. Once, of course, she recuperated from Cupid's open heart surgery. No telling how long that would take.

Expression puzzled, Emily glanced back and forth between them and finally gave up trying to worm any more information from Annie.

"How are you getting home?" Wyatt asked as Emily gathered her belongings and prepared to leave.

"Toby gets a dinner break soon and he's running me home."

"Toby-the-tiger, huh?" Head waggling, Wyatt shot her a lopsided grin.

"See what I have to put up with?" Emily asked Annie.

"I know just how you feel." Though Annie could commiserate, his teasing was one of the things Annie had most missed about Wyatt. Carl had never been much on teasing.

"Good night, you guys." With a last, curious wave at the two of them, Emily disappeared into the night.

Snake Eyes twisted the brown paper bag away from the rim of his bottle and, tipping it back, took a hearty swig. The whiskey was cheap and gave him a virtual tonsillectomy as it seared its way down his throat, but he didn't care. A buzz was a buzz, and until he was paid another payment on his retainer, he'd just have to settle. He'd gone to the bank earlier today, but the teller told him that there had been no deposit activity on his account.

His rude snort stopped the late-night cricket's song for a moment. No deposit activity meant no Snake Eyes activity. He would just have to outwait that Colton broad. Eventually, she would pay.

One way or another.

He cursed the questionable parentage of a mosquito that had been buzzing in his ear, then slapped it dead, leaving a streak of blood across his cheek. Twigs crackled as he searched for a more comfortable position in the sticker-filled brush that surrounded the brat's rental.

But there was none.

Blackberry brambles and bugs and a bunch of wild animals—

Snake Eyes took another long pull on his bottle. Hazard

pay. He was gonna collect some of that, all right. He checked his watch. The brat should be home real soon now.

Earlier that day, after some covert questioning of several regulars at the greasy spoon where the brat worked, he felt he had a pretty good handle on her schedule. She worked the lunch rush, then, when things died down, she came home for an couple hours, then went back for the dinner shift. So, with nothing better to do with his time, Snake Eyes had followed Emily to her motel-style cottage after lunch. When she'd gone back to work, he'd let himself into her place, done some snooping, a little pilfering, a bit of snacking—unfortunately, she used that snooty brown mustard that he hated—and then craftily adjusted her bedroom curtains and blinds to afford the best view for that evening.

Now he sat in the thicket just off the driveway enjoying a pre-show cocktail, some of her crackers and a few chunks of some kind of stinky, fat-free goat cheese—*man,* how he detested fat-free cheese—and planning her demise.

Killing her was going to be one of his more attractive assignments. She had a great little body, that was for sure. Made his job a helluva lot more fun. The whiskey was beginning to warm his brain and fuzzy feelings toward little Emily began to fill his mind. She was a pistol, that one. He'd have to be on his toes the next time he got into the ring with her.

As he sat ruminating, headlights swung around the corner, flashing into Emily's driveway and briefly illuminating Snake Eyes's hiding place. He dove down into the blackberry thicket and was rewarded with multiple stab wounds to the bare flesh of his face, hands, arms and lower back.

Profanity rang out and next door, a dog began to yap.

Snake Eyes took an extra long swig of rotgut, this time for the pain. He was bleeding like a sprinkler. The sound of car doors slamming reached him, then that canine rodent's high-pitched bark, then her soft voice.

"Rrrrrrr arrrp! Arrrrp! Arp, arp, arp!"

"Fifi! You be quiet!"

"Rrrrrrrr! Arp! Arp!"

"Fifi! Hush! You'll wake the whole neighborhood."

Snake Eyes peered through the brush at the groomed and ribboned rat that someone had tethered to a small doghouse. It was sounding louder. Probably smelled his blood.

"ARP! ARP! ARP!"

"That's the neighbor's poodle. She must not recognize you." Footsteps clip-clopped to her front door. "Thanks for the ride home, Toby. You really didn't have to do that."

"Rrrrrrrr!"

"My pleasure."

"GRRRRrrrrrrrrrrrrrrrrr!"

"Fifi! Shush! You're giving poor Toby a complex. Toby, why don't you come in for a cup of coffee? I have lemon bars."

Toby sounded eager. "Sure. I have time left on my break, you bet." The front door clicked shut and the bolt lock followed as they moved inside.

Snake Eyes gritted his teeth and groaned deep in his throat. He loved lemon bars. Where the hell had she kept the lemon bars? After a bit of a tussle, he got out of the blackberry thicket and rolled to the edge of her driveway only to come face-to-face with the irate Fifi. Snake Eyes promptly dove back into the thicket, but it was too late. Fifi, swifter and sober, had the advantage of night vision and a fur coat.

The streets had long since rolled up and darkness had descended over the sleepy little town of Keyhole. Hours ago, the street lamps buzzed on, and it seemed to Annie that they were the only two people awake within a hundred mile radius.

"You have really done a great job with this place," Wyatt murmured, lifting his mug and blowing across the rim of his second cup of coffee.

They kept their voices deliberately low, even though the twins had slept through the popping bubble wrap, the silly play and Emily's visit. Annie had scoured up some cookies from a cabinet in the boy's playroom, and they were enjoying a dessert, of sorts. She tilted her head and followed the drift of his gaze with her own.

"You think? I don't know. I've grown up here, and any changes I've made have come so slowly, it's hard to tell." She took a cookie and settled into the chair next to his.

"You can take my word for it. This—" his arm swept the area they'd just spent the evening cleaning "—is a cool store. You have some neat stuff here. And your art has really improved through the years."

Annie felt a flush crawl up her neck and burn in her cheeks. "No," she murmured and ducked her head. He was simply saying these things because he was a bigshot and he could afford to be magnanimous to the struggling backwater artist.

"Yes. Take that one, for instance." He nodded to a pastoral scene she'd done last year. "The way you've captured the reflection of that barn in the puddle...brilliant. You were always really good, but now—" he shrugged, his eyes never leaving her painting "—you're great. I know galleries in the city that would kill for your stuff."

Annie gave her head a modest shake. "No thanks. I have quite enough to keep me busy these days."

"That's true. But still, selling a few works in a city on the coast wouldn't take all that much of your time. Especially if you had help with the marketing end. You'd have to have help." His gaze shifted to the boys and a soft look settled behind his eyes. "As it is, I don't know how you do it. These guys are enough to wear a triathlete out."

She laughed. "Luckily, I don't have to play space monster every day."

Pulling a foot up over his knee, Wyatt leaned back and studied Annie through the steam of his cup. "You did a good thing by leaving school to come here, Annie. Even if I didn't think so at the time."

"It was really hard to know what to do."

"I'm sure I was no help."

"In your own way, you were." Her smile was wan as she reflected on their past. "Right after Daddy had the first stroke and ended up in the hospital, I came here to the store to call you, because it was quiet here and I could cry and stuff. Anyway, you can imagine my surprise—" She looked away, swallowing and blinking. Shooting him a bleary smile, she fanned her flaming face with her hands. How silly that this memory still choked her up.

"Ahh, Annie, honey." Wyatt heaved a cross between a sigh and a groan. He set down his cup and picking his chair up, moved right next to her and gathered her in his arms.

"When that girl answered and said you were in the shower, I—" Her laughter was strained. "I didn't know what to think."

Wyatt dragged a hand over the five o'clock shadow on his jaw. "Oh, sweetheart. I'm so very, very sorry about that. It was all a big mix-up."

"Mix-up?"

"That's what it was."

"To you, Wyatt. Not to me." She hated the plaintive quality in her voice and the fact that her eyes were filling with tears. "Too me it was a lie."

"Now that I'm older and wiser, I can see how you

wouldn't believe my explanation. But, Annie girl, after all these years, I have no further reason to lie to you." He cradled her head against his chest and she could hear his pulse pounding nearly as quickly as her own. With his thumb and forefinger, he tipped up her chin and forced her to meet his gaze. "So here's the honest truth. That girl in my room was just a study partner. Pure and simple. I give you my word that nothing was going on. Nothing. Annie, I was madly in love with you."

Annie drew a deep breath and held it. In her heart, she'd known. But her world had been so violently rocked by the near loss of her father, and then, the feeling of betrayal. A sigh shuddered through her.

"I guess it was the part about you being in the shower that threw me."

"And I can understand that. But there were a bunch of us. It was dead week. We'd study, then catnap, then take cold showers to wake up. I didn't even find out you'd called until after the test. Unfortunately, by then, the damage was done."

Annie lifted and dropped a shoulder. "It was all for the best. Your betrayal—"

"Alleged betrayal."

"You are such a lawyer." She fixed him with a bemused expression. "Anyway, that 'mix-up' was just the catalyst I needed to throw myself back into my life in Keyhole. To give up all those silly dreams of becoming some kind of fancy big-time artist—"

"They weren't silly!"

"Compared to my father's life, they were, Wyatt."

He sighed. "You're right. Back then, I just didn't understand. I'm only just now beginning to get the meaning of family. And what I've missed out on over the years."

His gaze wandered back to her sleeping sons. "Annie, I don't think I ever got over losing you."

She closed her eyes. *Nor I, you,* she wanted to say. But that would be just plain stupid. They'd gone on with their lives. Gone in polar opposite directions. No use going there. "There's nothing we can do about any of that now. It's over. Done with."

"I can apologize. I can beg your forgiveness. I will be able to sleep better, knowing that the wedge between us is gone. That the future will be—"

Frustrated, Annie leaned back and plunged her fingers into the springy coils of her hair. Elbows akimbo, she stared at him. "*What* future, Wyatt?" she cried, then leaning forward, lowered her voice to the intimate whisper they'd been sharing. "You live so far away. You've built a life for yourself. A good and important life. But so have I. I love it here. I need my family, especially where my boys are concerned. A long-distance friendship of any kind would be pointless."

Annie knew long distance had done them in once. What made them think it would be any different now, as friends?

Wyatt was quiet for a very long time before he spoke again. "Annie, are you really happy here?"

"Of course. How could you even ask?"

"Because once upon a time, being an artist and illustrator was everything to you."

"And now I'm just somebody's mom, moldering away in some middle-of-nowhere town."

"I didn't say that."

"It's what you meant."

Annie stood and began gathering the paper plates and other mess from their impromptu meal. As far as she was concerned, this discussion was over. Arms full, she marched over to the garbage receptacle under the cashier's desk and dumped her load. She gave her hands a savage dusting and turning, nearly bumped into Wyatt.

He grasped her arms to steady her, and didn't let go. "I didn't come here to cast aspersions on your lifestyle. To be honest with you, I'm a little jealous of all you've done for yourself."

"Sure." Head tilted back, she cast him a derisive smile, then allowed her eyes to slide shut. "Wyatt, I know I err on the side of playing it safe. Too safe, sometimes." She lifted her gaze to his. "That for all my fine talk, when we were kids, I probably would have hated the city and the dog-eat-dog artist community. I'm comfortable here in Keyhole. This is where I want to be."

"You've never tried anything else."

"I don't have to try it to know that I'd be miserable."

"You're hiding behind your family."

"No, I'm not! Wyatt, you are the risk taker, not me. You are drawn to new and challenging worlds. If we'd have married back when we were kids, I'd—"

He tightened his grip on her arm and pulled her close. "What?"

Annie gulped back the tears. Tears that she'd thought she'd been through crying years ago. "I'd have held you back."

"Is that what you think?"

"That's what I know." She glanced away. The boys were still snoozing, and the only sounds in the store were the occasional chime or cuckoo of an antique clock, and the gentle whir of the heater clicking on. Other than this, the world was silent.

"You'd never have held me back. Don't you see? You were everything to me. Annie, I'd have done anything for you."

"Except give up your career."

"Then."

"You mean to tell me you'd give it all up now? For me?" Her gaze shifted over his face and settled on his mouth. A pensive quirk pulled the corners tight.

"Are you asking me to?"

"No," she whispered, not knowing what she wanted anymore. A week ago she thought she had her future all figured out. Run the shop, raise the boys, send them to college, enjoy her grandchildren, putter in the garden, do a bit of painting. Now she wasn't so sure.

"Annie," he whispered, cupping her cheeks in his hands and looking deeply into her eyes, "I gave up a future with you because I thought it was what *you* wanted. I would do anything to make you happy. Anything." Eyes flashing, he brought their noses together. "Annie, girl, don't you know, I'd die for you?"

Annie's heart thundered and she clutched his arms as he sought her mouth.

"That I *am* dying for you?"

He closed his mouth over hers in a kiss that stripped Annie of any sense of reality and zapped her back to a more carefree time. A time when she had her whole life ahead of her. A time when she could be anything she wanted. Live where she wanted. Make a life with whom she wanted.

And right now—again, always—she wanted Wyatt.

Bruised and bleeding from his stint in the brambles with the hydrophobic Fifi, Snake Eyes hobbled back to his rent-a-wreck and, holding one hand over his eye to better discern the number of lanes that swam before him, drove to Main Street to find a pay phone. He managed to successfully land between two cars and the curb, doing only a minor amount of damage to each bumper. Throwing open his door, he fell out to the sidewalk and lay there for a moment, breathing hard.

Chasing runaways was hard work.

Nicotine. Yeah. A cig would give him the energy he needed to drag himself to his feet, so he rolled to his side, fished in his pockets for a moment, then fired up a smoke and filled his lungs.

A couple out for a moonlight stroll stared as they approached.

"Herb, isn't he the man who was laying on the floor at the restaurant the other night?" the woman wondered.

"Looks like him." Herb grunted. "Evenin'," he said as he towered over Snake Eyes.

Hat askew, flesh clawed, clothes covered in blood, Snake Eyes squinted up at them through a cloud of smoke.

"Are you all right?" The woman's pity made Snake Eyes mad.

"Yeah. Why? You own this ssidewalk, lady? Cuz if you don't, then you can go straight to he-*ic-up*—" He burped and waved drunkenly.

"Why, you ill-mannered—"

"C'mon, Gert. Leave him be."

"I think we should call the sheriff..."

"Why? He's done nothing wrong."

Their voices trailed off and when they were a good two blocks away, Snake Eyes gripped his car door and hauled himself to his feet. He stood swaying for a minute, then staggered to the phone booth on the corner. After taking his ill-humor out on a perfectly nice operator, he was eventually connected to Prosperino.

Meredith picked up on the first ring. "Why are you calling me so late?"

Snake Eyes could feel her fury vibrating across the lines.

So what? He didn't give a rat's patoon-ya. "Where's my money?"

"What money?"

"I went to the bank today. No deposit activity."

"Did you do the job?"

Snake Eyes banged the receiver against the wall a few times for good measure. "Not till I get paid."

"You'll get *paid* when you do the *job!*"

"I'll do the damned *job* when I get *paid!*"

"Don't mess with me, you disgusting, low-life reprobate." Her voice shook with anger as she drew in a deep breath and muttered, "If you don't finish what you started, you odious pig, you'll see no more money."

"I'll visit the bank again tomorrow and we'll see." Bored with this conversation and needing fortification and more than a few stitches, Snake Eyes hung up and headed across the street to the one joint that stayed open all night.

Wyatt had no idea how long they'd been standing there, bodies pressed together, hands caressing, mouths locked and seeking, communicating without words the feelings they still harbored for each other. He knew he could go on like this forever and never look back.

But could Annie? She'd found love again. Made a life with another man. Created life with him, for pity's sake. That was heavy stuff.

And then there was the minor problem of their living arrangements. He had a new and already thriving family law practice with his brother Rand. She had a thriving family business, handed down from her father. And in between lay a couple thousand miles. Hard to be a good husband with that kind of a commute.

Wyatt couldn't think with Annie so near. The smell of her, the feel of her, the taste of her were all too intoxicating.

When they were together this way all rational thought fled and he dreamed of fathering two little redheaded boys and refinishing furniture for the rest of his life. But that simply wasn't realistic.

Taking Annie's hands in his, he gently tugged them from where they were locked around his neck and, lips still touching, took a small step back.

She moaned, echoing his own dispossessed feelings when their bodies parted company.

"It's getting late. I really should go," he murmured, kissing the corners of her suddenly downturned mouth.

She pouted. "I wish you wouldn't."

"And how would we explain that to your mother? To the boys? To yourself, in the morning, after you've had time to repent in leisure?"

A tortured groan rumbled from deep within her throat. "Isn't that my line? When did you turn so darned practical?"

"The lawman in me, I guess."

"Well, tell him to shut up and kiss me."

Wyatt did.

And then, after a kiss that was filled with a desperate yearning on both parts, he let go of her and took several big steps back. Breathing hard, he dragged a hand across his face and stood staring at her for a moment.

"I'll, uh, I'll help you load the boys in your car, and then I'll follow you home and help you put them to bed."

Dazed, Annie nodded.

Seven

The boys were heavy as lead rag dolls. They stirred only briefly as, one at a time, Wyatt hauled them from the car and up to their rooms. Chopper staggered to his doggy bed in the front room and, with a tired groan, circled several times, flopped down and was asleep.

"You gonna stay all night with us?" Alex murmured against his neck as Wyatt carried him up the stairs.

Wyatt darted a wistful glance over his shoulder at Annie, who carried her son's shoes and jacket.

"I'm afraid not, cowboy," he said to the child.

"Darn."

"I'll come play with you tomorrow, how's that?"

Alex responded by tightening his grip around Wyatt's neck and burrowing against his chest.

Noah didn't rouse until he was being tucked in. "Hi, space monster." His voice was so small. He was still such a baby, really, plump cheeks, pudgy little fingers, smooth, lightly freckled skin.

"Hey, rascal." Wyatt perched at the edge of his bed. Annie hovered at the end, folding his comforter and straightening the stack of clothing they'd just stripped off the boys.

Holding out his arms, Noah tugged Wyatt close for a hug. "G'night." As the boy yawned, sleepy, warm breath tickled Wyatt's face and before the child let him go, he planted a noisy kiss on the edge of his stubbled jaw. "Ouch. Stickers," he mumbled.

Wyatt felt a lump the size of Wyoming settle in his throat and it was then and there that he lost his heart to Annie's boys.

"Sorry about that, buddy." He smoothed back the copper hair and kissed the freckled forehead.

"Tomorrow you'll read us a story?"

"I promise."

"Goody." Noah rolled over and was instantly back asleep.

As he sat, watching the child sleep, Wyatt felt Annie's arms slide over his shoulders and lock over his heart. She stood behind him, her voice low in his ears.

"Thank you."

"No problem." He kept his voice soft. "Besides, they're getting too big for you to lug around by yourself."

He could feel her smile grow against his cheek. "True, but that's not what I meant. Thank you for being their buddy. They need a man's influence."

"I remember dying for my dad's attention when I was their age."

"I'll bet you do." Annie sighed and squeezed. Wyatt reached up and closed his hands over hers.

"At least their father wasn't some old drunk who'd come home and beat on 'em for sport."

Annie was silent.

"I'm sorry. I didn't mean to bring their daddy into this. I know you really..." Wyatt licked his lips. Why was it always so blessed hard to talk about her late husband? The poor guy was no longer even around to compete with, and yet he felt the jealousy roil every time he thought of him. "I know you really cared for him and it must be so hard on you, raising them without his support."

She tilted her head, resting his against his. "Every child should have a good and loving father. I know that my dad made a huge difference in my life."

"Just as Joe did in mine."

"He's a good man."

"The best." Joe had a passel of children of his own, but somehow Wyatt was made to feel that even though he'd been fostered into the family when he was a school-aged boy, he was no less a member of the clan than if he'd been born a Colton.

"He did a pretty good job with you."

Wyatt leaned back and smiled. "I'll tell him you said so."

"Are you going to see him soon?"

"This weekend. My cousin Liza—"

"The singer?"

"That's the one."

"I've seen her on PBS. She's good. Really good."

"Isn't she? Anyway, she's getting married on Saturday."

"So you're flying back?"

There was a note of melancholy in her quiet voice that did his heart good.

"Mm-hmm. But then I'm coming back here."

"Why?"

"I have some vacation time to burn. One of the advantages of the bachelor life, I guess."

"No, I mean why *here?*"

Wyatt stood and led her to the door. "Must you ask?" he whispered, and then kissed her good-night. And, in doing so, came to realize that they'd begun something that would tear him up to finish.

The following morning Wyatt met Emily at her tiny cottage apartment for breakfast. Sunlight streamed in through a bank of windows in her dining area. Containers of all kinds, including old shoes, cluttered a card table and were filled with the first flowers of spring making the small area a veritable botanical bower on a shoestring. Emily had inherited—as much as an adopted daughter could—her mother's love of gardening, it seemed. Wyatt couldn't help but smile. Clearly, she'd spent all of her tip money on plants over the past months.

As he stood in the kitchen, helping her chop ingredients for an omelet, he could see why she loved it here in Keyhole. This was a great place to live. To run a business. Raise a family. With each day that passed he found he was increasingly reticent to leave.

But leave, he must.

He glanced at Emily, hesitating to bring Patsy's name into the quiet serenity.

"You have time to take a look at that stuff that Austin sent?"

She looked up at him, tears in her eyes.

"That bad, huh?"

"No." She cast him a watery smile. "It's the onions."

Wyatt laughed.

She pressed her wrist to her nose and sniffed. "Actually, it *is* that bad, but I'm not really surprised. I've read it all at least a half a dozen times. Austin did a great job. Talk about in-depth.''

''Mmm.'' Wyatt scooped up the onions that Emily'd been chopping and added them to the tomatoes and mushrooms that sizzled in the frying pan. ''Austin is nothing if not thorough.''

''I'm glad he included a lot of Patsy Portman's history. Did you know that she had a baby by some guy named Ellis Mayfair when she was only eighteen?''

''Yup. From what I gather, old Ellis was a used car salesman—a married one at that—who would blow through town twice a month and visit our Patsy. When she turned up pregnant, he wanted her to get an abortion. She said 'no way,' thinking that, get this, she could *hide* the pregnancy from her mother and Meredith.''

''Yeah, but the weird part is, she was successful. How could her mother not notice that she was pregnant?'' Emily shook her head in disbelief. ''Some of the reports say that she had her baby in a motel room with only this Ellis character to attend her. Can you believe that?''

''Bizarre, huh?'' Wyatt gripped the frying pan by the handle and flipped the browning vegetables. The aroma of caramelizing onions filled the air.

''Did you know that she murdered him?''

''Um-hmm.''

''With a pair of scissors.''

''Brutal.''

They were silent for a long moment. Butter hissed as Emily added a pat to the second frying pan and she adjusted the heat as it skittered across the iron surface. Outside her kitchen window, birds twittered. Fifi barked and the sounds of mail dropping through the slot in the door filtered back to them. The conversation, it seemed to Wyatt, was surreal in this happy, normal environment.

"Wonder what her motive was." Emily began cracking eggs and a shell fell into the bowl. Deep in thought, she fished it out with a spoon.

"Apparently, he stole the baby from Patsy while she was asleep."

"Did you know the baby was a girl? Jewel."

"Yeah. Wonder where she is."

"Well, the stuff Austin sent says that Ellis *sold* her."

"I know."

Emily stared up at Wyatt, her plaintive expression reminding him of the kid he used to push in a swing not so very long ago. "He sold his own daughter, Wyatt. What kind of a man would do that?"

"One that would date Patsy."

Her snort was mirthless as she cracked another egg. "Do you think Patsy knows I'm here?" Worry marred her delicate brow and Wyatt's heart went out to her.

"No. I don't think so, honey. But, as you can see from her history, she's very clever. I wouldn't put anything past her. That's why I'm such a nag about your safety."

"And I thank you." A small smile nudged at the anxiety in her expression and she set back to work. "You know, there were some really interesting records about Patsy's mental state as a child. From what I've read, I get the feeling that a lot of her problems stemmed from her father's rejection."

Wyatt snorted. "Yeah, well, just because daddy wasn't Mr. Sensitivity is no reason to go all postal."

"Of all people, you should know about a father's rejection."

"Yeah. I should know."

While Emily whisked the eggs, he dug around in her cabinets until he came up with some paper plates and two ugly mugs, which he set on the kitchen's tiny eating bar.

Considering she'd lived here less than a year, this place was outfitted with everything a person would need to survive quite comfortably. She'd been hitting the garage sales, he noted, taking in the mishmash of thrift shop kitchen utensils. Impressed, Wyatt gave his head a small shake. Even though she'd grown up in the lap of luxury, Emily was not afraid of hard work. Joe would be very proud.

Emily paused to pour the eggs into the frying pan. "Did you read the part where Patsy tried to frame Mom for Ellis's murder back in 1967?"

"Wasn't she just precious? No wonder Mom never wanted to talk about her. What a piece of work."

"I just hope you guys are able to prove that she's behind Dad's murder attempt, and mine—and possibly Mom's—and put her away once and for all."

Wyatt took the now screaming kettle off the burner and filled their mugs with hot water and instant coffee. "We're working on it, kiddo. Night and day."

"I know. And I appreciate it more than you'll ever know." Emily reached for the mug Wyatt handed her and blew across the rim. "So. On to more pleasant conversation. You and Annie. What gives?"

Wyatt threw back his head and laughed. "Women. You're all alike. All conspiring to end my carefree bachelor days."

"Has Lucy been matchmaking?"

"You could say that. She called this morning. Wanted to know how you were doing and to find out if I've decided to marry Annie yet."

Emily laughed. "Have you?"

"How the heck should I know?"

"Are you in love with her?"

"More now than ever."

"Then what's holding you back?"

"Well, for starters, several thousand miles and the ghost of a loving husband and father."

"Oh." She took a thoughtful sip of her coffee. "For you, that should pose no problem."

"Emily, I'm not Superman."

"To me, you are."

After several botched attempts at remembering his PIN number, Snake Eyes finally managed to get the ATM machine at the Wyoming Federal Savings and Loan on Main Street to begin the litany of hoops he needed to navigate, in order to check his balance.

Welcome, Silas Aloysius Pike.

He stared at his name and remembered he hated his mother all over again. Even his initials screamed under-achiever.

Okay. He squinted at the swimming screen, moving his lips as he read. Did he wish to: check the balance of his primary checking, primary savings, secondary checking, secondary savings, withdraw money from his primary checking or savings, make a deposit, request further information or exit?

How in Sam Hill should he know?

Cursing roundly, Snake Eyes punched the button that best seemed to correspond with moving this damned process along and the machine beeped at him, causing a stabbing pain to sear his brain. He should know better than to do this after a breakfast of Bloody Marys. Then again, having to do this sober would only make him mad. Why couldn't Marilyn or Muffy or Meredith or whatever-the-hell-her-name-was just send him a suitcase full of money the way they did in the movies?

Again, he punched a series of buttons, following the flashing cursor to the best of his ability and the machine spit his card back out at him. He stared at it for a moment, knowing that his PIN number had slipped once again into the muzzy recesses of his gray matter and *bam, bam, bam,* out of frustration, he gave the machine a couple of rapid-fire right crosses to the key pad, and some left-handed jabs to the tiny little TV screen with the picture of the happy, smiling teller. He cursed her perky face and decided that after Emily, this broad was next.

Much to his amazement, a receipt spewed forth from the bowels of the bank and the perky teller thanked him for using the Wyoming Federal Savings and Loan ATM machine. Snake Eyes grunted and held the receipt out at arm's length. When he was finally able to decipher the numbers that swam before his eyes, his jaw sagged.

The Colton broad had finally come through. There was money in his account. A lot of money. Not as much as he'd asked for, but enough.

Time to get to work.

After a little celebration, of course. After all, it wasn't every day that Silas A. Pike's ship pulled into the harbor.

A little skip in his stagger, Snake Eyes headed toward the local watering hole for some libation and to strategize. He needed to form a game plan for tonight. His fingers itched and his stomach tingled at the thought.

"Bye-bye, little Emily," he muttered, then threw back his head and howled with laughter.

"So. Mom tells me that Wyatt is back."

Annie took her younger sister, Brynn's, grim expression and critical tone to mean that she was not pleased at this news. Annie sighed. Brynn was always such a little freedom fighter. Truth, justice and the American way. With Brynn, everything was just so danged black and white.

"Yes. He came to town two days ago and decided to look me up while he was here."

"I can't believe you'd even speak to him, after what he did to you."

As they'd done every Monday morning at ten since Annie could remember, they were in her antique store sharing a cup of coffee and a small bag of donuts. This morning it was soft, warm maple bars, gooey with frosting and baked an hour ago at the bakery across the street. They had the place to themselves as it was still a bit early for the tourist crowd to begin filtering in and the boys were in preschool until noon.

"He didn't *do* anything to me. It was simply a misunderstanding."

Donut poised at her lips, Brynn stared at her sister. "Since when?"

"He explained everything. And, now out from under the stress of Daddy's illness, I can see that I jumped to conclusions. Conclusions that made it less painful to stay home and run the business. The girl in his shower was a study partner. Nothing more."

"And you believe that?"

"What reason would he have to lie to me now? It's not like we're still dating or anything."

Brynn waved her mug under Annie's nose. "Hello? Wake up. Smell the coffee. He just *happens* to be here in Keyhole of all places and decides to look you up? He's got some kind of motive."

"As a matter of fact, he does. His sister lives here now."

"You're kidding. Here? In Keyhole? Well, now there's a happy accident." Clearly, Brynn was skeptical.

"It's not that hard to believe, Brynn. His foster father grew up down the road in Nettle Creek. He wanted to visit some family and, since I lived here too, he stopped by. And

I'm really glad he did.'' Annie broke off a piece of her donut and fed it to the salivating Chopper.

Brynn's heavy, world-weary sigh amused Annie. ''Annie, I just hate to see you get hurt again. Your marriage to Carl left you with a broken heart.''

''Who said anything about marriage? Besides, he's different now.''

''How?''

''I don't know. More mature.''

''Which is just another way of saying he's pruney and gray.''

Annie laughed at her sister's puckered expression. ''He is not.''

Brynn grinned and laughed too. ''Okay. He's not gray because he's bald.''

''Hey now, he looks great in those Bermuda shorts and black socks. His wing tips are new and very shiny.''

''Eeewww!'' Brynn hooted. ''He sounds just like Dad. Does he have big old bushy eyebrows, too?''

''Why don't you judge for yourself? Here he comes now.'' Through her front window Annie watched Wyatt come out of the Mi-Ti-Fine Café and instinctively knew he'd just dropped Emma off at work and was coming to spend the morning here in the shop.

''No thanks. I'm gonna skedaddle. I have a house to show. Besides, if you want to make a mess of your life, that's your busin—'' Brynn's head swiveled and she followed Annie's gaze with her own ''—esssss. Oh, my,'' she murmured, as Wyatt strode toward the store. ''I'd forgotten how cute he was. He looks just the same. Better even.''

''I told ya so,'' Annie sang under her breath.

''No wonder you're all gaga over him.''

''Would you shut up? I'm not 'all gaga.'''

"You must be. How could you not be? You're only human. I hear wedding bells."

"Don't be ridiculous."

"Don't let him get away."

"Hey, weren't you the one, not five minutes ago, telling me to wake up and smell the coffee?"

"That was then." Brynn tucked in her blouse and inspected her teeth with her tongue for stray bits of donut. "Back when he had Bermuda shorts and a bumper crop of ear hair."

The front door opened, and there stood Wyatt.

"Wyatt!" Brynn gushed.

"Brynn? Is that you?"

Brynn fell all over herself as she stood and attempted to smooth the wild coils of her distinctive Summers hair. "Long time, no see!" She twittered like MaryPat and held her hand out in a most coquettish manner.

Annie rolled her eyes. Where was her freedom fighter when she needed her? She'd been counting on Brynn and MaryPat to shake some sense into her when it came to Wyatt. Instead, it seemed she was the one who might end up having to do some shaking.

Annie looked on as Wyatt ignored Brynn's hand and pulled her into his embrace. The soft flannel of the plaid shirt he wore muffled Brynn's breathless giggle and she seemed positively dwarfed by his solid build. After he rocked her back and forth for a moment, he set her away from him and looked her over.

"Tin-grin Brynn! Last time I saw you was back when I was in college and I came to Keyhole for Christmas. You had braces on your teeth. And now look at this smile. Nearly as beautiful as your big sister's."

"Oh, stop." Blushing, Brynn batted at his arm.

Annie rubbed her temples. For the love of Pete. Was

there a single member of her family that didn't lose all sight of reality the moment Wyatt walked into the room? She motioned to the door. "Brynn, don't you have to be going?"

"In a minute." Eyes as glazed as the maple bar she'd abandoned, Brynn stared up at Wyatt. "So, I hear your Dad grew up not far from Keyhole and you have family in the area. Isn't that a co-inky-dink? Does this mean you'll be visiting Wyoming more often?"

"I'm hopeful." He shot a meaningful glance at Annie.

"Brynn, don't you have a house to show?"

"Yes, yes, whatever."

"So Annie tells me you're in real estate now."

"Mm-hum." Brynn wrapped a ginger coil of her hair around her finger and cast a sly glance at her sister. "I'd be happy to show you around, if you decide for, you know, whatever reason, that you might want to buy a piece of real estate in this area."

Wyatt pinched his lower lip between his thumb and forefinger. "You just never know."

"Really? That's great!"

It seemed that if Brynn had her way, Wyatt would be moving in next week. Mortified, Annie gave her throat a noisy clearing.

"Brynn?"

"Right, right. I have to go. But listen. It was wonderful seeing you again." She rummaged in her purse and withdrew a business card. "Call me. If you ever want to get out of that nasty old city, I'd be delighted to help."

An awkward moment passed after Brynn breezed out. It was a while before either of them spoke again and in that time, memories of last night's all-too-brief good-night kiss filled Wyatt's mind. He knew that if he could feel the heat that shimmered between them, she could too. The temperature inside the store seemed to suddenly rise ten degrees, and Wyatt shucked out of his jacket and tossed it behind the counter that held the cash register. He cocked a hip against the counter and crossing his legs at the ankles, shot her a tentative smile.

She answered with curved lips and slowly sank back into her chair.

A certainty that there could never again be happiness without this woman in his life suddenly filled Wyatt's belly with dread. Somehow, they had to figure out a way to be together. They had to finish what they'd started so many years ago in the shadows next to the campus library when, with one heart-stopping kiss, she'd become a part of his very soul.

Wyatt had to admit that coming to Keyhole and falling back in love with a woman who lived in a different world was sheer folly. But folly or not, the wheels were set in motion and he was helpless to stop.

Realizing he'd been staring, Wyatt pushed off the counter and moved to stand behind Annie. He placed his hands on her shoulders and bent to kiss her neck.

"Good morning," he whispered against the smooth, warm column of her throat.

"Mmm, morning." Annie clasped her fingers around his wrists and lay back against his chest. "Sorry about my sister. She tends to be a little zealous when it comes to her work."

"Don't worry about it."

"I just don't want you to think that I'm plotting to get you to move to Keyhole."

"I don't think that." He wished she was. "You know me. There's nothing I admire more than a solid work ethic."

"Just as long as she remembers what's really important in this life."

Wyatt had an uncanny feeling that this speech might be directed at him, and he grinned. Annie never forgot to put her family at the top of her list and was not shy about demanding that others do the same. How she managed to keep this place running so smoothly and at the same time keep her children happy and well adjusted was a testament to her determination.

"With you as an example," he murmured against her neck, "I don't see how she could fail."

He tipped her chin up with his forefinger and lowered his mouth to hers for the kiss he'd dreamed of ever since last night, when he'd left her standing at the top of her stairs, the feel of her lips still burning on his. He'd known that if he didn't leave at that very moment, there would be emotional hell to pay. So he'd gone. But to what end? His emotions were in a tangled knot anyway. All night he'd tossed and turned, anticipating the next opportunity to kiss Annie.

Annie seemed to sense what he was feeling and responded in kind. She turned in her chair and then slowly rose to stand within his embrace, wrapping herself around him like a honeysuckle vine, delicate, yet strong and oh, so fragrant. Together, bodies entwined, they stood, lungs heaving, hearts pounding, mouths searching, seeking.

Since before he'd arrived, Wyatt had known it would be like this between them again, a long smoldering ember, flaring to life, burning out of control when given the tiniest bit of oxygen. He filled his hands with her wonderful hair and pulled her closer still, kicking a chair out of his way. Never breaking their kiss, he lifted her up onto the table and pulled her thighs around his hips. She locked her legs around his at her ankles and circled her arms around his neck. One palm on the tabletop, he cradled her back in his other arm, pressing against her, thrilling to the feel of a physical closeness that mirrored their emotional bond.

Wyatt was home.

Once again.

For home, family and future were all in Annie's arms.

It was very unfortunate, to Wyatt's way of thinking, that the first customer of the day would choose this precise moment to arrive. Luckily, they were shielded by a bank of china cabinets. With a tortured groan, he pulled her off the tabletop, stood her on her feet and kissed her nose.

"Later," he whispered.

"Mmm," she answered as she let her hands slide slowly over his chest. With a deep breath, she set about straightening up the breakfast mess she'd made with Brynn.

Having nothing better to do now that Emily was safe and sound next door, Wyatt put himself to work.

"Hi!" He held up hand and gave a jaunty little nice-to-see-you wave to the two customers, a middle-aged woman and the elderly lady she referred to as "Mom."

"Hello." The ladies smiled.

Wyatt advanced. "Is there anything I can help you with today?"

"Yes. Do you have any Madrilla vases? We have a friend from Spain who collects them and her birthday is this Saturday."

Wyatt nodded, mentally searching the myriad shelves he'd dusted for Annie. "Come with me," he advised. "I know we have a lot of vases back here, but if you ask me, they're all pretty ugly." He ignored Annie's strangled gasp. "Now, I know we have one of those washbasin-type pitcher and bowl sets. You could stick some flowers in that and pretend it's a vase." He climbed onto a chair and retrieved a pitcher, hand painted with delicate roses and gold trim.

"Wyatt!"

Wyatt sighed. Annie's face was all scrunched into a wad of concern. "Relax, Annie." To the women he said, "She hates it when we jump on the furniture. Could you catch?" He gently lobbed the pitcher into the daughter's waiting arms.

Annie covered her face and emitted a guttural squawk.

"Oh, yeah. Mom, this would be perfect for Carmen's entry hall."

"But Carmen collects Madrilla."

"Madrilla, Shramilla." Wyatt waved an impatient hand and let the bowl dangle from the other. "You don't want to give her an ugly vase, do you?"

Annie's exhale hissed though her lips like a leaky balloon.

Mom shrugged. "No…"

"He's right, Mom. I always thought those Madrilla vases were hideous." The daughter grinned at Wyatt. "We'll take the pitcher."

Annie looked up, eyes wide.

"Cool! But wait! There's more! The little washstand that goes with the pitcher set is on sale." Wyatt remembered Annie telling him about a lot of these pieces as he'd carted them hither and yon the other night. He leapt off the chair, handed the bowl to "Mom," vaulted over a love seat and lifted the washstand into the aisle. "It was made by some pioneer or other from around here, I think. Or maybe that was that funky little stool over there."

Again, Annie's head flopped into her hands.

"Look at the dovetail work in the little drawers. Made with dowels and square nails. Don't see that anymore. If you ask me, we're giving the dumb thing away."

"We'll take that," the daughter said, "and the funky little stool, too. I've been looking for a stool exactly like that for my pump organ."

Before they'd paid, arranged for delivery and left, more customers had arrived.

"Hi there," Wyatt greeted the young couple before Annie could make it out from behind the cash register and deliver the lecture he sensed poised on her lips. "Whatcha looking for today?"

"We're looking for a pane of old style bubble glass to replace a broken window in our home."

"Hmm…bubble glass, bubble glass. Never heard of it."

"I don't know if that's the exact name of the stuff, but it looks like glass with little bubbles in it."

"Sounds weird. Are you sure that's what you want? I mean, now that it's broken, I say good riddance." Again, he ignored Annie's indignant cluckings and flabbergasted gasps. He grinned. At times, she sure sounded like MaryPat. "Come with me and check out these really old stained glass windows. They'll knock your socks off."

When he'd sold the window, he approached another customer that Annie was now too busy to take on. "Hi. Whaddya need? We've got it."

"I don't know what I'm looking for, actually," the befuddled woman said. "I need a little something or other for this corner in my dining room and I thought about putting a hat rack or something…I don't know."

"A hat rack? Tacky."

"Tacky?"

Annie moaned.

"Trust me. You don't want a hat rack. Come here. You have to see this really cool Victrola that comes with an assortment of ancient records."

When he'd sold the Victrola, he went on to sell two of

Annie's paintings, a settee, a pair of really old oak and wrought iron school desks and a hurricane lamp. All before noon.

Annie sighed, blowing her bangs out of her eyes as she checked that morning's totals. "Wow, this was a bell-ringer day," she murmured. "The totals are more than twice my average."

"So. Do I get the job?"

She glanced up. "Are you applying?"

"You never know."

Her dimples bloomed as she glanced up at the ceiling. "Well, I don't agree with all of your sales tactics, but I guess I have to say you sell circles around me."

"Aww, shucks, ma'am. Yer just sayin' that."

"You ever think about leaving law and going into sales?"

"Sometimes."

"Yeah?"

"Yeah."

Their gazes locked and held for a long, electric moment, and Wyatt wished he knew what she was thinking.

"Not antique sales," she hedged, flustered. "You know, any kind of sales. You'd be good at anything you set your mind to."

"I know what you're trying to say. And thank you." Again, they stood and simply smiled at each other.

Outside, the noon whistle sounded down at the Keyhole fire station.

"I have to go get the boys. Want to come?"

"Yes. Put up the Gone Fishing sign. I'm taking you guys on a picnic."

"Wyatt, I can't just up and close the store."

"Why not? You made twice as much money as usual this morning, you said so yourself."

"Yes, but—"

"No buts. I'll come back this afternoon and help you make another killing."

Eight

"**H**igher!" Noah squealed. Head back, mouth wide open and filled with laughter, he hung on for dear life as Wyatt pulled the boy's swing back over his head and allowed him to hover.

"I can't hold you any higher than this," Wyatt protested. "I'd need a ladder."

"Then go get a ladder!" Noah dangled backward and giggled like a loon.

"Are you ready?"

"Yes!" Noah shrieked.

Wyatt released the swing and Noah flew. Excited, Chopper barked and wagged his tail.

"Weeee ahhh ha ha haaaaaaaa!"

Noah laughed so hard, Annie feared he'd fall. Although, she could hardly interfere. For the last four hours, her boys had giggled and laughed and squealed with the unmitigated joy of children who'd discovered Disneyland personified.

Wyatt wrestled them, swung them, pushed them, chased them, galloped them around the small delightful, tree-filled park in Keyhole's town square, and gave them his undivided attention.

And she'd never seen them happier. She'd never seen Chopper happier, for that matter.

"My turn, my turn!" Alex flung his arms around Wyatt's waist and tugged. "I want to swing, Wyatt. Please?"

"Just a minute, spaceman. You just had a long turn. It's your brother's turn."

"But he's already been up there forever." '

"Spacemen don't whine, buddy."

Alex laughed and waved his arms at his mother. "Mom! Come here and push me. We'll race these guys."

Annie shook her head. "Alex, you've had your turn. As soon as Noah's turn is over, I want you guys to let Wyatt rest for a while. You guys can push each other. He's tired."

"No he's not, Mom. He wants to play with us." Alex looked up at Wyatt. "Doncha, Wyatt?"

"Yep. I love to play with you guys, but we have to obey your mother."

"You don't have to obey her. You're a grown-up."

Wyatt winked at the child, then shifted his gaze over to Annie and grinned. "Alex old man, one of these days you're going to learn that all us guys have to obey the girls. That's life."

"Awh."

Amid much protest, Wyatt managed to extricate himself from the boys and the dog and make it back to the picnic table where Annie waited with an ice-cold glass of milk and a tin of home-baked cookies.

"Tired?" Annie reached out and gave his arm a squeeze. Wyatt looked as if he'd met his match in her sons.

"Umm." Wyatt flopped down on the bench and mopped

his brow with a napkin. "Pooped. Those guys wear me out."

"I know. I just wish I had half their energy. I could run the world."

"You already do, trust me."

They smiled at each other, the way parents smile when they've spent the day enjoying their children. She sat down next to him as he dug into the pie and a sense of serenity washed over her that she hadn't felt since she used to lie in the Memorial Union Quad with Wyatt and pretend to study biology while she actually studied his body and dreamed about their future together.

A future filled with love and laughter and their children. A future not unlike today. Only in this fantasy, Wyatt stayed.

The noon hour hand come and gone long ago and Annie had ignored the inner voice that urged her back to work. Wyatt was right. The store would still be there when she got back.

But Wyatt wouldn't.

Not after this week, anyway. And, even if he came back after the wedding, which Annie highly doubted, he would eventually have to leave Keyhole. Go back to being a mover and shaker in the nation's capital. The boys needed this time with him. She would have the rest of her life to run the store. She only had the rest of the week to spend with Wyatt.

The thought made her melancholy and she stared off through the trees. Behind the rugged, snow-tipped mountain peaks that surrounded Keyhole, the sky was a deep, cloudless blue. Over the western horizon the sun hovered high, but it wouldn't be long before it began its nightly descent. In the shade, the temperature was already growing cool.

Annie glanced at her watch. There were only a few hours of daylight left. By the time she got the kids home, bathed and fed, and helped them clean up after the tornado that had touched down in their room that morning, it would be bedtime. Wyatt had promised to read to them tonight after he checked on his sister and made sure that she was home, safe and sound.

Annie rested her chin in her hands and watched him as he ate. She couldn't help but notice that he was unusually adamant about Emma's safety. It was odd. Especially here in Keyhole, where the crime rate was practically zero. Something was going on there, Annie guessed and, when they had a few uninterrupted moments together, she was going to come out and ask.

The little lines at the corners of Wyatt's eyes forked as he sensed her staring. Angling his head, he gave her a smile that had her palms suddenly clammy.

The years had been very, very kind to Wyatt. He was far better-looking now, in his thirties, than he'd ever been in his early twenties. He'd been such a cute boy, but now he was a man. Everything about him screamed power. Position. Self-assurance. Sex appeal.

Annie swallowed.

"Penny for your thoughts," he murmured in that silky voice she remembered from a long ago night under the trees next to the campus library.

"Me? My thoughts?"

"Mm. I'm sure they're much more interesting, not to mention less exhausting than their thoughts." He pointed at the boys who were hanging by their knees from the monkey bars.

"No comment." Annie laughed.

He arched a brow and studied her from beneath lazily

hooded eyes. "That's interesting. So you have some thoughts about wearing me out?"

"I thought after all the furniture I made you move the other night that you'd run screaming."

"That's not what I'm talking about."

"I know what you're talking about."

"What am I talking about?"

"You know." Annie felt the laughter well.

His grin began at one corner of his mouth and slowly spread to the other. "No, I don't."

"Yes, you do."

"No, I don't."

"Yes. You do."

"Kiss me." Wyatt pushed his plate away and turned to face her on the bench.

"See. You know."

"Are you gonna kiss me?"

"Here? In front of the boys?"

"I doubt that it'll traumatize them too badly."

"But what if someone sees us?"

"So what?"

"Well, I—"

"Would you shut up and kiss me?"

Annie inched forward on the bench and slid her arms up over his chest and around his neck. "Mm-hmm." She sighed and settled her mouth against his and filled her fingers with the hair that curled at his nape. Her heart picked up speed and her whole body began to pulse. To come alive. To sing.

When she was with Wyatt like this, it was as if the rest of the world just dropped away, leaving the two of them completely alone to drown in the very essence of each other.

Or not.

"Eeeeew! Mush! Yuck! Look, Alex, they're kissin'!"

"Yech!"

Making tremendous gagging noises, the boys ran up and tugged on their clothing. Wyatt ignored them, and refused to release Annie.

"Blach!" Alex yelled.

"Gross!" Noah shouted.

Annie could feel Wyatt's smile against her mouth.

He pulled back just a fraction and scowled at the boys. "If you guys don't back off, I'm gonna kiss you next."

That was all it took for the boys to bolt, screaming and howling with laughter as they went.

"Scuse me, but what the hayell do you think you're doin'?"

Snake Eyes started. "Uh, hiya." After a deep drag on his cigarette to regain his composure, he scrambled down the ladder he'd been using to peer into Emily's cottage and backed onto the sidewalk.

He bared his teeth in a false-smile at the bathrobe-and-slipper-clad woman who stood on the front porch next door. Pink sponge curlers sprouted from her head like Medusa's snakes and her frown was feral. Like owner, like dog, the animal in her arms was also frowning.

Fifi. The dog struggled in her arms and growled, as if he remembered their tussle in the blackberry bushes the other night.

"Is the landlord here?" Snake Eyes improvised.

"Who the hayell wants to know?" the woman shouted, reminding Snake Eyes of his mother. Fifi barked and snapped, also reminding him of his mother.

His pulse went thready and he began to sweat. He was five years old all over again, and in trouble.

"I—I—I'm here to clean the gutters." He pulled out a

credit card receipt from last night's debauchery at the all-night saloon on Main Street and held it out. "I got a work order here, says this place got a gutter leak."

The woman cackled and shook her head. "What the hayell?"

Snake Eyes froze. She was onto his scheme. He considered bolting, but knew that, in his condition, he wouldn't get to the end of the sidewalk before he passed out. Then he considered shutting her up with physical force, but the dog scared the pea-waddin' out of him.

Much to his surprise, she turned and, with a dismissive wave of her hand, shuffled back into her apartment.

"You go 'head and fix the gutters and then you tell that jerk Simmons to get his butt out here and fix the damn roof. I never heard of anything so bass-akwards in all my born days. Fixin' the damned gutters while the roof leaks like a bloody sieve."

Fifi growled and snapped as his owner slammed the door behind her.

Snake Eyes breathed a sigh of relief and crammed his credit card receipt into his pocket. That had been just a hair too close for comfort.

He needed to get inside and out of sight. He glanced at his watch.

Five-thirty. He was early. She wouldn't be home till seven, which gave him plenty of time to prep for the job. There were bushes by the door that would shield him as he picked the locks on her front door. He'd let himself in and make a sandwich. After all, killing on an empty stomach had never been his bag.

Wyatt helped Annie unload the boys and their stuff and the trunk full of groceries they'd shopped for on the way home from the park. Traipsing back and forth between the

car and the house, they soon had it all carted inside. When
Annie flipped on the kitchen lights, the shadows fell away
and a cluttered warmth filled Wyatt with a feeling of right-
ness. Of belonging. Funny how he'd been here in Keyhole
for less than a week but already felt more at home here in
Wyoming than he had in all the years he'd lived in Washington, D.C.

"Mom, I'm thirsty."

"Me too, Mom."

"My hands are full. Ask Wyatt."

"Wyatt, I'm thirsty."

"Me too, Wyatt."

As the boys and dog bobbed about underfoot, Annie
glanced at him and it was almost as if she'd reached out
and touched him, so great was his awareness of her lately.
He could tell the feeling was mutual as their gazes connected and held over the heads of her boys.

"There's ice water in the fridge," she told him and in-
clined her head in that direction.

The boys pointed out the sippy cups and he awkwardly
fixed them drinks. Then, he refilled Chopper's water bowl.

"Thank you," Annie murmured, brushing by him, catching his eye, smiling meaningfully and setting him on fire.
"Can you stay for dinner? I'm making spaghetti and meat-
balls."

"Spaghetti? Yuck!" Alex clutched at his throat.

Exasperated, Annie shifted her gaze down to her son.
"What are you talking about? You love spaghetti."

"I hate it!"

Wyatt palmed the child's head as if it were a basketball
and waggled it back and forth. "All the more for me, then,
I guess. Plus, if I eat all my dinner, I bet I'll be able to
really chase you. And catch you."

"Nuh-uh!" Alex's laughter rang out as he threw his

arms and legs around Wyatt's legs and hung on for dear life. "I'm eating *all* the spaghetti!"

"Alex, get off him." To Wyatt she said, "I take it this means you'll stay for dinner."

"I'd love to. Give me an hour or two to run back to the hotel for a shower. While I'm there I want to check my messages and make sure that Emma made it home safely."

"Oh." Her brows knit thoughtfully.

As Wyatt peeled the giggling Alex off his legs and set to stowing milk and eggs into the refrigerator, he could tell that Annie wondered why he would even question Emily's safety. By the curiosity behind her eyes, he knew she was brimming with dozens of unasked questions. Questions that he couldn't answer. Not yet. Though he longed to tell her the truth and knew he could trust her with his life, at this point he felt that keeping her in the dark on this subject was safer for all involved.

"Okay." Arms loaded with salad makings, Annie gave a little shrug and glanced at the clock. "That'll give me plenty of time to get dinner ready and bake a pie too. You can be here by seven-thirty?"

"I get to sit by Wyatt!" Noah shouted.

"Me too!" Alex jostled in front of his brother.

"Sure. I can be here by seven-thirty." He shut the refrigerator door and in two steps was standing behind Annie, arms around her waist, chin resting on her shoulder. "On the dot."

"Are you gonna kiss my mom again?" Alex wondered.

"Blach." Noah clutched his throat.

Wyatt could feel the heat rise in Annie's cheeks and couldn't hold back his amusement. "Do you guys think I should?"

Giggling, Alex and Noah whispered to each other, jostling and peeping up at the adults.

"Well?" Wyatt wondered.

"Yes," the boys shouted, punch drunk with hilarity. "She *likes* it!"

"Is that true?" Wyatt murmured against her ear.

Annie sighed and leaning back, relaxed into his embrace. "Busted."

Thus encouraged—and amid much laughter—Wyatt gave her the kiss they'd all been waiting for.

Snake Eyes polished off the last of a pan of Emily's lemon bars and belched. Nothin' like home-baked goodies. His mother never had been much on baking. Then again, his mother had never been much on getting out of bed. Just liked to lay there and shout at him to bring her a fresh bottle or a new pack of smokes or a light. Speaking of which…Snake Eyes patted his chest, feeling for his cigs. Time for a little after-dinner smoke and a drink.

Little Miss Priss didn't keep anything stronger than a diet soda in her fridge and his flask was nearly empty. Absently, Snake Eyes wondered if he had time to make a run to the convenience store down the street before she got home. He shoved the empty baking pan out of his way and, feeling around in the dark, crawled to the stove, gripped the countertop, and hiked himself up. Swaying like a poplar in the autumn breeze, he squinted at the illuminated numbers on the clock and cursed them for swimming.

Six-fifty-nine.

Okay, okay. He did some calculations on his fingers. She'd be home by seven. He still had an hour. Damn, the time was dragging. Definitely time for a party run. He shoved off the counter and staggered toward the front door. Just as he reached out to yank on the knob, the sound of a key sliding into the lock and turning the tumblers had him recoiling in surprise.

She was an hour early?

Fifi's crazed barking rang out and Emily paused to glance over at the excited animal before she pushed her front door open.

"Hey, Fifi." Emily knew the animal was high-strung, but the past few days she'd been more agitated than usual. "What's wrong, girl?"

Like a yo-yo on amphetamines, Fifi strained at her leash, leaping, barking, twisting and boinging about on the porch till Emily was sure her neck would snap.

"Fifi! Shadup!" Gruff voice leading, Fifi's owner shuffled out onto her porch, still wearing her robe and slippers.

"Hello, Mrs. Flory," Emily called.

"Oh, it's you."

"I think I scared Fifi."

"Nah. She's been like this all day. Ever since that bum showed up to fix the gutters over at your place."

"My place?"

"Simmons didn't tell ya?"

"No." Emily felt the hairs at the nape of her neck rise.

Mrs. Flory harrumphed. "Figures. Well, anyway, I found this idiot up on a ladder, lookin' into your place. Says he's gonna fix the gutters, but that's a laugh if you ask me. Rain don't make it all the way down the roof to reach the damned gutters. Too many damned holes in the damned roof. Why the hayell they're fixin' the gutters first is beyond me."

As Mrs. Flory nattered on, Emily took a deep, calming breath. It's okay, she told herself. It was simply a handyman, here to repair the gutters. Heaven knew that the quaint old place could use an overhead overhaul. No use letting her anxiety get the better of her. When the curmudgeonly

Mrs. Flory had finally run out of steam, Emily bid her good evening and slipped into her home.

Just inside the door, she flipped the light switch on and a solitary bulb in the foyer sent long, eerie shadows dancing across the walls and floor. Spooked, she spun and shut her front door, shot the bolt, secured the chain and twisted the lock on the doorknob. There. No one could get through that.

Nervous laughter bubbled past her lips and the hollow sound reverberated off the walls of the sparsely furnished apartment. She was being such a ninny. Even the evening shadows had taken on a menacing quality. What a boob.

Shucking out of her jacket, Emily tried to rid herself of the ever-present feeling she had of late that someone was watching her. Just nerves, she mentally chided herself. And was it any wonder? After what she'd been through, a few nerves were normal, she was sure.

But still…

Knowing that someone had been looking into her little home through the front window was unsettling.

It was cool in the house, so she decided not to put her jacket in the closet, and instead draped it over her shoulders. Heat cost a fortune and on her limited budget it was a luxury she could not afford. Rubbing at the gooseflesh that covered her arms, Emily moved to the window that overlooked her porch and peered out. Clouds flitted in front of the full moon, and there was a breeze that ruffled the branches of the giant oak tree in the yard and caused them to scrape against the side of the house. *Scrape, scratch, scrape.*

Head cocked, she grew very still and listened.

There was another sound. But what? She strained to hear, but it was elusive. Tingles skittered up her spine and her breathing became shallow.

Something was not right.

She could feel it in her gut.

It was the very same feeling of foreboding she'd experienced the night in her room, back in Prosperino. Rattled, Emily moved as quickly as possible through her tiny living room area and over to the kitchen to make a check of the premises. She would feel much better once she reassured herself that she was alone. That she was simply being silly. That there was nothing to fear and that she was safe here, in her little home, miles from Patsy and her hired thug.

The dim bulb of the lone hallway fixture cast just enough light for her to make out her kitchen. And the kitchen floor. And the baking pan that lay in the middle of the floor.

She stared at the empty pan as if it might leap up and strike.

What was that pan doing in the middle of her floor?

And why was it empty?

On her break that afternoon, she'd baked Toby lemon bars as a thank-you for checking up on her, and put them in the refrigerator to cool. Hadn't she?

There was a clicking sound that Emily slowly realized came from her chattering teeth. Terror gripped her and she stood frozen to the spot. Someone had been in her house. Eating her food. No doubt going through her things.

The phone. The phone. She needed to get to the phone and call Toby. Yes. This was a good plan. If only she could move.

Woodenly, Emily forced herself to take the few steps needed to reach her phone. Backing into the shadows of her living room, she lifted the handset and with shaking fingers, punched in Toby's cell number. He picked up on the first ring.

"Toby Atkins here."

"Toby!" Hand cupping the mouthpiece, Emily's voice was hushed and frantic.

"Yes? Emma?" His immediate concern bolstered her slightly, giving her the confidence she needed to remain upright.

"Toby, someone's been in my place." Her voice was high and tinny and it was all she could do to catch her breath. "They ate the lemon bars! The pan...the pan was on the floor! In the middle of the floor! Toby, I baked those for you, but they're gone!"

"Slow down, honey. I'm having trouble understanding. Someone was in your house?"

"Yes!"

"Is he still there?"

Emily froze. Was he? There weren't that many places to hide. Just the bathroom and that little closet by the front door. From where she stood, she glanced into the bathroom and didn't see anything. But that didn't mean she was alone. "I don't know! Toby, you have to come over here! Now! Right now!"

"I'll be there in a minute."

"Hurry! Oh, hurry." Her teeth were now chattering so violently, her neck began to ache. Pulse roaring, Emily groped for the back of one of the plastic patio chairs she'd been using as living room furniture, to keep from falling down. "My n-neighbor told me that there had been a man here, to fix the gutters, and he was looking in my windows and now my lemon bars are gone. Why would someone steal my lemon bars?"

A muffled noise sounded from inside her hall closet and Emily swallowed a scream.

"Toby?" she whimpered.

"Yeah?"

"Ummm, uh, I think... He's here. In the house. With me."

"Can you get out of there?"

"He's in the hall closet. Next to the front door. I don't have a back door."

"What the hell kind of apartment doesn't have a back door?"

"A cheap one. I-I could jump out a window maybe. If I can get one open."

She could hear the squeal of the sirens over the phone lines. "Emma? Stay on the line, honey. I'll be there in a minute. Do you have a weapon?"

There was a sound, near the front door. Emily sucked in her breath and held it. Was he coming out?

"Emma?"

Emily clutched the phone, but for the life of her, she couldn't speak. She stared hard at the closet door, and sure enough, it was slowly opening.

"Are you still there?"

She didn't know if she was still there. The lone hall light began to sway, and the room, to spin. Her legs tingled and she wasn't sure they were still touching the floor. Beads of sweat broke out on her upper lip and at the same time, she shivered. She couldn't move her jaw to form the words to tell Toby that a man was indeed coming out of her hall closet.

The same man who'd chased her out of Prosperino just seven months ago.

Phone jammed between his shoulder and ear, Wyatt sat on the edge of his bed at The Faded Rose hotel and listened to the busy signal yet again. When he'd finished strapping on his watch, he checked it once more for the time. Emily had been on the blasted phone for nearly twenty minutes now. At least he had the satisfaction of knowing that she was home. Even so, he wanted to touch base with her and knew he couldn't do it over at Annie's without arousing her curiosity.

Feet up on the bed, Wyatt leaned back against his pillows and dropped the phone's handset back into its cradle. He'd try again in a minute. His cheeks puffed as he emitted a heavy sigh. He hated keeping secrets from Annie. That had never been his style.

Back in college, he'd relished having that one person in whom he could confide everything. Annie never laughed at his dreams. His fears. She was always supportive and understanding. Until he'd blown it by not being there for her when she'd needed him the most.

But he'd learned his lesson. Big time.

Because of that lack of understanding, now, more than ever, he wanted to make sure that there was no miscommunication between them. They'd wasted far too many years, laboring under false assumptions.

Again, he glanced at his watch. If Emily didn't answer soon, he was going to be late for dinner. Annie was expecting him. Her boys were expecting him. He couldn't let any of them down. Picking up the phone, he decided he'd call Emily one last time. If she didn't answer, he'd simply have to assume she was gabbing on the phone to a girlfriend, or maybe that Toby character, and had forgotten to check in with him. He punched in her number and waited.

Busy signal.

Wyatt hung up. Okay. He was outta here. He'd call Emily when he got home tonight. Snatching up his keys, he shrugged into his jacket and grabbed a couple of colorful kids' books he'd bought for the boys.

Just as he was about to leave, the phone rang. Emily. It

was about time. He crossed to the phone and lifting it to his ear barked, "Hey, gabby. Wha'd you do? Forget me?"

"Wyatt?"

Wyatt frowned. This was not Emily. Instinctively, he knew it was serious. "Uh, yeah?"

"Toby Atkins."

Wyatt froze. "What? What's wrong?"

"There's been an attack. Emma needs you over at her place. As soon as you can get here."

Annie stared in dismay at the coagulating spaghetti sauce, the rubbery noodles and the candles that had burned low and dripped wax on her best linen tablecloth. Wyatt was now officially two and a half hours late. She was torn between anger and worry, but the minute one would rise to the forefront, the other would take over.

She'd tried calling his room at the hotel, to no avail, left several messages, and finally gave up.

Maybe he forgot.

Maybe he didn't.

Maybe he'd decided that all this reminiscing and apology stuff was getting a little too heavy for him, and he'd opted to bug out before he became any more deeply involved. With her. With her kids.

Annie propped her elbows on the table and cradled her head in her hands. Try as she might to believe this, she simply couldn't. It simply didn't ring true. Wyatt was not the kind of person who'd abandon her. Ever. Deep in her soul, she'd known this years ago. Deep down, she'd known that he still loved her. That even if he had dallied with another girl, that she, Annie, was his true love. And always would be.

But, back then, believing that he didn't care anymore made it so much easier to stay here in Keyhole and help take care of her dying father. Made it easier to turn him loose and let him become everything he was so very capable of becoming. Without her, and her family, to hold him back.

Wispy tendrils of hair fluttering with her sigh, Annie pushed herself away from the table and began gathering the dishes. The boys had picked at their food, claiming that if Wyatt didn't have to suffer through his spaghetti, then why should they? After a torturous meal spent bartering and cajoling and threatening, just to get a bite or two of food into their bellies, Annie excused them from the table to play in their rooms and wait for Wyatt.

Then, later, getting them into the tub, when they'd *known* he was going to show up and chase and toss and tickle them ''any second, Mom! Give him a chance to get here!'' was also a test of her parental mettle. Once they were scrubbed and dressed in Batman and Superman pajamas, she'd allowed them to sit up in bed and wait for Wyatt to arrive, so he could read them a story. After a solid hour of waiting, the boys had drifted off and Annie had removed the books from their arms and tucked them in.

For a long while, before returning downstairs to wait at the table, she'd stood in their doorway, watching them sleep and thinking that Wyatt had better have a pretty damned good excuse for letting them down.

Nine

The sound of a sharp knock at her front door, coupled with Chopper's frenzied barking, woke Annie with a start. Pushing herself to a sitting position on the couch, she squinted at the clock and was shocked to note that it was after midnight. Who on earth...? Groggy, she wrapped an afghan around her shoulders, shuffled to the door and peeked through the leaded glass panels.

Wyatt?

"Chopper, hush!" Annie grabbed the dog by the collar and pulled him back behind her.

What in heaven's name was Wyatt doing here at this hour? Suddenly, the haze began to lift and she remembered that she was furious with him. And, frantic with worry. She gave the bolt a vicious twist and yanked the door open, hoping the scowl she wore was enough to say it all.

That she was hurt.

That the boys were hurt.

That he could have at least called.

That was, until she noted the strain in his eyes. The tension in his posture. The way the tendons in his neck and jaw bunched. Something had happened. Something terrible. She could sense it in his despondent smile. Afraid to know, she closed her eyes against the visions she'd been entertaining all evening. Leftovers from the day Carl died.

He stepped inside and drew her into his embrace. He held her with a desperation that took her breath away. She coiled against him, and held him back, drinking in his warmth, his scent, his solid build, the steady beat of his heart.

Thank God, he was here. He was all right. That was all that mattered. As long as he was alive and well, she could deal with the rest. In that moment, all the wonder and worry about his feelings for her vanished, and instead Annie resigned herself to the fact that they'd picked up where they left off a decade ago. And they still had no future together.

After they'd held each other for a long, silent moment, Annie leaned away and looked at him. He was tired. World-weary. Afraid. She knew the feelings so very well. Taking his hand in hers, she drew him into her living room and tugged him down next to her on the couch. Because the room had taken on a bit of a chill, she offered him half of her afghan.

Finally, she summoned the courage to speak. "What happened?"

"My sister was attacked."

Annie stiffened and her gaze flew to his. *"What?"*

Wyatt inhaled deeply, held it for a beat, then slowly released the breath through his lips. He gathered the afghan up over his shoulders, then reached for her hands and cradled them against his stomach. "When she came home from work tonight, there was a man waiting for her, in her apartment.''

"No! You're kidding."

"No."

"Is she all right?"

"Physically, yes. Toby arrived in time to scare the creep off, but not before she'd been pretty badly traumatized.''

"Traumatized?"

"He didn't rape her, but I get the feeling that it was on his agenda, among other things.''

"Oh, no. How awful.'' Tears welled in her eyes and the back of her throat burned with a fear that radiated throughout her body. Annie suddenly felt violated, herself. "How could this happen here? Things like that just don't happen in Keyhole.''

He drew her hands up to rest against his heartbeat. "Honey, I'm afraid they can happen anywhere these days.''

"Not *here!*'' Her vehemence came from feelings of powerlessness as her illusions about the complete safety of this small town shattered. "No. That just can't be right.''

A lump crowded into her throat and she blinked back the tears. That was one of the main reasons why she still lived here. Her boys were safe here. Nothing bad could happen to them if she stayed right here in Keyhole. Safe, old-fashioned Keyhole. An innocent town filled with innocent people. Crime was for cities. Big places, like the one where Wyatt lived.

"I'm sorry,'' he whispered against her temple as the tears rolled down her cheeks.

He released her hands so that he could take her in his arms, and she leaned into his chest, loving the comfort. The strength. She scrubbed at her face with the fuzzy hem of the afghan and felt like a little kid again. Safe and protected. The way she had with Daddy.

It had been so long since she'd had anyone to hold her when she was upset. Her sigh was ragged as she leaned her cheek against the soft T-shirt he wore stretched over his chest, and slowly, she felt her body begin to relax.

Tears dripped off the end of her nose, making little dark patches just over his heart. She knew she must be a mess. Her cheeks had to be splotchy—they always were when she cried—and her nose must be as red as a tomato. What with her messy hair and rumpled clothes, she knew she had to look a sight. Even so, something about Wyatt always made her feel unconditionally accepted.

"Where is she?" she asked.

"With your mother."

"*My* mother?"

"I called her—"

Annie levered off his chest. "Let me get this straight. *You* called *my* mother?"

"Yep. And I asked if she'd mind taking Em in for a little while. Since she lived alone and all, I figured she might have the room."

"And she said yes?"

"Sure. Just until we get this thing straightened out, of course. Your sister is going to help, too, staying with her when your mom can't."

"You called my sister?"

"You have a very nice family, Annie."

"Yeah, well, I knew that. I just didn't know you knew that."

"They've forgiven me."

"I guess so."

Annie curled her feet under her body and snuggled closer. Leaning her head back against his arm, she peered up into his face. "She'll be safe with Mama."

"I thought so."

"Did they catch him?"

Wyatt gave his head a single shake and rested his chin on the top of her head. "No."

"Oh."

"He got away, just before Toby arrived. Seems he'd been hiding in her apartment a while, waiting for her to come home."

"But why? Why he would break in and then *wait* for her? Was he some kind of stalker?"

Wyatt was silent, but to Annie, it spoke volumes.

"This has happened before, hasn't it?"

In a surprise that was dulled by fatigue, Wyatt stared at her. "How did you know?"

"You've been as protective as a henhouse rooster with a fox on the loose. Wyatt, I know it's a cruel world out there, but this is Keyhole. The one town in this country where keys, until today, were never really needed."

He closed his eyes and let his head loll against the back of the couch. "I'm not supposed to talk about this."

"But you are."

First he shrugged. Then he nodded.

"Am I going to need a cup of coffee and a brownie to hear this?"

For the first time that evening, there was a small spark of interest in his eyes. "You made brownies?"

"Yes."

"With fudge frosting and walnuts?"

She laughed. "Yes."

"I love fudge frosting and walnuts."

"I remember."

He was quiet for a long moment. His Adam's apple bobbed as he swallowed and glanced around the room. Annie could tell he was battling old tapes that played in his head and knew that the attack on his sister brought up strug-

gles he'd had with his own childhood. Feelings of being
out of control. Feelings of powerlessness. Defenselessness.
She could tell he wanted to exact revenge, but couldn't and
that left him frustrated and angry. Gently, she brushed his
hair back out of his eyes and then let her fingers stray down
the sides of his face to cup his jaw.

She wanted to tell him she loved him. But instead she
simply said, "I could whip up a fresh pot of decaf."

Without ceremony, he shoved Annie off his lap. "Let's
go."

In the deep of the night—over warm brownies topped
with heaping scoops of vanilla bean ice cream—Annie and
Wyatt sat in her breakfast nook, eating, sipping decaf coffee
and talking. Wyatt had finally begun to relax. The brownies
were ambrosia and the homey, warm kitchen, a safe haven
from life's cruel realities. He savored every moment, stor-
ing away this secret time with Annie together with the rest
of the memories of her that he held in his heart to see him
through future lonely times.

"So, you're telling me," Annie paused and pointed at
Wyatt with her fork, "that the woman I met, back when
we were in college, wasn't really your foster mother, but
an impostor?"

Mouth full, Wyatt nodded, then swallowed. "Weird,
huh?"

"It's like something out of a soap opera. Tell me. How
come not one single one of you ever realized she wasn't
Meredith?"

"Well, first off, she didn't look any different. Secondly,
Meredith had never told anyone that she'd had a twin sister.
Thirdly, she'd been in a pretty bad car wreck. We just figured that the change in personality had come from that
nasty bump on the head."

"Okay, let me see if I'm following you. Patsy is Meredith's twin sister—"

"Yeah."

"And in a crime of passion she stabbed the father of her baby to death with scissors after he sold the baby into the black market, and then she tried to blame the whole murder on her sister, Meredith, but when that didn't work she went to jail and then to a mental ward and when she escaped from there, she ran your foster mother off the road and killed her."

"We don't know that for sure."

Annie squinted. "Are you making this whole thing up?"

"I wish."

"Okay." She waved her fork in a loose circle. "We'll give her the benefit of the doubt on your mother's murder. Now, where were we?"

"She ran Meredith off the road..." Wyatt blew across the rim of his mug and smiled at her avid interest in the history of his family.

"Oh, right. And Emma-Emily, actually, remembered seeing 'two' mommies at the crash site before she passed out." Annie stabbed at her pie. "Wow. An evil twin. The stuff of all the really good fairy tales."

"Kinda makes you wonder which one of your boys is the baddy, huh?" he teased, lightening the mood.

"They take turns." Annie chuckled with him for a moment, then sobered. "So, since Emily might blow the whistle on Patsy, her life is in danger?"

"Looks like it."

"And the shooting at Joe's birthday party? That was her, too?"

Wyatt shrugged. "Don't know about that. We do know that Patsy's not keen on giving up her lifestyle. Maybe she felt Joe was getting too close to the truth."

"She's crazy."

He nodded. "Like a fox."

"Tell me you did it."

Snake Eyes took a long, steadying drag on his cigarette and brushed the tickling fingers out of his free ear. "Not—" he exhaled a long, gray stream and coughed "—yet."

"Not yet? Not *yet?*" Patsy's shrill voice filled one of his ears and the whispered giggles of a barfly filled the other. "What am I paying you for?"

Snake Eyes winced as he shifted his battered body to better accommodate the not-so-slight woman on his lap. Leaping out the brat's window probably hadn't been such a good idea. He had the battle scars and the dog bites to prove it. Not to mention the walloping he'd gotten from the brat. But the cops were coming and the front door was covered with a jillion damned locks and so what the hell was he supposta do?

He ducked his head to keep the drunk that was slobbering on the back of his neck from hearing. "I tried to do the job tonight, but she came home an hour early and caught me by surprise." He lowered his voice to a whisper. "The cops showed up, so I had to get out of there."

"You id-i-ot!" Patsy fired the three separate syllables as if they were bullets in a semi-automatic. "Now she knows you're in Keyhole! Now the cops know you're in Keyhole!" Snake Eyes could practically hear her face turning red and the phone felt suddenly hot. "This is twice, now, that you've dropped the ball! This is a simple job! Just do it!"

Snake Eyes sucked his cigarette down to the butt and clouds of thick smoke belched from nostrils. "I have to lay low for a few days. Give things a chance to cool down around here.''

''You have until the end of the week. Then I want results.''

Hands shaking, Snake Eyes slammed down first the phone, and then a shot of whiskey with a beer chase. That witch reminded him just a little too much of his mother. When he got a hold of her, he was gonna do to her what he shoulda done to his mother a long, long time ago.

And it would feel good.

''Mom? I had to go potty and the lights were on down here and I— Oh! Hey, Mom! Wyatt's here!''

''Hey, Sport-o!''

As if he couldn't believe his good fortune, Alex ground his fists into his eyes, then peered again at Wyatt. ''Look, Mom! It's him! See? I told you he'd come!'' Alex shuffled over to Wyatt and standing next to his chair, leaned against his arm. ''Wyatt, are you here to read us a story?''

''Is your brother awake?''

''Yeah. He's up in the bathroom now.''

''Okay, then. You go hop back up in bed. I've got two new books we can read, if it's okay with your mama.''

Annie nodded, loving the exuberant expression on her son's small face. ''It's okay. I'm just going to straighten up down here. I'll be up in a few minutes to kiss you guys good-night.''

''All of us?'' Wyatt asked.

Alex looked at his mother with interest.

''Yes, all of you.''

''Promise?'' Wyatt gave his brow a rakish waggle.

''Promise.'' Laughing at his comical expression, Annie waved them off and set to putting their coffee cups and plates in the dishwasher. As the guys moved from the kitchen and through the living room, she could hear Alex chattering away at Wyatt, and the sounds of Wyatt locking the front door.

"Sean Mercury came over to borrow some eggs for his mom after you left tonight. He says you're probably gonna marry our mom pretty soon, cuz you guys been kissin'."

Annie froze, listening for Wyatt's response.

"And how does this Sean kid know I kissed your mama?"

"I told him."

"That so?"

"Yep."

"So. When do you suppose Sean thinks I ought to ask her?"

"Pretty soon. You could do it right now, if you want to."

"I thought I was supposed to read you a story now."

"Oh. Yeah. Well, then, you can ask her tomorrow."

"You'd like that?"

"Sure! Then you'd be our dad. We never had a dad before."

"You had a dad, kiddo. He just had to go to heaven a little bit earlier than he'd planned. But he's still your dad."

The boy's voice grew faint as he reached the top of the stairs and moved down the hall. "Well, then he can be our heaven dad, and you can be our real-life dad."

"You have it all worked out, huh?"

"Yep."

Blinking back the tears, Annie stretched plastic wrap over the pan of brownies, put it in the refrigerator, then wiped down the counter tops. More than anything, she wanted her children to know the security of a father's special brand of love. But not if it meant uprooting their life and making everyone unhappy in the process.

She was needed here in Keyhole. She had a mother to look after. Friends. Family. History. There was a business to run. A business that had been in the Summers family for generations.

Plus, the big city did not hold the allure it used to, when she was a kid. Unless she pictured that city as Wyatt's home. Then—she sighed and stared unseeing at her blurry reflection in the window—the thought of living in the city took on a whole new excitement.

But still. It wasn't just herself anymore. She had her boys to consider. MaryPat. Brynn. What was left of Carl's family.

Oh. Confusion made her head ache. She wadded up a pile of kitchen towels and cleaning rags and, moving to the service porch, started a load of laundry. Just last week her life had seemed so uncomplicated. Now everything was upside down. She had the strangest feeling that terminally snoopy Sean Mercury might just be right. What if Wyatt did indeed want to pick up where they left off so many years ago and marry her? Build a family with her? What then?

She pulled a load of whites out of the dryer and began to fold them on the top of the chest freezer, her mind clicking away like the keys on a computer.

Damn him.

She rolled pairs of socks together and fired them into a laundry basket. Damn him for waltzing back into her life and making her vulnerable all over again. It had taken her so long to recover from all the loss she'd suffered, and now, thanks to him, another loss hovered on the horizon.

If she decided to follow him, she lost her family.

If she sent him away, she lost her heart.

Laundry basket propped on her hip, Annie moved down the hall to her son's room. The deafening silence puzzled her. She'd have thought that the sounds of space monsters on the loose would have been rattling the rafters by now. She set the basket on a marble-topped washstand and stepping to the doorway stopped and took in the scene before her.

Wyatt, far too long and lanky for Noah's kiddie bed, was leaning back against the headboard, his head cocked at an angle that would require a chiropractic team first thing in the morning. One leg was propped on the floor, the other on the footboard. His mouth hung slack and he snored ever so slightly. Her sons, one tucked under each of his arms, were also in dreamland, their heads rising and falling with his chest as he breathed. The book they'd been reading lay cockeyed on Wyatt's stomach.

Chopper was curled at the end of the bed, against Wyatt's leg.

Annie gripped the door frame and, as she gazed at the poignant scene before her, was filled with a strange combination of peace and melancholy. In just a few short days he would be leaving for Liza's wedding in Prosperino. After that, he might come back to check up on Emily, but surely, he couldn't stay. Just like her, he had a business to run. Friends. Family. A life of his own. A life she knew nothing about.

Swallowing back the myriad feelings that she was too tired at—she glanced at the Mickey clock on the nightstand—3:00 a.m. to sort out, Annie padded across the room. As promised, she bent and kissed all three of them on the forehead. Gently, she lifted the book and set it aside, then straightened the covers to better keep them all warm.

Wyatt shifted in his sleep, not disturbing the boys in the least as they all rolled over, a tangle of arms and legs. Chopper stood, circled twice, and fell back to the bed. Hand over her mouth, Annie stood a while longer, watching and loving so hard, it hurt.

Over the next three days, Wyatt spent all of Emily's free time together with her at MaryPat's house. Sometimes, he could coax her out for a walk, or over to Annie's place, but emotionally, she was a bundle of nerves, starting at every loud noise and having trouble sleeping because of the nightmares. The only place she felt truly safe was at the café, she claimed. Wyatt wanted her to take some time off and get some rest, but Emily said that at least at work she didn't have time to dwell on the memory of the second attack.

Again, she'd been lucky and only suffered minor cuts and bruises as she'd scuffled with the man who she was positive had followed her to Keyhole from Prosperino. He, on the other hand, had been brutalized by her phone, a potted plant, a lawn chair and the business end of a golf umbrella.

Wyatt couldn't begin to find the words to describe the pride he felt in Emily. She was a scrapper. Even so, she needed protection.

Each day, after he'd seen Emily safely to work for her morning shift—and exacted promises from Roy, Geraldine and Helen that they wouldn't let her out of their sight until he could take her back to MaryPat's—Wyatt would wander next door and help Annie out at the shop.

In a very short amount of time he'd learned a great deal about antiques and, though his methods were slightly unorthodox, his sales record was impressive. Of course, being the type-A personality that he was, there was a friendly, not-so-subtle sales competition between him and Annie. And between him and MaryPat, when she would come in for her part-time shifts. And between him and Brynn when she would pop in to relieve Annie for lunch.

That Thursday evening, Brynn dropped by as Wyatt, Annie and MaryPat tallied up their sales receipts. The boys shot Matchbox cars under their mother's desk while the adults worked. It was a drizzly spring day there in the little town of Keyhole and mist clung to the mountain tops and drifted between the trees. It was so incredibly beautiful here. As Wyatt stared out the window in Annie's office, he could understand so perfectly now why Joe had such blissful memories about his childhood years here in Wyoming. Though it was growing dark outside, inside Annie's cluttered office, it was bright and cheerful and cozy warm.

Wyatt shifted his gaze from the window to Annie's desktop, where he squinted at the tidy columns in her accounting book. Fingers flying over the ten key, she tallied their individual daily totals.

"I'm winning," Wyatt bragged. "Brynn, I hate to say this, but I embarrassed you all over the place today."

"Oh, no you didn't!"

"Yes indeedy." He pointed to his column. "Read 'em and weep, sister."

"Yeah, you think you're pretty tough, don't you? Well, after I sold that butter churn during lunch hour today," Brynn boasted, "I went out and sold the old Cooper farm to a couple from L.A. It's been on the market for *five* years!"

"Butter churn? Big deal. And the Cooper farm doesn't count." Wyatt waved a dismissive hand. "I sold an armoire and a dresser during lunch and still had time to eat sandwiches with Emma and the boys."

A small smile played at Annie's lips as she listened to his silly banter with her mother and sister.

"I ate a whole one," Noah bragged.

"So did I," Alex put in.

"You didn't eat the crust," Noah accused.

"Did too!"

"Did not!"

"Did too!"

"Boys, please. I'm trying to point out that I kicked your Aunt Brynn's butt today."

"You did?" Noah asked, jaw slack.

"Where was I?" Alex wondered aloud.

Brynn planted her hands on her hips. "Did I mention that I also sold a hundred-year-old soup tureen?"

"Ooooo. I'm scared."

Brynn blew a raspberry at him.

"Listen, sonny," MaryPat warbled, "you sell a puny armoire and a dresser and you think that makes you somebody. Well, I'll have you know I sold two—count 'em, two—of those ugly Madrilla vases."

Wyatt quirked a brow. "You did? Which ones?"

"That hideous yellow one with the pink and orange flowers and the green sort of art deco thing with the garish burros."

"Get outta here! You sold those?"

"Before 9:00 a.m." MaryPat huffed on her nails, then burnished them on her vest. "So, I ask you, who's number one?"

"You are. I'm definitely not worthy."

Brynn and MaryPat hooted as he bowed down.

"Actually," Annie said, "Wyatt comes in first with nearly three thousand dollars—"

Wyatt jumped up and jammed an imaginary basketball through an imaginary hoop. "He shoots, he scores!" His silly antics got the boys all riled up and they danced about at his feet, jabbering and laughing and pawing at his clothes.

"I wanna play basketball," Noah screamed.

"Let's play!" Alex squealed.

Annie had to raise her voice to be heard above the hub-bub. "I came in with nearly fifteen hundred. Mom, you did a little over five hundred, and, Brynn, you did two fifty. All in all, a blockbuster day. Thank you very much, you guys."

"Yeah, well, tomorrow I'm gonna be the queen butt-kicker, buddy," Brynn blustered at Wyatt.

"Oh, no, you're not." Wyatt picked up the boys and began to gallop around the office.

"And why may I ask not?"

Wyatt stopped and let Noah slide to the floor. "Because I have to go back to California tomorrow morning."

At this announcement the room went suddenly silent. Wyatt and Annie exchanged glances, then regarded the be-wildered faces of the rest of her family with trepidation.

"You're leavin'?" Alex's voice quavered as he leaned back in Wyatt's arms and looked into his face.

"But you just got here," Noah protested from where he clung to Wyatt's legs.

Brynn and MaryPat remained quiet but were obviously curious.

"I have to go to my cousin's wedding."

"Do you hafta?"

"I'm afraid so, buddy." Wyatt slowly lowered Alex to stand beside his brother.

Noah's eyes filled with tears. "But you can't go away. You kissed my mom."

"And you still have to ask her to marry you." Doing his best to remain stoic, Alex too, battled the tears. "Re-member?"

Brynn and MaryPat looked at each other with wide-eyed expressions and Annie's hands flew to her face.

Another horrible, awkward moment of silence passed. Then the boys began to cry.

"I should probably get going." Brynn reached for her purse and MaryPat, clearly sensing the tension, followed suit.

"Yes, me too. I'm going to have dinner at the café and then take Em home with me. Care to join me, Brynn?"

"Love to."

Within the moments it took to share a flurry of kisses and knowing looks, they were gone, leaving Wyatt and Annie to deal with the boys' disappointment.

"You don't have to go, do ya?"

"Tell 'em you don't want to. Tell 'em you want to stay here. With us."

Wyatt hunkered down, in order to be at eye-level with the boys. "That does sound really tempting, partner, but she's kinda countin' on me."

"But so are we." They moved into the circle of his embrace and, draping their skinny little arms over his shoulders, leaned against his sides.

Wyatt shot Annie a helpless glance which she answered in kind. The look of pure sorrow on their innocent faces tugged at his heartstrings and brought back all kinds of memories of abandonment. By the death grips they had on his shirt, Wyatt could feel the strong attachment they'd formed for him. Though he was not their father, somehow—in the accelerated five-year-old time and space continuum—he'd become a surrogate of sorts. A kind of uncle-daddy-buddy guy. And, as such, he knew he couldn't simply waltz off to Liza's wedding without somehow making the boys feel a little better.

But how?

He racked his brain for answers, but none were forthcoming. "I'm going to come back, just as soon as the wedding is over. I'll only be gone for the weekend. I'll be back Sunday afternoon and we can play and I can read you bed-time stories.''

By the expressions on their faces, Wyatt could see that this wasn't cutting it.

''Why don't we come with you?'' Noah suggested.

''Yeah. That way you won't have time to miss us.''

Mind churning with the possibilities, Wyatt looked back and forth between the two boys. ''You know,'' he mused aloud, ''that's not a half-bad idea.''

''Oh, no. I don't think—'' Hands up, Annie took a step back and shook her head.

''But why not? There's plenty of room at the house and Liza would be thrilled. Trust me on this, if I show up with a date, *everyone* will be thrilled.''

''Who said anything about a date?'' The tiniest trace of a smile crinkled at the corners of her eyes.

Sensing that there might be a chance, Wyatt pressed on. ''Come on, Mom,'' he cajoled, looking up at her with the same puppy-dog expression the boys wore, ''give a guy a break. I don't want to be the only goofball there without a date.''

Alex sniffed.

Noah rubbed his eyes and a tentative smile flirted with his lips.

''He doesn't want to be a goofball, Mom.''

''Yeah, Mom. Without you, he'll seem stupid.''

Alex knew he wasn't supposed to say the word stupid, but obviously felt this situation called for strong language.

Not to be outdone, Noah tossed out another forbidden term. ''He'd be an idiot, Mom.''

''Boys…'' She raised a censorious brow.

Wyatt patted his chest. ''My treat.''

''It's not the money, Wyatt.''

"Then what?"

"I just don't know about..."

"About what?"

"You know. Meredith."

"Who's Meredith?"

"Meredith is my mom," Wyatt explained to Noah and then glanced back at Annie. "Well, considering her henchman is here in Keyhole, we'd probably be safer in Prosperino. Besides, there will be a ton of kids there. And a ton of security."

"What about Emily?"

"Your mom and sister and Roy and Geraldine and Helen and Toby and the entire Keyhole police force will all be looking out for her."

"But what about the store?"

"Ask Brynn or MaryPat to sub for you on Saturday. If they can't, close it."

"But what about Chopper?"

At the sound of his name, Chopper's tail thumped on the floor.

"He stays here. In a kennel. Also, my treat."

"But—"

"C'mon, Annie, quit grasping for excuses. When was the last time you got out of town and had some fun? When was the last time you took the boys anywhere?" He could sense that she was weakening. "You know it's already warm there. Last weekend the temperature hit the high seventies. We could take the boys to see the ocean."

"The ocean?" Noah bobbed excitedly.

"We never been to the ocean," Alex told him.

Wyatt thrust out his lower lip. "Annie, they've never been to the ocean."

"Yeah, Mom."

She sighed, opened her mouth to speak, but then closed it.

"Everyone would be really happy to see you again." Wyatt played his trump card. "And it would really mean a lot to me and the boys if you would say yes."

The boys turned in his arms and the three of them looked up at her with pleading eyes.

Ten

"**O**h, all right." Annie moved to her desk and dropped into her seat. "I know when I've been outvoted."

The boys gaped at her for a moment before the facts registered.

"We get to go?"

Annie nodded.

The celebration was deafening. The boys jumped and shouted and hugged Wyatt, and then their mom, and then each other.

"I'm gonna go pack!" Alex ran to the play area and began to gather an armload of toys. Noah joined him and soon they had enough stuff to fill all of the luggage their mother owned.

Annie couldn't help but smile. Wyatt was right. She hadn't taken time to go on a vacation in far too long. In fact, the only place she'd ever taken them was on a car trip to visit Judith and her family in Iowa for Christmas when they were three. She doubted they even remembered.

A tiny thrill began to burn in her belly and spread up her spine, sending gooseflesh in all directions. She was going back to Prosperino with Wyatt. She hadn't been there since before her father died. The idea of walking barefoot along the surf with Wyatt and watching her children frolic in the waves of the Pacific Ocean was a dream come true. A dream that she hadn't dared, until this very minute, to admit that she'd even harbored.

The boys' wild excitement was contagious.

Annie looked up into Wyatt's broad smile and began to tingle with excitement all over again. "How are we going to get plane tickets at this late date?"

"I'll call my travel agent in the morning. If you can't get on my flight, we'll take another route or something. Don't worry, it'll all work out." He took her hand and drew her to stand against his body, then locked her there with his arms. "Before we can go there's something you have to do for me."

"What?"

"I need you to add five hundred dollars to my earnings today."

Annie reared back and stared up at him. "Five hundred dollars? Why?"

"Because I'm buying the painting you did of that basket of grapes." He gestured to a lovely sepia tone and dark eggplant-colored painting Annie had done years ago, to remind her of her life in Prosperino. And of Wyatt.

"You're buying that picture? Why?"

"Liza and Nick need something very special to commemorate the beginning of their marriage and this painting is just the thing. It's part Prosperino and part Wyoming, and part you."

Annie could see the tears rise in her eyes, sparkling, re-
fracting light. Feeling foolish, she blinked them away.
Wyatt never ceased to amaze her with his thoughtful ways.
Arms circled securely around his waist, she stood on tiptoe
and he lowered his mouth to hers in a tender, gentle kiss
that had her suddenly weak in the knees.

Then and there, she made up her mind to worry about
the future later. For now, she—like her excitedly thrashing
sons were doing at the moment—was going to enjoy whatever came her way and deal with separation anxiety when
it eventually happened.

And it would happen.

She could see no happy way around that.

Bracelets jangling, Patsy tippity-tapped away on her lap-
top computer. Her tongue peeked out of the corner of her
mouth as she pursed her ruby lips in concentration. Occa-
sionally she stopped to sip on her latte and listen to the
hum of activity beyond her bedroom door.

Dullsville, baby. Yet another wretchedly tedious pre-
wedding party to endure. All those trying conversations
with the banal Colton family. All those phony sentiments,
all those tiring smiles. She got exhausted just thinking
about it. Didn't these people have anything better to do with
their time than gush on about forever and happy-ever-after,
and loving, honoring, obeying, worshiping each other? It
was sickening.

Downstairs, in the elegant courtyard, the preparations
were in full swing for Saturday's wedding. Florists bustled
about, delicious smells wafted from the kitchen, and trucks
arrived by the dozens with tables and chairs and linens and
large white lawn tents.

Knowing that she was neither wanted nor needed, which
was more than fine with her, Patsy decided the time was

right to do a little office work. To get the proverbial ball
rolling on Jackson's murder rap. Ahh. The thought of Jackson laboring over license plates in the state pen spurred her
to heretofore unrealized cerebral heights and as she typed,
she was summarily impressed with her own brilliance.

Dear Detective Law:
I am a concerned citizen wanting to make you aware
of a situation I have inadvertently discovered just recently. In regards to the attempts on Joe Colton's life,
please check Grimble's Insurance Company of L.A.
policy 1762529 and lawsuit titled: Amalgamated Industries vs. Jones.
For reasons of my own safety, you'll understand why
I wish to remain,
Anonymous

Patsy reread her missive several times before deciding it
was deliciously perfect. After the cops checked out this
lead, they'd have to turn a suspicious eye to Jackson. Poor
baby. Never should have messed with Auntie Meredith. She
tapped the print button on her computer, and as she sat
back to wait, the cell phone rang.

She snatched it up and jerked an earring off her ear.
"What now?"

It was clear from the background noises that Snake Eyes
had been biding his time in a bar.

"I'm just callin' to tell ya that I didn't do it yet. She got
more people watchin' her than a circus act. She moved in
with some ugly old goat, and the cops are crawlin' around
there like termites, I tell ya."

Patsy rolled her eyes. "Silas, Silas, Silas." She took
pleasure in using the name she knew he hated. Leaning
back in her chair, she studied her flawless manicure and

toyed with him. "You were supposed to have been done with this job by now. Isn't that what we agreed upon when I sent you more money?"

Snake Eyes was silent for so long, Patsy feared he may have dropped off to sleep.

"Silas!" she shouted.

"Yes," he growled back.

"Okay then. When do you plan on doing your job?"

"Her brother's been stickin' to her like glue."

"Her brother?" Patsy froze. She'd thought everyone was here for the wedding. What brother? She racked her brain. There were a jillion damned Colton foster kids running around the countryside and they were multiplying like rabbits.

"What's his name?"

"Wally or Whippet, or something."

"Wyatt?" She tried to swallow, but couldn't. That's right. Wyatt had left a few days ago on some kind of a secretive business trip. Now, she knew the "business" had been in Keyhole, with Emily. Her heart stopped beating for an alarming moment.

Could this mean that Wyatt was onto her?

Her mind raced. How would he have known that Emily was holed up in Keyhole? Unless... Her blood ran cold. Had someone overheard one of her phone conversations with Snake Eyes? Had Emily kept in contact with the family, unbeknownst to her? Had she, Patsy, somehow messed up and left a clue behind?

Tiny beads of sweat formed on her upper lip and she felt simultaneously hot and cold and quite suddenly nauseated. How many people suspected that she might be behind Emily's murder attempt? Or Joe's, for that matter?

Patsy fumbled for her cigarettes and, after breaking a

record number of matches, finally got one lit and took a deep calming drag. She had to stay cool.

She'd always been the cool one. She could be cool now. Cool, cool, cool.

She carried the phone with her over to her private liquor stash. Using silver tongs, she loaded a crystal tumbler with ice and splashed in a generous amount of vodka. She held the glass first to her molten cheeks, then, to her lips. The fiery liquid burned a wicked trail down her throat and set her empty stomach aflame. As she listened to Snake Eyes blather on incoherently, her brain began to fuzz, and some of her jangled nerves began to gel once again.

She cradled the rim of her glass against her lower lip.

No, no, no.

She was fine. Once she set the wheels in motion, nobody would be able to pin this whole mess on her. But she'd have to hurry. She'd mail the message she'd just typed to Thad-odious Law this very afternoon. That, coupled with the other plans she had for Jackson... Well, it wouldn't matter that Silas A. Pike was a blithering idiot. She would be in the clear, and Emily would be dead. Maybe Joe, too.

The burning sensation in her stomach settled down to a teensy pile of glowing embers. Umm, yeah. She'd be okay. If she just kept her wits about her. She was always okay, as long as she stayed steely calm.

She tapped her ash into a heavy crystal ashtray. "So Wyatt has been visiting with our Emily."

"Yeah. Anyway, he's leavin' for some weddin' tomorrow and he's taking his friends with him, so I'll take care of business then."

"Wyatt is coming back here to Prosperino, and bringing friends?"

"Uh-g huh." He snorted and spat. "Should be there by now. And the brat will be stayin' behind with that old broad, but that should be no problem-o. If the old lady gets in the way, I'll just get ridda her, too.''

''Ah, lucky me. A two-for-one sale. Listen, you dolt, just do the job we agreed upon. I don't pay by the pound!'' Molars grinding, Patsy plunged a hand through her hair. ''At this rate, just taking care of the one problem should take the rest of your life.''

''Saturday night. It'll all be over by tomorrow night.''

''It had better be. If you ever want to see the rest of your paycheck.''

''Hey. Speakin' of my paycheck—''

''No! Not another cent until the girl is history.'' She slapped her phone off and marched back to her computer.

After she slipped on a pair of latex gloves, she folded the letter and stuffed it into an envelope. She used her left hand to scrawl the address to Thad Law's office. Then she affixed a stamp and slipped the letter into her purse.

Now off to town to post this little gem.

This was the beginning of the arrogant Jackson Colton's demise. A tiny smile clung to the edges of her mouth.

Only the beginning.

Early that Friday afternoon, Wyatt and Annie and the boys landed in San Francisco. They rented a car and took the scenic route up the coast and over to Prosperino. On the way, of course, they had to stop and buy kites, run on the surf, dig deep, pointless holes in the beach, search for seashells, and eat blackened hot dogs and marshmallows with a healthy dash of sand sprinkled in.

Smelling like campfire smoke and covered from head to toe with sand and ocean water and heaven only knew what, they loaded their impromptu picnic back into the trunk of the car and enjoyed the back roads that wound through the beautiful California wine country to the Hacienda de Alegría.

The day was warm and cloudless and, while the boys slept in the backseat, Annie got a chance to spend uninterrupted time talking with Wyatt.

"I'm nervous." She smoothed the wisps that escaped from her thickly corded French braid.

"Why?"

"What if it's supposed to be a private, intimate, family-only gathering?"

"So?"

Annie huffed. "You don't understand."

"I do more than you think. But, Annie, if I love you, they'll love you."

She stilled at his use of the word *love*. He couldn't mean that he *loved* her, loved her. He probably only loved her euphemistically speaking. In the loosest, most old-girlfriend sense of the word. Certainly not the undying variety of love she'd harbored for him all these years.

As if sensing her anxiety, he took her hand in his and pulled her to sit next to him in the seat. Just like the old days.

Slowly, her eyes traveled to his and they held for an intense moment before he had to turn back to the road.

Her heart turned over. He was such a wonderful man. How had she ever had the strength to go on without him and marry Carl? She'd been a different person back then. So young. Headstrong. Like Brynn. Life had been so black and white. Now life wasn't so simple. There were infinitesimal shades of gray everywhere. In everything. Nothing was clear to her anymore.

Except the unfortunate fact that she still loved Wyatt. Maybe more than ever. He was older, wiser, more mature.

A real man. Someone she could count on. The way she used to count on her father.

As the car traversed the miles, her mind traveled back to her own wedding day. When she'd married Carl, she'd been dead inside, with the exception of the place in her heart that still bled for Wyatt. But Carl hadn't seemed to notice. Since grade school he'd been eager to claim Annie for his own, and their eventual marriage had seemed inevitable to everyone in Keyhole, except Annie.

For Annie, it signified a way to forget about Wyatt.

She figured if she stuffed her feelings way down inside, perhaps she could forget about Wyatt, and maybe, in the process, fall in love with her husband. Unfortunately, Carl's myriad problems—many of which had not become evident until after the wedding—had made it easy to withdraw even further. So, forcing herself not to feel was the only way she'd been able to survive until the boys' birth had coaxed her to life once more.

Knowing that she'd been staring at Wyatt's face for a long while, Annie turned her focus to the road and worried her lower lip with her teeth.

When he went back to his life in Washington, D.C. again, how would she cope with this new emptiness she was sure to feel in her heart? It had been easy to retreat inside herself back when she was responsible for only herself. But now she had two little boys who wouldn't let her die to the pain. She couldn't even bear to think about their pain at Wyatt's departure. Surely their anguish would only compound hers.

Like a divining rod to water, her gaze steered back to Wyatt. She studied the sensitive curve of Wyatt's mouth, the smile lines at his eyes, the dent that she'd kissed so many times as a girl, the muscle that would sometimes

work in his jaw when he was worried. Or feeling possessive.

He was as familiar to her as her own heartbeat. Yet in
many ways, he was different altogether than the boy she'd
once known.

Instinctively, she knew their breakup had been hard on
Wyatt. Workaholism had been his coping skill of choice.
By proving to the world that he was somebody, he could
forget that he had nobody. Annie shifted her gaze past
Wyatt to the seemingly endless Pacific Ocean.

It couldn't have been easy for him to be the one to make
the first move, and re-establish contact after all these years.
Then again, for him to admit that he'd been wrong about
her need to be there for her father. And yet, he had. And
he'd done it with such grace. Such maturity.

She glanced into the backseat at the cherubic faces of
her slumbering sons. The fact that he'd been so kind, so
loving to her little boys, children she'd borne with another
man, was simply additional testament to his character.

And now, he'd put his career on hold in consideration
for his sister's safety...Annie swallowed against the lump
that was forming in her throat.

Whether he knew it or not, he'd become a man Joe Colton could be proud to call son.

When they pulled onto the Hacienda de Alegria's long,
tree-lined drive, Annie was again astounded at the massive
estate that spoke of a family imbued with such privilege.
Such power. It was almost chilling, in a way that she'd
been too naive to notice back when she was a girl. Then
again, it probably had everything to do with what she knew
about Patsy Portman and nothing to do with the imposing
structures laid out so grandly before her.

She hadn't been here since her college days and Annie

drank in the awesome sights. Memories of happier times came flooding back. She glanced back at the boys, who were awake now and staring agog, out their windows. She shifted her gaze to Wyatt and they shared a smile.

Rolling hills surrounded the multi-level house—nay, mansion. Stucco and brick pillars flanked the road where the line of trees ended and allowed access to the grand estate through a set of ornate iron gates. Then, drawing closer to the house, a stucco wall, ornamented by a series of massive Mediterranean-style arches gave the whole affair the secluded feel of a fortress in the waning afternoon light. Impenetrable. Strong. Safe.

Annie knew the feeling was only an illusion.

Exactly like the feeling in her own hometown now. For as long as Emily's attacker was there, Keyhole was no safer than Prosperino.

Beyond the seemingly endless fields, the mountains were a light plum-colored backdrop. Sunlight slanted through the grove of trees that sheltered the house, casting an ethereal golden glow over the terra cotta roof. Overhead, the sky's cloudless blue was deepening, preparing to showcase the stars that would be visible all too soon.

Annie couldn't imagine a finer place in all of God's heaven, it was so magical. Just like something out of a Maxfield Parrish painting.

As Wyatt had predicted, they were met at the Prosperino ranch with open arms by Rand and Lucy and assorted other Colton family members, foster and otherwise. Within minutes, Liza heard the commotion and rushed from her last-minute meeting with the wedding planner to hug Wyatt and greet the infamous Annie. Ever since they'd heard that Wyatt was bringing an old flame, the family—chiefly Lucy—had been abuzz with speculation.

When they'd all been roundly kissed and hugged, Liza

grasped Annie's hand in her own. "Annie, though I never got to meet you while you and Wyatt were in college, I have heard so much about you over the years. I'm honored that you would come to my wedding."

"The honor is all mine," Annie murmured.

To the boys, Liza said, "Hey, guys, did you pack your swimsuits?"

Shy, they could only nod, but their expressions held vast interest.

"Great. Your bags are being delivered to your suite now, right next to Wyatt's. He and I will show you the way. If your mom says it's okay, you can go put your suits on and swim in the pool out back."

Annie smiled. "It sounds wonderful."

Together, they all moved through the grand foyer and toward the large courtyard garden that sat in the very center of the house. The sky itself acted as the ceiling allowing sunlight to stream in and plants to flourish. A stunning fountain burbled at one end of the yard, and before it, a smallish, gazebo-like tent, draped with yards of mosquito netting had been erected and under that, an altar.

"This is where Nick and I will say our vows tomorrow afternoon," Liza explained as they all stopped and gazed and the lush atrium-style courtyard. "It's going to be a small wedding, friends and family only for the ceremony."

Annie sent Wyatt a narrow gaze.

He winked and rubbed the small of her back, and suddenly, Annie felt included. Especially since Liza was smiling so happily, lost in her little dream world, moving through the garden, envisioning her wedding.

"After the ceremony, the reception will include about two to three hundred more guests, and be held in the great hall that faces the south hillside garden and lake. We are going to open up that wall of glass doors that lead to the patio, to sort of bring the outside in. If you get a chance later on, you should go see it. The designers have outdone themselves.''

She continued to chatter, as she led them out of the court-yard and off toward Wyatt's suite.

''I just hope the weather is gorgeous, just like this, to-morrow,'' Liza mused. ''Although, we do have a ton of tents set up. There will be a sit-down dinner and after that, dancing until the wee hours, and of course, Uncle Joe is cracking open some of his private reserve, so the toasting should go on forever.'' She laughed. ''Oh, I'm so excited. I've looked forward to this moment for so long, I can't even begin to tell you.''

Wyatt glanced at Annie and in that instant, she knew he was thinking about their own missed opportunity. And her wedding to Carl. And the improbable chance that they might have their own wedding in the future, and all nature of wonderings. She knew, because she was having the exact same thoughts.

They wended their way through the opulent interior of the house, and off toward the wing where they'd be staying. Once again, Annie was reminded of the few times she'd come here to visit, back when she was a student. Wyatt's girl.

As they passed Joe's masculine study, Annie peeked in, remembering the rich smell of freshly polished wood and cigar smoke, and the hours spent there, studying with Wyatt. Studying Wyatt. A tiny smile twitched. She was looking forward to seeing Joe once again.

Meredith, however, was a different story.

Her gaze shifted to her sons. What with the beefed-up security, Annie knew that they were probably safer here in Prosperino than in Keyhole with the actual attacker. Even so, this Meredith person was disturbed. Hopefully, she'd spend most of her time out of the way and off doing her own thing, as she was now.

Annie nudged Wyatt, and being that he'd always been able to read her mind, he glanced around and asked, "Liza, where is Meredith?"

"She was holed up in her room all morning, and then she went for a drive this afternoon. Haven't really seen her all day. But I know Joe is eager to see you both. He's in the wine cellar and should be back any minute."

It was obvious that Liza was acting as hostess for her uncle in her aunt's absence. Liza's warm expression included Annie and made her feel welcome and at home. And for that, Annie was grateful.

"Now, are you hungry?"

Wyatt scratched his stomach and answered for them all. "Yes. We had a picnic on the beach, but that was hours ago."

"Well, good. I'll have something light sent to your rooms and then we're having a giant family dinner at eight, right after the wedding rehearsal. A last supper, so to speak." Liza laughed and took Wyatt by the arm. As they led Annie and the boys to their room, the bride murmured to her cousin in that intimate way that spoke of a long history together. "I'm so glad that you made it back in time for my wedding, cousin."

"I told you I would."

"True, but you've been known to let work interfere with your plans before."

"Those days are over."

"Really?" Liza peeked over her shoulder. "She must be good for you."

"She is."

"Good. She's really lovely, Wyatt."

"I think so too."

"So, do I hear wedding bells?"

"Yes, you do, but I'm afraid they're yours."

Much later that evening, while the children frolicked outdoors, the adults rehearsed Nick and Liza's ceremony with the wedding planner and the minister in the large garden courtyard. There was much laughing and teasing; Joe caught the bouquet and ran, Wyatt picked up Liza and ran, Lucy and Rand grabbed each other at the altar and smooched noisily every chance they got and more than once had to be dragged away and reprimanded.

No one missed Meredith.

After Noah and Alex had worn themselves to a fare-thee-well in the pool and then attended a pizza and movie party with the other Colton-and-friends small fries in the home theatre, Annie put them to bed and joined the rest of the family for the dinner that followed the rehearsal.

Joe was in fine fettle, cracking jokes and making toasts. As she had remembered, he was still every bit as sweet and gentlemanly as he'd been when they first met. He treated her like a long-lost daughter and ribbed Wyatt about locking her up and not letting her go this time.

Wyatt had taken the teasing good-naturedly, but there was nothing offhand about the possessive look in his eyes that had the family whispering and smiling.

During dinner, Meredith put in a brief appearance and, when she had endured as much of the festivities as she could, she excused herself and turned in early. The party went on without her, much the way it usually did. The only person who appeared even remotely troubled by her absence was Joe.

Seeming to notice Joe's sudden melancholy at Meredith's departure, Jackson sprang to his feet and offered yet another ridiculous toast designed to distract.

"Here's to Uncle Joe, foster son, foster brother, foster father, second foster cousin twice removed from Foster Grant!"

Joe grinned and slowly tore his eyes away from the door Meredith had just exited.

Annie couldn't help but feel sorry for Joe. No doubt he was reflecting on his own wedding. On the love he'd lost.

On his vows to stay with Meredith, until death parted them.

Annie shook off the eerie thought. There were plenty of guards on duty. Surely Nick and Liza's wedding would go off without a hitch. Certainly, with all these people around, not to mention the raft of security guards, no one in the Colton family had anything to fear from Meredith.

"May he continue to live long and prosper," Jackson went on. "May we all."

After dinner, Wyatt took Annie for a moonlight walk around the ranch. Hand in hand, they wandered around the property and looked back at the house, lit up and sparkling, a gem at the top of the hill. From where they stood, they could hear voices and laughter mingled with live music.

Liza had hired a small jazz ensemble to perform on the back patio and many of the family's couples had drifted outside to dance under the stars. Wyatt took Annie in his arms and they danced, cheek to cheek.

"Remember when we used to slow dance in the dormitory's cafeteria on Friday nights? Everybody from our five dorms would push back all the tables and turn out the lights and we'd play records till some house mother or somebody would chase us out. Remember that?"

"Um-hmm." A husky laugh burbled from deep in Annie's throat. "I remember the first time you ever asked me to dance."

"You do?"

"Yes. I'd just been asked to dance by the cutest ROTC boy with a buzz cut."

Wyatt snorted.

Annie ignored him. "I said yes, so he turned to lead me to the middle of the dance floor. But before I could get all the way out there with him, you saw me and grabbed me and pulled me off to the middle of the dance floor without even asking. I barely knew you, and—" her laughter rose and Wyatt found himself chuckling "—it took the poor ROTC guy several minutes to realize that he was dancing with both of us."

"So? He didn't have anything to complain about. As I recall, I was a pretty good dancer."

"Then why did I have to carry a box of Band-Aids in my purse every time we went dancing?"

"Blisters from trying to keep up with old Mr. Foot-loose?"

"No. Mashed toes."

Wyatt chuckled. "Am I mashing your toes now?"

"You seem to have outgrown that habit."

"Ah. Good." He nuzzled her neck. "Having fun?" He hoped that he hadn't commandeered her all the way to California only to realize that she was having a terrible time.

"Mmm. Heavenly," she murmured into his shoulder. "Your family is just as lovely as I remembered. Liza and Nick's wedding is going to be so beautiful. I got all choked up at rehearsal tonight when they were saying their vows, and he was looking down into her face and promising to love her until death parted them. It was...very touching."

He hated himself for asking, but he'd been so good for so long and he was dying of curiosity.

"This remind you of your own wedding?"

"No."

"No? Why not?"

"I don't have particularly fond memories of my wedding."

"Oh."

They were silent for a very long time and Wyatt feared that he'd overstepped his bounds. Brought up a painful memory and she probably thought he was prying, which he was, but still...

"Why were the memories of your own wedding so unhappy?"

Annie didn't respond.

Wyatt waited, wondering if he should backpedal. Apologize for asking such an insensitive question. But something made him hold his tongue. He wanted and needed to know.

Annie took a long, deep breath, then seemed to resign herself to the fact that it was time she finally opened up about her life with Carl.

"Well, for one thing," she murmured and stopped moving to the beat of the music and looked down at the ground. Her voice grew soft. "I was not in love with my husband."

Eleven

Annie knew that once she'd confessed this much, Wyatt wouldn't be satisfied until he'd heard the whole story. Unable to meet his piercing gaze, she turned and began to meander toward the house. She knew that Wyatt was staying just a step behind her, giving her the space she needed to formulate what she wanted to say. Trouble was, she'd never let herself dwell on the subject, so the words came hard. She snapped a dead twig off a tree and rolled it between her fingertips as she strolled along.

"Do you ever remember me talking about how I grew up with Carl, back when you and I were in college together?"

"Your late husband, Carl?"

"Mmm."

"Uh...kind of. I guess."

"I didn't talk about him all that much. I had my reasons for not dwelling on him."

"Hey, now, wait a minute. Come to think of it, I vaguely remember you telling me about how some kid named Carl gave you your first kiss. I remember that now, because I remember I hated him."

Annie tilted back her head and let the laughter flow. "I only told you about him because you were bragging about what an experienced kisser you were and I was feeling a little abashed."

"I was no doubt lying. Guys do that stuff, you know."

"Now you tell me. Anyway, yes, he was my first kiss. Sort of. We were in the fourth grade and Carl had been chasing me around the playground all during recess, just as he had for grades one through three, and finally, I just ran out of steam. I let him catch me."

She stopped walking for a moment and gazed up at the fantastic Hacienda de Alegria and marveled at the romantic picture it made against the night sky. To the west, there was a great wash of inky blackness. Void of all light, Annie knew it was the Pacific Ocean, and she could feel the marine breezes as they lifted the hair off her neck, smell the salt in the air and hear the eternal roar of the sea.

Wyatt stood behind her, hands on her shoulders, chin rested lightly on her head. "What'd he do?"

Annie grinned. "I think he went into shock. After years of chasing me, to finally have me in his clutches was so exhilarating. Everybody in Miss Dalberg's fourth-grade class was watching. He knew he had to do something big. A grand gesture, so to speak. So he kissed me on the lips real hard—in fact I thought for a minute he broke my tooth—and announced that someday he was gonna marry me, whether I liked it or not." She heaved a heavy sigh. "And he did."

"I'm sure there was more to it than that."

She lifted and dropped an arm. "Not really. From that day forward, everyone just assumed that I was Carl's girl."

"I didn't."

"I know. But you were different."

"I wasn't from Keyhole."

"And I liked that about you." She smiled and continued to try to paint a verbal picture of the boys' father for Wyatt. "Carl was…he was single-minded, I guess you could say. Proprietary. Not to mention huge, and a bit of a bully." She held up a finger and tilted her head. "Albeit a likeable bully."

"The best kind."

"I didn't have a chance with any of the other boys in Keyhole. They were all scared of Carl when it came to me. And, considering the rather awkward, skinny, shy and geeky-haired stages I passed through as a kid, I guess I was glad for the male attention. Because of Carl, I always had a date to the prom, so to speak."

"How did you ever get away from him long enough to end up at Prosperino State?"

"In my senior year of high school, I told him I was going, and that was that. I think he was in such shock at my sudden display of backbone that he didn't know what to say. But I knew deep in my heart that I had to get away from Keyhole, where I was Carl's girl, and figure out who I really was."

"And sunny California seemed a long way from Carl's influence."

Annie snapped the twig she carried in two and tossed half of it away. Slowly, she turned toward Wyatt and searched his face with her eyes. It was evident that he understood. She only wished that she'd discussed her marriage with him earlier.

"Exactly right. Ever since the fourth grade when I made

the mistake of letting him catch me, he'd had a hold on me." She took a deep breath, then let it hiss. "Anyway, even though I told everyone I was going away to college, nobody, especially Carl, took me seriously. People in Carl's and my families didn't go to college. They thought it was just a phase with me. A passing fancy. Everybody just figured I'd outgrow the idea and realize that my proper place was with Carl. He'd run his daddy's auto parts store and I'd have the babies. But when I got a job at my father's store and started a college fund it raised a few eyebrows. Even so, Carl just figured I'd use the money for our future together."

"That was big of him."

"That's who he was. He always just took it for granted that the shy, awkward, redheaded girl would be overjoyed to be his woman. I wasn't so much an individual as a trophy. Or a status symbol or something. You know, I don't think we ever discussed love back in high school. But, because of my own mom and dad, I knew there had to be more to love than just…I don't know…being there."

"And there was." Wyatt pulled her into his arms and kissed her temple.

"Umm." She nodded and slipped her arms around his waist, loving his gentle touch. "So much more."

"I have a hard time believing you were ever shy."

"I was until I met you. Something about you just made me…I don't know…"

"Mad," Wyatt supplied.

"Yeah." Annie giggled. "With you, I forgot to be shy."

"I'm glad." He turned her around, draped an arm over her shoulder and began to steer her back toward the house. "C'mon. We can finish this discussion in the house. It's getting a little chilly out here. You have goose bumps."

Annie leaned against him as they walked. "You've always given me goose bumps."

"I'm not sure how to take that."

"It's a good thing."

Arm in arm they strolled slowly around to the more secluded front of the house. Light strains of a party still in progress reached them from out back, but here, it was quiet. Just the two of them. They moved through the shadows of the portico and up to the massive front doors that swung silently open, at the lightest touch, into the house. Wall sconces glowed in the foyer and, just beyond, the courtyard, where Nick and Liza would take their vows in a matter of hours, was a fairyland.

Votive candles from the wedding rehearsal still burned in small crystal glasses that lit the pathway to the altar. From above and below, indirect lighting illuminated the gauzy tent and garden's lush plant life. Behind them, the fountain bubbled quietly. It was incredibly beautiful. Annie only wished her own wedding had been half so nice.

Still holding hands, she and Wyatt were drawn slowly, quietly down the flickering path and up to the altar.

"It's so magical here." Annie kept her voice low, so she wouldn't somehow ruin the holy feel of this place.

"The perfect place for a wedding." Wyatt nodded in agreement and turned to face her.

Annie could fairly hear the wedding march echoing throughout the courtyard. Wyatt would look fantastic in a tuxedo, she was sure. And she'd always wanted a real wedding dress. Florist flowers. A professional photographer.

"I got married in Carl's parents' backyard," Annie murmured, fingering the ribbons of the altar's fabulous bouquet. "It was a casual affair with one of Judith's cast-off, ivory prom dresses and Mama's garden flowers. Daddy's brother, Uncle George, took pictures with his Instamatic.

Afterward, we threw a barbecue for all of our friends and family and Carl's hunting and fishing buddies. His idea.''

"I take it this was not your idea of a wedding reception." Wyatt's tone was dry.

"Hardly. But I really didn't care." She shrugged. "I didn't care about anything."

"Then why did you marry him?"

"I thought I could learn to love him. We'd been together since we were babies in preschool." Annie's gaze traveled to the candles that still flickered on the table in front of the altar. "Daddy really wanted to know that I'd be taken care of after he was gone, and he knew his time was short. He knew Judith was married and Brynn was a go-getter who could take care of herself, but for some reason, he worried about me. I was always sort of his favorite."

"I can see why," Wyatt whispered.

Annie grabbed his hands and lightly, playfully, rocked him back and forth. "You're prejudiced."

"No. I just have good taste in women."

She snuggled closer, entwining their arms between them, still remembering. "Daddy thought it was a good idea that I marry Carl, because Carl was basically a good kid. Carl thought it was a good idea that I marry Carl." Her laughter held a brittle edge. "Everyone thought it was a good idea that I marry Carl." She tried to swallow. "Except me."

"Annie." Wyatt tilted her chin and looked deep into her eyes and whispered. "Why on earth did you go through with it?"

"Tons of reasons." Tears pooled at her lower lashes. She blinked and one, and then another, began to roll down her cheeks. "I married him because I felt sorry for myself. For him. For you. I married him because I knew I had to let go of you once and for all. I had to sever that connection so that you could realize your dreams. A wife—and maybe kids—would only hold you back, and I knew how important proving yourself to the world was to you.''

When Wyatt started to protest, she held a finger to his lips. ''That was only part of it. I married him because I had to stay near my family. They needed me. I saw no other way out.''

''So you married a man you didn't love.''

''I never said it was smart.''

Wyatt was silent for what seemed to Annie like an eternity. She could see his mind working, backtracking, trying to figure out exactly where they'd gone wrong. The look in his eyes was tortured, as if he were battling age-old demons.

''I'm so sorry, Wyatt,'' she whispered, feeling the need to apologize for her own part in their breakup. ''My unhappy marriage wasn't your fault. I made my own decisions. And something wonderful came of it in spite of everything. You got your career—''

Wyatt winced.

Reaching up, she smoothed the furrow between his brows with her fingertips and bestowed him with a watery smile. ''—and I got two beautiful little boys.''

''And the tough role of a single parent with a full-time job.''

''That's life, Wyatt. That could have happened to you and me.''

Slowly, Wyatt cupped her face in his hands and traced the tear streaks on her cheeks with his thumbs. ''Rand told me that Carl had died, but not until months after it happened. He'd heard it from someone in the McGrath family, who heard it from someone else. No one knew any details, so I was afraid to call.''

''It's all right. I understand.'' Annie closed her eyes. ''It was a boating accident, right after the boys were born. He and two fishing buddies drowned in Willanoon Lake, about fifty miles south of Keyhole. They'd all been drinking and horsing around and they collided at top speed with a floating dock. Carl drank a lot. Especially after we had the kids. I think he was afraid of the responsibility of twins.''

A telltale muscle jumped in Wyatt's jaw. ''My old man used to drink and then take his troubles out on my mom.''

Annie blinked and covering his hands with hers, pressed his palms to her cheeks. She knew that his statement contained a question and she didn't know what to say. It didn't seem fair, discussing Carl's foibles when he wasn't here to defend himself.

''He...never hit me. He just didn't have the first idea of how to be a loving husband or parent. He never really had any kind of example growing up. His father was a real—'' She waved her hand. ''He was hard on Carl and Carl's mother. Expected a lot. Used to smack them around. I think that a lot of my feeling for Carl was wrapped up in pity. And wanting to please my own dying father.''

''Ah.'' Wyatt sighed. ''You ever notice how the whole father thing can really screw you up?''

Annie emitted a strangled sort of combination sob and laugh. She nodded. ''It seems to be a trend for you and me. And Carl.''

''And Noah and Alex, and Joe.''

''And Meredith.''

''And Meredith,'' he whispered. He dragged a hand over his mouth and jaw. ''Man, I hope when the time comes for me to parent that I don't make the same mist—''

Annie interrupted by pressing a finger to his lips. ''No. No. You won't.''

''How do you know?''

''I know because I've seen the way you are with my boys. They don't remember Carl or my dad. You are the closest thing to a father they've ever had. And in the short time you've spent with them, I've seen positive changes. I know you're going to make a wonderful father someday. Already my kids love you to pieces.''

"I love them too," Wyatt whispered, and pulled her hands up to rest against his steadily beating heart. He looked deep into her eyes. "And you. I never stopped loving you, Annie. I know I never will," he vowed.

As she looked into his eyes, Annie felt just as though she were standing at the altar in her own wedding to Wyatt. Heaven help her, she loved the feeling, even though she knew that it was an impossible dream, considering their vastly different lifestyles. She could feel her mouth quivering as she bit back the never-ending flood of tears and heartbreak that had been threatening again since she'd said goodbye to Wyatt seven years ago. Long-distance relationships never worked. She and Wyatt had proved that true once already.

Even so, it was lovely to dream. If only for a moment.

"Oh, Wyatt. I love you, too. I never stopped." Her heart was thundering. What on earth was she doing, flirting with disaster this way? Reaching up, she traced his lips with her fingertips and said with a sigh, "Suddenly, I can't breathe."

Wyatt dipped his head and kissed her so tenderly, she knew that he'd forgiven her all of her stupid mistakes. And she had forgiven his. In that regard alone, Wyatt's trip to visit her had been a wild success.

The next morning, thousands of miles away in a small Mississippi town, Louise Smith awoke from a deep sleep, and for the first time in ten years felt supremely happy. Like a purring tabby, she stretched in her bed, yawning, enjoying the patch of sunlight that streamed through her window and heated her back. Eyes closed, she strained to grasp the fleeting remnants of a truly lovely dream.

What was it, she mused as images flitted through her head. Mmm. Yes. There was a garden. But this was not just any garden. This was a special garden. One she'd dreamed of before. One she'd had a hand in creating, she was sure, as the flowers and plants all pleased her sense of color and fragrance. And there was the sound of water. Bubbling water.

She placed a hand on her furrowed brow and forced herself to remember. Why was this place so familiar? She knew this was a recurring dream, but that couldn't be all there was to it. She'd actually been there, she felt quite certain.

"...anyone fitting this description, please notify the authorities immediately. And now for the top-of-the-hour traffic and weather scene here's mean Jean Greene. Hey thanks, Bob, and a good morning it is, too. Right now it's a balmy seventy degrees outside and climbing. We've got a warm front moving..."

The rude blaring of her alarm clock's radio distracted her for a moment until she could disentangle herself from her covers and slap the snooze button. Once she'd accomplished that, blessed silence reigned once more. Now, where was she? Oh, yes.

The garden.

She settled back into her pillow and upon closing her eyes, the garden came alive in her mind's eye once more. The tall, dark man was there again. That, she remembered. She always remembered the tall, dark man, because he gave her such a feeling of peace. Security. Happiness. Could this man represent her father? No...but whom?

Every time she had this dream, a powerful sense of relief

filled her, as if she'd been traveling for a long time and had finally arrived at her destination.

Outside her window, the trash men were kicking up a ruckus and she put her fingers in her ears and swallowed a shriek of impatience. *Auugh!* Why couldn't she get a handle on this elusive dream? Surely it was a key piece to the puzzle of her true identity.

Just as she was about to give up, toss back the covers and head for the shower, the fleeting image of the tall, dark man standing beside her in the garden materialized. She pressed her palms into her eyes and she could see him holding her hand. Yes, that was it! He was holding her hand and slipping a ring on her finger!

A ring?

She could recall the feeling of pure joy and utter contentment as she looked down at the two hands, hers and whose? Her husband? What else could it be? She strained to remember but, like an out-of-focus picture, she couldn't spot the details.

However, the feelings were suddenly acute. Nearly palpable.

Love. Deep, abiding love. She could feel it even now. This blurred man was her other half, her partner, the part that was missing from her heart. She yearned for him with a longing so strong her body physically ached.

Drawing her legs up under her chin, she lay curled into a fetal ball, fighting to remember.

Remember. Remember! *Remember,* damn it!

The last vestiges of the dream began to dissolve. Like a bad television signal, everything was breaking up. But before the image faded completely to black, she could tell that they were not alone in the garden. There were people gathered around her and the tall, dark man. Many people, enfolding them in warmth. In happiness. In love.

* * *

As Liza had hoped, the day of her wedding arrived in the tradition of California's sunny best. Temperate. Cloudless. The merest hint of an ocean breeze. The Hacienda de Alegria's lush central courtyard was a peaceful haven, fully decorated and ready for the impending nuptials.

A harpist was seated off to the left of the first row of seats and, as her fingers danced over the strings, Nick and Liza's family began to filter into the garden. Ushered to their seats by two of Nick's gangly, red-faced, tuxedo-clad, teen-aged cousins, the crowd grew until there were at least fifty family members and just about that many more friends. The excitement was electric and the audience buzzed quietly among themselves. For a moment, the murmurings stopped as Joe arrived with Meredith on his arm, and then, as they took their seats up front, the murmurings began again in earnest.

Annie felt almost as if she were hovering over this blessed occasion, rather than sitting on the bride's side, next to Wyatt, near the back. Heart pounding, head buzzing, stomach roiling, she clutched his hand until her knuckles turned white.

Wyatt looked at her with concern but Annie could only manage a weak smile in return. She glanced at her boys and gave silent thanks that, for once, they were exhibiting model behavior. There was absolutely no way she could handle it if they acted up now.

She took a deep, cleansing breath, hoping to somehow orient herself. It was the oddest thing. Almost as if she were having some kind of out-of-body experience. Near as she could figure, the raw terror that had invaded her body arrived last night, when Wyatt confessed his deep and abiding love.

With that pronouncement, he'd brought them to a "Y" in the road. It was him or her family and Keyhole.

Either way, a broken heart of gargantuan proportions was staring her in the face and she simply did not know if she had the strength to navigate another loss. Only in the last couple of years had she begun to live again. The boys were less work, the store was flourishing and she'd moved beyond her grief and into a rather bland, but nonetheless, peaceful existence.

Try as she might to calm herself, the more she thought about her own future, the more panicky she became. It was a horrible feeling and she was utterly helpless to control it.

Peering through her tunnel of fear and depression, she watched as Nick and his best man, Jackson, moved to stand under the gauze wedding tent. Moments passed and then the bridesmaids followed a tiny set of flower girls down the aisle. Behind them, a darling ring bearer, no older than three and clutching a heart-shaped pillow, stumbled up to stand by the girls.

The harpist began the wedding march and a sea of happy faces rose. Annie watched herself being propelled to her feet by some autopilot life force that seemed to be standing in for her at the moment. The only thing holding her upright was her death grip on Wyatt's steely bicep.

"You okay?" he murmured.

"Mmm."

"This bring up too many bad memories?"

"It's not that. I'll be okay. I just feel a little weird. Jet lag."

"Oh." Wyatt was not convinced.

Looking the picture of serenity, Liza floated down the aisle on her father's arm. Annie envied her this strength. This calm. This certainty of family and destination.

Why couldn't it be this simple for her and Wyatt? Why did life always have to be so blasted hard? Tears burned at the backs of her eyes and she struggled to fill her lungs with air. Sometimes it felt like all she ever did was fight the good fight.

But damn it all, she was tired of fighting. Tired of healing. Tired of making decisions that were right for everyone but herself.

She rummaged through her purse and withdrew a tissue and joined a number of other people who were dabbing their eyes and discreetly blowing their noses. Fortunately, for different reasons altogether.

Annie shuddered with the heaviness of her sigh. She hadn't been this miserable since her own wedding.

The ethereal harp music reached a conclusion and Liza, looking for all the world like one of Grimm's beloved royal heroines, bestowed her father's ruddy cheek with a light kiss, and then turned to face her prince. Expressions glowing with love for each other, she and Nick moved to stand together before the altar.

Amid rustling and whispering, the audience was once again seated, and Liza and Nick began the journey that would take them through the rest of their lives together.

Annie fished her purse once more for tissues and came up with an empty tissue package, a ticket stub, a grocery receipt and some empty gum wrappers. Great. Running mascara went with her unruly hair, and that panicked deer-in-the-headlights expression she was sure she wore on her face.

Luckily, a woman seated at her side, who'd introduced herself and her husband as Elizabeth and Jason Colton, was on the ball and pressed a handkerchief into her hand. Her nine-month-old son reached for the lacy scrap, but missed and began to fuss. His father took him into his lap and the baby immediately quieted.

"Keep it," the woman whispered. "I have a feeling you're going to need it."

Annie nodded and, feeling utterly foolish but unable to control her emotions, dabbed and sniffed and blew her way through the minister's opening remarks. Coltons to the left and right of her sent knowing smiles and she returned them to the best of her ability with trembling lips. Luckily, they had no idea that her heart was breaking.

When the time came, Nick winked at the little ring bearer who labored to untie the ribbons that contained Liza's ring. When he'd accomplished his mission, he stood right there, between the bride and groom, staring straight up, absorbing the solemnity of the moment, as the groom slipped the small circle of gold on the bride's slender finger.

Neither Nick, nor Liza, seemed to notice the small child hadn't moved away.

Nick's mellifluous baritone resonated strength as he began to recite the vows he'd written for Liza.

"I, Nick Hathaway, take you, Liza Colton, to be my partner and wife. I promise before God and these witnesses to be your loving husband and friend. I will comfort you in sickness, rejoice with you in health. I will share in your happiness and success, and uphold you in sorrow."

Temples throbbing, Annie ducked her head and watched her tears splash off her purse and drip onto her raw silk skirt. Wyatt squeezed her hand, but she was too weak with emotion to return the favor.

"I want," Nick began, then took a deep breath and slowly exhaled as if he couldn't quite believe that this moment had finally come. The deep love in his eyes for Liza was evident, even across the room, "I want to provide loving and sensitive leadership in our marriage that will leave a lot of room for individuality. I will help and encourage you in achieving the dreams and goals that God has given you. I pledge myself to you alone as a loyal companion. I will hold you in my heart as long as we both shall live. I love you, Liza.''

Except for the occasional sniffle, for which Annie was mainly responsible, the room was silent. Holy. Filled with joy.

After helping the little ring bearer—who hadn't strayed from where he stood, directly between them—with Nick's ring, Liza looked up at her beloved and, in a voice strong and clear and filled with vitality and health, began her own vows.

''I, Liza Colton, do give myself to you, Nick Hathaway, before God and these witnesses, to be your wife and receive you as my husband. I promise you tenderness and love. I want to always treat you with sensitivity and understanding. I desire to always make decisions in your best interests. I promise to always be faithful and loyal, no matter what circumstances we may face.''

Annie bit back a sob.

''I want to dream your dreams, to be your best friend and loyal supporter and companion, to comfort you in sickness, rejoice with you in health. I will share your happiness and uphold you in sorrow. I pledge myself to you alone and trust you and hold you in my heart as long as we both shall live. I love you, Nick.''

The minister nodded, satisfied that the vows were completed, and the rings exchanged. ''By the powers vested in me by the great state of California, I now pronounce that you are husband and wife. If you like, sir, you may kiss your bride in celebration.''

As Nick swept her into his arms, the ring bearer disappeared among the folds of Liza's voluminous satin and lace skirts where he remained, amid much laughter, until the ardent kiss was over.

Twelve

The reception was being held in the great room, which truly lived up to its name in every sense of the word. A high stone hearth formed the room's central focal point and casual leather couches and mission-style furnishings created a comfortable atmosphere for entertaining. Today, every spare square foot was set with lavish tables, both inside the great room and on the giant patio beyond the dozens of wide, glass doors.

Annie watched her boys join some other children who were darting through the milling throng and normally, she would have cautioned them to be careful, but she simply did not have the energy. The mental fortitude. The will to drag herself through the rest of this extravaganza, let alone scold her rambunctious offspring.

Fantastic floral arrangements, ice sculptures, champagne fountains, along with endless buffet tables loaded with every conceivable delicacy decorated the filled-to-bursting

great room and patio. Already several hundred people had
arrived after the wedding, and more were expected as the
evening progressed.

Nick and Liza had been hugged and kissed within inches
of their lives in the receiving line, and were now moving
about the dance floor, lost in a haze of their love. Over in
one corner an orchestra played lively music from the Big
Band era, and already, the party was hopping. Waiters and
waitresses worked the crowd, delivering fluted glasses of
champagne to the adults and sparkling cider to the children.
Gourmet hors d'oeuvres designed to tickle the most distin-
guishing palate were also making the rounds, while those
with a heartier appetite jumped into the buffet line.

Rumor had it that the party would be going on until well
past midnight, which was not unusual, given the history of
social events at the Hacienda de Alegria.

Annie only hoped she could make it through an hour or
so without coming completely unglued. By sheer grit alone
was she holding onto her fragile sanity. She knew she had
to get away. To be completely alone to think and pray and
grope for answers to her future before she would begin to
feel even a tiny bit better.

At the moment, however, that was impossible.

People were interested in meeting and carrying on meaningless conversation with Wyatt's date, and so she had to
rally. To rise to the occasion. To discuss the beautiful
weather with the best of them.

"Actually, I think the horizontal stripe on the mother of
the bride's dress is quite flattering."

"Yes, I love living in Wyoming. And yes, we have a
car. It's actually quite modern."

"No offense taken. I know people are curious about the
circumstances of my late husband's death. But no, he was
much closer to my age than that."

"Why, thank you. But, no. Wyatt is not their father."

"Hard to tell in this light. You might want to have it appraised. Unless it's a costume piece, antique stones any larger than a walnut are usually kept in a vault."

"No, I'm not insinuating that your grandmother's brooch is fake. Only that you take great care with a jewel of such size."

"Yes, I've seen the way he looks at her."

"I'm sure they will live happily ever after."

She wanted to scream.

And, when she caught Wyatt's eye, she knew he was concerned. He was so sweetly solicitous, and rescued her from more than one endless conversation, but she didn't want sympathy. She wanted answers, damn it. She wanted to know what the heck she was supposed to do with Wyatt's undying love when he lived halfway across the stupid country.

She needed an aspirin.

She sighed.

She needed a shrink, but she'd settle for an aspirin. Tapping Wyatt on the arm, Annie politely excused herself and headed for the nearest powder room.

"Enjoying yourself?"

Jackson looked up from the hors d'oeuvre tray to see Meredith sidle up next to him, wearing a phony smile. She was carrying two glasses of champagne, which he figured might account for the flush in her cheeks.

"It's my sister's wedding. Of course I'm having a good time." He eyed her with suspicion. "Why?"

"Just wanted to make sure you were enjoying yourself. That and to take a moment to bury the hatchet between us."

Between us, Jackson wondered sourly, or in me? "Why?" he asked again.

"Because," she simpered, pouting, "I hate it when there are hard feelings. We are usually such a close-knit family."

"Meredith, I hardly know you anymore."

She lifted a delicate shoulder. "Be that as it may, I still want for us to be bosom friends. The way we used to be. When you were a little boy. Here." She held out one of the glasses she carried.

Jackson stared at her.

"C'mon," she cajoled, "take it. Drink with me. To friendship. To family."

Jackson ground his back teeth and forced himself to mentally count to ten. He could hardly refuse her when they were surrounded by so much happy family. Besides, making a scene on her wedding day would hardly be fair to Liza. Hating himself for giving in to this viper's wishes, he took the glass from her and waited.

Meredith pouted. "Forgive me?"

"For what?"

"For our little disagreement the other morning. You caught me at a rather bad time, and I'm so sorry. I simply don't know what has come over me lately. I think I'm just so terrified of hurting Joe." She pulled a full, rosy lip between her teeth and studied her glass for a moment. "I'd do anything to protect him. That includes making sure that he never finds out that our son is really—" she lifted her lashes and glanced over the rim of her fluted glass until her gaze landed on Graham "—his."

Jackson snorted. "Blackmail is not the answer."

"You're right, of course." Carefully arranging her face to appear contrite, Meredith nodded. "There's a better way of handling all this, I'm sure." She held up her glass. "In any event, I'm sorry. For everything. I made a terrible mistake, and I'll spend the rest of my life dealing with the consequences. I can only beg your forgiveness.''

Jackson glanced away from Meredith and watched his sister glide around the dance floor on a cloud of love. The last thing he felt like doing was bestowing this witch with his forgiveness. But it was probably the right thing to do. This day, of all days, was a day to unite families. Feeling as if he had no choice, he gave a curt nod.

Meredith held her glass to her lips. ''Thank you,'' she murmured, then took a sip. ''To friendship and new beginnings.''

Jackson brought his own glass to his lips as he continued to watch Liza flirt with Nick. ''I'll drink to new beginnings.''

Annie returned from the rest room to find Wyatt deep in conversation with Lucy and Rand. Deciding not to interrupt, she forced a bright smile to her lips and stood just far enough away to give them privacy, but close enough to still feel as if she were part of the group. She took this quiet opportunity to further attempt to collect her runaway emotions.

It was the wedding.

It had to be.

Weddings always brought out the high emotion in people. Annie was no different. Worse, maybe, considering her own unfortunate foray into matrimony. But still, none of that explained the nausea, the dizziness, and the inability to simply breathe.

In the powder room, she'd run cold water on her wrists and taken the quiet time to give herself a pep talk, but it wasn't really working. If anything, she was more of a wreck than ever. Last night, as she'd lain tossing in her bed she'd considered each possible scenario and come up wounded at every turn.

She could feel Wyatt getting ready to propose, and once he did, there were only two answers she could give.

Yes, she could rip her children away from her mother and sell the store that had been in her family for generations and follow Wyatt to the big, scary city and miss Keyhole for the rest of her life. Or no, she could stay single and spend the next two or three years climbing back out of a pit of depression over another broken heart. And then, miss Wyatt for the rest of her natural life.

She needed to go lie down. And stay down until she woke from this nightmare.

"Excuse me…"

Annie looked up at Jackson Colton's rather wobbly approach, and at first she thought he was trying to make the melancholy girl in the corner smile with his silly antics. He held his hand out in front of his face and stared intently at it for the longest moment, then held it out to her.

"Can you tell me, does my hand look really huge to you?" He glanced up at Annie, concern lying just under his lopsided grin.

Annie returned his silly grin. "Is this a trick question?"

Jackson pushed his hand right up under her face. "For pity sakes, woman, look at it! My fingers are Polish sausages! My palms are like—" he stared intently at his palm "—they're like hams. Say, look at that! They are so far away. And huge. They sort of have a life of their own." He grew pensive. "I'd never really noticed that before this very minute. Our hands have lives of their own." Slowly, his gaze floated back to Annie's face. "My hands have left. I have to go follow them now." He paused. "You are really beautiful, did you know that? Really, really beautiful. Like an angel."

"Uh, thank you." Annie stared uncertainly at him. She didn't know Jackson very well, but this did not seem at all right. Yesterday he was the picture of charm and success, and now... It was almost as if he were having some sort of breakdown.

She knew she should be grateful. By comparison, she seemed to have it all together.

Jackson staggered forward and draping himself heavily over her shoulder, began to root around in her hair with his nose. Like a dog in search of a bone, he snuffled and emitted noisy guttural groans of pleasure. "You have great hair. Really, really wonderful stuff. Smells like...a meadow."

"Oh, Wyatt?" Annie hated to break into whatever deep discussion he was having with Rand and Lucy, but she figured that at the moment, this was more important.

Still speaking in hushed tones, Wyatt turned and blinked, as if suddenly remembering Annie was there. "Hey, sweetheart. I was just talking about you." He frowned as he noticed Jackson's face buried in her hair.

"All good, I hope," she chirped. She batted at Jackson and attempted to shrug him off her shoulder. Jackson's hand roved down to settle at her hips. She smacked them off. "Jackson. Jackson, dear, I think I've found your hands." Eyes wide, she mouthed a message to Wyatt. *I think he's drunk.* She lifted a worried brow.

"You found my hands?" Jackson's voice was dreamy.

"Yes, and they are being a little naughty. Perhaps you'd better put them away."

"Can't."

"Why not?"

"They are too big for my pockets. And they keep getting out. They are growing boys." Jackson's hands snaked around Annie's middle. "See?"

At the narrow look in Wyatt's eyes, Annie gave her head

an imperceptible shake. Jackson was out of it. Trying to reason with him on any normal level would prove fruitless, she was sure.

Rand and Lucy exchanged puzzled glances with each other, and then with an unamused Wyatt.

"Jackson, honey, why don't you show your hands to Wyatt?"

"I love it when she calls me honey," Jackson announced. "Isn't she beautiful? Hair like fire. Fire. C'mon, baby, light my fire."

"Jackson, Wyatt wants to see your hands." Annie pulled her lips into her mouth. It looked as if Wyatt wanted to lop his hands off.

"Why? Is he a doctor?"

"I'm a lawyer, cousin." Wyatt took a step closer.

"Oh, right. So am I! I'll sue! I'll sue the hand people. I haff defective hands. Jus look ah tha damned things. They're huge! Like a couple a damned Christmash turkeys." Jackson frowned. "Do my slurs sound word to you?"

"Jackson?"

"Yesh, Dr. Wyatt?"

"How much have you had to drink, guy?"

"One li'l glass of champagne. Thass all. I think…"

Luckily, no one but their immediate group seemed to be paying the slightest bit of attention to Jackson's antics, with the lone exception of Meredith.

"Hello." Her smooth, beautifully modulated voice took sudden command of their little group as she approached. Smile wide, her gaze flitted about, bouncing off Jackson whenever he managed to stumble into her sightline. "So, I see our Washington D.C. faction is huddled over here, sticking close together."

"Just enjoying each other's company, Meredith," Wyatt said with a grim smile.

"I'll bet." Meredith tipped her head and tapped a cherry nail on her chin. "So, what have we been talking about?"

"Oh, this and that."

"And my freakin' hands," Jackson put in, once again lost in the enormity of his appendages. He fell off Annie and wobbled over to Meredith. "Look at 'em! They're huge. And so far away! I could get you thumbthing from tha food table, if you want. I don' even half to walk over there. My hands will go."

Annie glanced at Wyatt, then to Rand and Lucy.

"You don't look so good, honey." Meredith placed a delicate hand on Jackson's flushed brow. "Perhaps you should go lie down."

"You'd like tha, wouldn' ya?" Jackson nuzzled her neck. "My auntie Meredith. Wants to take a nappie with her boozoom buddy." He reared back and looked at her, then allowed his eyes to take a meaningful dip. "Speaking of huge, my, what big—"

Abruptly, Wyatt reached for his cousin, supporting him and turning him toward the exit. "How about some fresh air, buddy boy? That might fix you right up."

Meredith placed a firm hand on his arm. "No, Wyatt, you have a guest. I'm the hostess. Jackson is my responsibility."

Jackson flailed about, throwing off Wyatt's hold. "I'm nobody's sponsor. I have to go find my hands now. The regular size ones. Sho, if you will all excush me, I'm just going to go to my room and get them now."

Meredith issued the little foursome a curt nod. "I'll find Joe and see to it that Jackson makes it to his room all right."

Mingling a little as she went, Meredith followed Jackson out of the great room and into the house proper.

"What the devil was going on there?" Rand stroked his jaw thoughtfully.

Lucy tsked in disgust. "She's clearly looking for an excuse to escape the party. Her drunk nephew was just the ticket."

Wyatt shook his head. "It's sure not like Jackson to get wasted like that."

"It could happen to anyone," Annie said in his defense. "It's his sister's day. He might be feeling a little lost."

"His hands certainly were, at any rate," Wyatt said and they all exchanged worried smiles. "I'll go check up on him after he's had a little time to sleep it off."

Save for a few servants rushing back and forth to the kitchen, the house proper was empty. Careful not to draw any undue attention to herself, Patsy followed Jackson at a discreet distance to his wing. After several botched attempts, he found the corridor that led to his room and Patsy was relieved to note that they were alone. Jackson ricocheted off the walls like an eight ball in search of a corner pocket, then finally stumbled upon his door and found his way inside.

Time was short. Patsy strode past his suite to a grandfather clock at the end of the hall. She checked over her shoulder to make certain she was still alone before she opened the small door that housed the clock's heavy weights and reached inside. After she'd withdrawn a black cloth bag, she set the clock's stalled pendulum in motion once more and hurried back to Jackson's room.

Wearing only his BVDs, Jackson was just staggering out of his bathroom as she arrived. He leaned against the door frame, planted his hands on his narrow hips and tried, to the best of his limited ability, to focus on her.

"Meredith?"

Patsy gently closed the door behind her and gave the lock a twist. She swallowed.

He was built the way she liked a man. Hard. Lean. Muscular. Far more to her taste than his fleshy-from-too-much-good-life father. And though she was reticent to admit it, being that she hated him and all, Jackson's powerful personality could be a real turn-on, too. When he was stone cold sober, there was a frightening edge to his demeanor that sent tingles up and down her spine.

She gave her head a little shake. Indulging in fantasy could wait. Right now she was here to do a job.

Delicious or not, this boy had to go bye-bye.

"Oh, Auntie. Look at you. Here to tuck me into bed." His eyes were fully dilated and he wore a dopey smile.

"Yes," she breathed, and clutched the cold steel of her revolver through the cloth of the bag. "Time for Jackson to go night-night."

"Are you gonna wear jammiesh, too?" He pointed to her black bag.

"No. No." She laughed and set the bag on his dresser. "Why don't we get you into bed?" Attempting to seem casual, she sauntered over to the bed and pulled back the comforter. The sooner he was unconscious, the sooner she could take care of business.

"I like that about you." He pushed off the door frame and negotiated the few steps it took for him to fall onto his mattress. "Alwaysh ready for bed. C'mom on in, the water'sh fine." His hand snaked out and he grabbed her wrist and tugged.

Not expecting this sudden action, she fell down beside him and, flailing about, struggled to right herself. But even in his inebriated state, he was too strong. Before she knew what hit her, Patsy found herself pinned beneath his body.

"Jackson! Let go of me this instant!"

He ignored her and shoved her legs apart with his knee.

"C'mon, Auntie. You know you want it. We're boozoom buddies, remember? Why don't you give me a little kissh? The way you used to, back when I was a little boy."

Patsy hated herself for the sudden rush of sexual excitement she felt at her predicament. Her wrigglings against him were a sorry attempt to free herself and, for a moment, she allowed herself to forget her mission.

"Mmm, baby." He playfully bit her earlobe. "That'sh right. Relax. Let'sh bury that hatchet now, huh?"

His breath was hot on her neck, his words irreverent, his body, hard. She wanted him. How entirely idiotic. She was old enough to be his...well, his much older sister. It was ridiculous. Not, of course, that she was anything to sneeze at. After all, she spent a small fortune keeping herself in shape.

But still. She didn't have time for this. She had to frame this jerk for murder, and then get the hell out of here.

"Auntie Meredith?" He pinned her legs beneath his and moved his arms between their bodies. "Hafe you sheen my hands? They sheem to be missin' in action."

Meredith gasped. Yes, his hands were most definitely enjoying being out on their own. "Jackson!"

"They're huge, huh? And you know what they say..."

His eyes rolled back in his head and he collapsed in a dead weight on top of her body.

"Jackson?" She lay silent, waiting, unbelieving. He chose *now* to pass out? Of all the— She grunted in exasperation and tried to thrust him off, but he was limp as a solid lead noodle. Clearly, she'd miscalculated the amount of drug she'd needed when she'd doctored his champagne.

Near as Patsy could figure, he outweighed her by sixty to eighty pounds. Getting out from under him with her party hair intact and still finding time to complete her business was going to be tricky.

"Noah and Alex seem to be having fun," Annie observed in a stilted voice as she and Wyatt took a stroll alone together through one of estate's many gardens. She'd been desperate for some fresh air, and Wyatt had obliged.

The twins were out front with the ushers, decorating the limousine with tin cans and shaving cream. So far they'd had a bell-ringer day. After a morning pony ride, they'd eaten a sumptuous breakfast, played with Joe's dogs, attended their first wedding and were now up to no good. It was a dream vacation from their vantage point.

"Mmm."

"I don't think they'll ever forget the pony rides." She wanted to keep the conversation superficial, the focus off her own problems. It seemed that as long as she didn't think about the future, she was able to fake normalcy.

"Mmm."

"Or the swimming pool."

"Mmm." Wyatt was clearly distracted.

"Or the space aliens that abducted them in the middle of last night and turned them into girls, which is okay, since I've always wanted daughters."

"I'm sorry. Did you say something?"

"No." She plucked a bright flower from an oversized azalea and tucked it behind her ear. "You seem to be lost in thought." After Jackson's display back there, it was no small wonder. No doubt he was wanting to go check on him and make sure he was okay.

Wyatt abruptly stopped walking and, pulling her off the pea-gravel path, led her to an ornate concrete bench that was situated in the middle of a rose garden. Angling his head, he gestured for her to sit down next to him. The delicate fragrance of rose blossoms scented the air and off in the distance, music and laughter and voices could be heard coming from the reception.

Annie's stomach grew tight at the suddenly serious expression on his face. Uh-oh. No. She wasn't ready for this.

"Annie, I have been doing a lot of thinking over the last couple of days and the wedding here today just seems to...I don't know, hammer the point home."

She felt herself growing cold. Then hot. Feeling dizzy, she unbuttoned the top button of her suit jacket, then buttoned it again. Something told her that he wasn't worried about Jackson's sobriety at the moment.

Wyatt dropped off the edge of the bench to his knees. He took her hand and all of the air was suddenly sucked out of her lungs.

"Annie, I know this is going to seem kind of sudden and all, but it doesn't feel that way to me. To me, it feels like I've been waiting all my life to do this."

"Oh, Wyatt," Annie croaked, beginning to panic in earnest. Not now. Not here. She wasn't even on home turf, where she could cry and fall apart among friends and family.

"Shh, let me finish." He touched her lower lip with his fingertip. "I only wish I'd had the good sense to do this when your father first got sick." Settling himself more comfortably on his knees, he took a deep, calming breath and then smiled. "Annie, I love you now, more than I ever have. You have grown and matured into such a beautiful, graceful woman. I'm so proud of what you've accomplished with your life. You are a wonderful mother, a hard worker, a good friend and daughter. You are talented beyond belief, and you make everything seem so easy. So comfortable. So safe.

"I'm the person I like to be, when I'm around you. You bring out the best in me. With you, I'm energized. Positive. Wanting to believe in the future. Happy."

Gently, he brought her fingertips to his mouth and kissed them one at a time while he formulated what he wanted to say next. Obviously, this was difficult for him. He was making himself vulnerable to her, and that only increased her angst.

"Oh, Wyatt—"

"Hold that thought," he whispered. "I couldn't love your boys more if they were my own, and I know that relationship will only get better with time. I want to parent them. To teach them to be men, the way Joe did for me. I know from personal experience that it's not biology that makes a father. It's love. And commitment."

Annie could not swallow past the lump in her throat. Tiny sobs backed up like a logjam behind her lips. Tears scalded her eyes and then her cheeks. Her breathing was as shallow as if she'd just run a mile. She felt light-headed. Faint. Her heart was thrumming a mile a minute, her arms were numb and she was sure she was in the throes of cardiac arrest.

He was so incredibly sweet. His words were what she'd waited her entire life to hear.

But the circumstances were still so wrong.

A keening wail sounded and Annie was dismayed to discover it had come from her own throat.

"No!" she gasped and leapt to her feet and began to stumble back to the path that led to the house. "I can't let you do this."

While Patsy listened to Jackson's slumberous breathing in the next room, she checked her makeup and hair in his bathroom mirror. Not too much worse for the wear, she decided. Baring her teeth, she made sure there were no stray streaks of lipstick and with a last appreciative glance, declared herself perfect and ready to return to the party.

But first, she needed to attend to a bit of a chore.

Patsy moved to the dresser and retrieved her black bag. Nudging Jackson's legs aside, she made herself comfortable at the edge of his bed and opened her bag removed the gun she'd found out by the cliff. Too bad it had been so dark that evening. All she remembered seeing was a black shadow.

Was there anything more beautiful than a 9mm automatic Luger? She stroked the dark metal shaft. Perhaps, but the sight of this key to her perpetual freedom excited Patsy nearly as much as the man who slept so soundly at her side.

She smiled, recalling Joe's birthday. Now *that* was a party. But not to worry. Soon enough, everything would work out to her advantage.

Once she had the gun polished and clean, Patsy slowly reached for Jackson's hand. When he didn't stir, she grew bolder and pressed his hand around the gun's barrel and stock, taking care to slip his finger over the trigger. Finally satisfied that she had all the incriminating evidence that she needed, for now anyway, she released his hand, slipped the gun back into the bag and after looking both ways down the hall corridor, returned to the grandfather clock to make her deposit.

Wyatt caught up with Annie just before she got to the path and dragged her back into the garden. And, just as he had done so many years ago, he completely ignored her cries of outrage, hauled her under a grove of trees and pressed her spine up against the nearest trunk. Even as she protested, she arched against him.

Heat flared in Wyatt's belly. Dipping his head, he nuzzled her neck and filled his hands with her thick, wonderful hair.

"No," she moaned and writhed, fighting to get away.

"Yes." Like a man starved for over a decade, he dragged her mouth beneath his and hovered over her lightly parted lips. As she whimpered, he tasted her bottom lip, pulling it between his teeth, nipping, nibbling, then muted her protests with his tongue.

He gripped her by the shoulders and pulled her flush against him so that every part of their individual bodies found its perfect counterpart. They fit together as well now, as they had when they were kids. Even better. His hands dropped to the gentle slope of her hips and he urged her ever closer.

Their kiss turned wild. Frantic. He spread his legs for balance and immobilized her between his body and the tree, as if by doing so, he could keep her from running. She clutched his arms for support and he had the feeling that his body and the tree were all that held her up.

"Wyatt, no," Annie whimpered. "We shouldn't. This will only make it worse."

Even as she protested, she kissed him back with all the desire he felt building within himself. Wyatt was breathing like a freight train chugging uphill as he kissed her mouth, her cheeks, her jaw, her mouth again. Annie's breathing came in labored puffs as ragged as his own.

He felt her hands rise to cradle his head and she responded to his kiss with the ardent abandon of a full-fledged woman now. Annie was no longer a girl, and that excited Wyatt more than he ever could have imagined possible.

Again, as he had a decade ago that night in the trees next to the college library, he lost himself in her and felt their souls melding together. There would be no other life for him now, without Annie. He'd lived long enough as only half a human. She made him whole. He could not—would not—go on, without her.

"Listen to me," he demanded against her slack lips. He dipped his head for another deep kiss that sent him to the edge of his control. "Just listen to me."

His words seemed to bring her back to the present and she sagged. He could taste the salt of her tears as she started to cry.

She twisted her mouth away from his. "No, Wyatt. You have to let me go!"

The knot in his stomach grew in proportion to the size of his desperation. "You haven't heard me out." He grasped her flailing wrists to keep from catching one in the face.

"I can't."

"Why not?"

"I'm scared."

"Of what?"

"That you…" She sobbed and looked away, "That you are going to ask me to marry you."

He froze. This was not the response he'd been living in his fantasy life all these years. In his dreams, he'd envisioned Annie falling happily into his arms at his proposal. The tears she shed would be tears of joy, not anguish.

She was slipping away once again, and suddenly he felt the same terror he saw lurking behind her eyes.

"No," he murmured and tightened his hold on her wrists. "No. You can't do this to me. To you. To us."

She closed her eyes and lashes, spiked with tears, rested

against her cheeks. "Damn it, Wyatt. Why did you have to come back to Keyhole and screw my life up this way?"

"What the hell are you talking about?"

"Starting up our relationship like this is futile. Pointless. I live in Keyhole, Wyoming, for crying out loud! You live in Washington, D.C.! Long-distance relationships do not work. We proved that once already. I can't afford the therapy bills." She was growing hysterical.

"But that doesn't have to tear us apart." Ignoring his protest, she struggled against him, frantic to escape. "Annie, please! We can work this out."

"No!"

"Yes!" He yanked her back up against his body.

This time the word was devoid of emotion. "No."

Desperate to make her see reason, Wyatt crushed his mouth to hers once again, but as he did so, he had the sinking feeling that he was kissing Annie goodbye. This time for good.

Thirteen

It wasn't until the plane had reached cruising altitude that the boys finally, blessedly, stopped crying. Annie was an emotional wreck herself, but she tried her best to be strong for them. Cheerful even. But she was failing miserably, and she knew it. She glanced over at their long faces. Though the tears had dried, the disappointment was still sharp.

"Mom, you guys said Wyatt was comin' back home with us," Noah moaned. Like most five-year-olds, it was hard for him to let a subject die. "Wyatt said he was gonna play space monster with us again."

"And read to us." Alex had thrust his lower lip out during takeoff and was still pouting.

"I've explained this to you both, over and over. Sometimes grown-ups change their minds. They realize that they have other important commitments and those things must come first."

"Sean Mercury's new dad didn't have other command-ments. He married Sean's mom."

"And now his new dad lives at Sean's house and some-day, he's gonna adopt Sean and maybe Sean will get a new name. His mom already got a new name."

"Cuz they were kissin' and junk," Noah reminded.

Annie closed her eyes as memories of Wyatt's last kiss threatened to tip her over the precipice of her sanity. Before she'd given him another chance to propose, and thereby confuse her any further, she'd broken away from him and rushed to the house. Once back in her suite, she'd hurriedly packed, called a cab, grabbed the boys and bid the Colton family a hasty goodbye.

Luckily, they'd all inferred, by the wild look in her bloodshot eyes, the tear stains on her cheeks, the tomato-esque nose, that she was mourning the loss of her own marriage and the ceremony had simply been too much for her. They'd been more than helpful and completely under-standing.

Wyatt, on the other hand, had not come to see her off. To try to talk some sense into her jumbled mind. Quite the opposite, in fact. As she hustled the boys out to meet the waiting taxi, she'd glimpsed him having drinks with Rand and Lucy back at the reception. He'd cast her a cool to-hell-with-you look and turned his attention back to Rand.

Life went on.

Whether she wanted it to or not.

As the tears came again, Annie pressed her face against the smooth glass of the jet's window and watched the mountains slowly pass by below.

"Mom?"

"Hmm?"

"You cryin' again?" Alex peered up into her face.

She pressed the back of her wrist to her eyes. "No,

honey. No. I'll be all right. I'm just feeling a little sad right
now."

"I really love Wyatt, Mom. I wish you did too."

"I do, honey." At this admission, Annie began to hy-
perventilate.

"Mom?" Noah craned his head past his brother for a
better view.

Annie struggled to breathe. "Yes?" she gasped.

"You okay?"

"I'll...be...okay..." Frantic, she loosened her collar
buttons, then dug through the back pocket of the seat in
front of her until she found an airsick bag. Flipping it open,
she held it to her face and sucked in great gulps of soothing
carbon dioxide.

This was ridiculous.

The bag snapped out, the bag whooshed in.

Noah stopped whining long enough to laugh at the funny
picture she made.

Snap. Whoosh. Snap. Whoosh.

"I wanna do that," Alex cried and grabbed his own air-
sickness bag and began to imitate his mother. Not to be left
out, Noah joined in. *Whoosh snap whoosh snap.*

Concerned passengers turned in their seats to stare. A
flight attendant approached after the elderly woman across
the aisle had signaled for help.

"Are you going to be all right, ma'am?"

Annie smiled weakly and nodded. "I'll be all right."
Flopping back against her seat, she took another deep drag
from the bag.

Whoosh. Snap.

"Would you like a glass of ice water?"

Bag bobbing, Annie said, "That would," *whoosh, snap,*
"be nice."

"Airsick?"

Heartsick, airsick, whatever. Annie nodded. "Something like that."

The flight attendant gave her shoulder a gentle pat. "Hang in there. It will all be over soon."

Annie knew the stewardess was referring to the flight, but she had to wonder if her present troubles would ever be over.

Was she going to spend the rest of her life hyperventilating every time she thought about how much she loved Wyatt? Was she going to have to explain to her children why she'd chosen to keep them fatherless and miserable? Was she ever again going to enjoy living in Keyhole, when her heart was in Washington, D.C.?

Whoosh. Snap. Whoosh. Snap.

As her breathing slowed, the fog began to lift and Annie, for the first time in over a week, was finally beginning to think clearly. She shifted her gaze back out the window and an amazing revelation began to slowly take shape in her heretofore muddled mind.

She, Annie Summers, had been given a second chance.

How about that?

Her boys had been given a second chance.

They'd been handed a loving husband and father on a silver platter, and here she was, throwing it all away over a silly pile of Madrilla vases and butter churns.

What on earth was she thinking?

If she and the boys moved to Washington, D.C., they were only a phone call away from her mother and Brynn. MaryPat could fly out and see them as often as she wished. Annie didn't know why she worried so about her mother. After all, it wasn't as if she'd laid down and died when Judith and her husband and kids had moved to Iowa.

"Here you go, ma'am." The flight attendant handed her

a soda water and packages of peanuts for the boys. "Please, let me know if there is anything else I can do for you."

Annie took the soda water and sipped. "No, no. Thank you. I think I'm going to be fine." As she recalled the wounded look on Wyatt's face, misery flared once more and she wondered if she'd blown it beyond salvation. "Eventually. I hope."

The first thing Annie wanted to do when she got home was to call Wyatt. They needed to talk. She needed to apologize for her abhorrent behavior just as soon as she had a few minutes to herself.

Dragging their luggage behind them, the boys slogged in a foggy depression into the house and up to their room to unpack. Annie was worried about them, but knew she had to sort her own problems out before she could tackle theirs.

Annie took her luggage to the laundry room and, once she'd started a load of her delicates, rushed to the phone in the kitchen. She located her address book and picked up the phone only to discover Alex on the extension. He was talking to Sean Mercury.

"Nah. He doesn't want to be our dad."

"How come?"

"I guess he had a bad time with us on the trip. Me and Noah helped make a mess of the bride's getaway car. Maybe that's why he's mad."

Slowly, Annie hung up the phone. Her eyes slid closed and she sagged against the counter. Boy, she'd really done it this time. By trying not to hurt anybody, she'd ended up hurting everybody. Dully, she looked up as a knock sounded at her front door.

Brynn barreled past as Annie pulled the door open. MaryPat shuffled in behind her.

"What gives?" Brynn demanded in her typical all-business style. "You weren't supposed to be back until tomorrow. I saw lights on over here and with what's been going on around here lately, I thought I'd stop by and see what's up. We're just coming from dropping Em off at work…" Her voice trailed off and she peered at her sister. "Good grief, woman. You look like you fell out of a pitiful tree and hit every branch on the way down."

"Mmm. Thank you." Annie shuffled to the living room and flopped into a recliner. She motioned for Brynn and her mother to take a seat.

"What happened?" MaryPat settled in next to Brynn on the couch.

Annie decided to ignore their questions and counter with a few of her own. "Mama, would you mind horribly if I wanted to sell the store?"

MaryPat opened her mouth to speak, but no words came.

Annie looked from her mother to her sister. "And, Brynn, if Mama gives me the thumbs-up, would you consider listing it as soon as possible? I'd be happy to pay the going commission rate."

For the first time in years, both women were completely speechless. They stared agog at Annie and then at each other.

"I—" Annie squirmed in her seat and twisted her fingers together. "I'm thinking of moving. To Washington, D.C. Over the last week, out of curiosity, I got on the Net and found out that there are some very nice, affordable neighborhoods with excellent school systems. And what with the Smithsonian and the monuments and the memorials, and that whole political scene, well, I just know it would be great for the kids, educationally speaking. And you know, without the burden of the store, I can focus on my kids. And my art. Which is something I've kind of always wanted to do." She shrugged.

"He's the one?" MaryPat asked with a smile.

"Mama, when he's in the room it's like there just isn't enough air."

"He's the one." She cackled like a turkey the day after Thanksgiving.

Brynn finally found her voice. "Wyatt has proposed?"

Annie shook her head. "No. But I'm going to. First chance I get."

Her chin propped in her hand, Emily leaned over the café lunch counter and starred dreamily at Wyatt who was seated on a stool and picking at his fries. "So it was really beautiful, huh?"

"You'd have loved it. I've never seen a more beautiful bride."

"I wish I could have been there."

"Liza sends you her love. I know she wanted you to stand up with her, but she understands."

"Why did you come back so early? I thought you and Annie were going to stay a couple extra days."

"Change of plans. She wanted to get back yesterday. So she flew out shortly after the wedding. At first I was going to stay in Prosperino and then go back to D.C., but I got to thinking—"

"Just couldn't stay away, huh?" Emily teased.

"Something like that." Wyatt poked a fry in his mouth, but he was so sick at heart, it tasted like a stick of fried cardboard. "Anyway, I hopped a plane this morning and here I am. Just in time for lunch."

Last night had been the longest night of his life. He knew he'd been a fool to chase her all the way here, knowing how she felt about marrying him, but he couldn't seem to help himself. Before he went home to Washington, D.C., he had to talk to her one last time. Get some answers. Answers that he could live with.

Hopefully.

Criminy. He couldn't think about this anymore. His head was killing him. Time for a change of subject.

"So." Wyatt dredged a fry through some ketchup. "How'd it go while we were gone? Toby any closer to catching that freak that broke into your place?"

Emily shook her head. "No, but *he's* a lot closer. Toby moved in with MaryPat and me for the weekend."

Wyatt hooted. "Sounds like a really weird *Three's Company* rerun."

Emily smacked him with a damp rag. "Funny boy. I have to say he did seem to love all the home cooking."

"That's the way to a man's heart, you know."

"Would you shut up? It's not like that between us." With her rag, she wiped up a dollop of ketchup off the counter near Wyatt's plate. "Although, it was nice of him to stay on MaryPat's couch all weekend. I felt safe with him so close. He's a special man."

"It's love, I'm telling you."

Emily giggled. "You're so weird. Speaking of love, when are you going to pop the question to Annie?"

"I did, this weekend. Or at least I tried." Wyatt sighed. Did he really want to go into this? Just talking about it made him feel as if his heart was a bloody ball of hamburger.

"You did?" Emily stopped cleaning the counter and gaped at him. "What'd she say?"

"No."

Emily's broad smile twitched, then faded. "No?"

"No."

"You're kidding."

"No."

"You're not going to let her get away with that, are you?"

"What do you mean, not let her get away with that? She's a grown woman. She can do what she wants. Marry whom she wants. She's proved that once already." Wyatt tossed his sloppy French fry back onto his plate and twisted his napkin in his hands.

"But you can't just give up."

"What would you suggest?"

"Fight for her this time! Last time you just let her walk out on you, without putting up a fight. Bad move, Wyatt. Women..." Emily said with a sigh. "We like our men to fight for us. Makes us feel wanted. Needed. Loved."

Wyatt grunted. "How do you know?"

"I'm a woman."

Wyatt stared at her in mild surprise. By golly, she was. When had his baby sister gone and grown up? "You think fighting for her is the answer, huh?"

"Yep. If it was me, I'd fight."

Beneath his ribs, Wyatt's heart began to pick up speed at the idea. Emily was right. He'd let Annie walk away once. It had been the worst mistake of his life.

She still loved him.

He knew it.

And he'd be damned if he was going to make the same mistake all over again.

Emily tossed her rag in the pail beneath the counter and, leaning toward him, took his hand. "Why don't you find a place here in town? Move here and court her the old-fashioned way. Prove that you love her by just not going away. Finally, she'll just get so sick of you hanging around that she'll marry you just to get rid of you."

Wyatt grinned. "You know, that makes a wacky kind of sense."

"Call Brynn."

He fished his cell phone and Brynn's card out of his pocket and dialed.

"Hello?"

"Yeah, Brynn? It's me. Wyatt."

"Hey, Wyatt. What's up?"

"I need a place to hang my shingle here in Keyhole."

"Gonna move to Wyoming, huh?"

Odd. She didn't sound surprised in the least. "Yup. So I'll need a place to live and a place to work." He winked at Emily who was crouching near, trying to follow Brynn's half of the conversation.

"Well, you're in luck. The Summer's Autumn Antique building will soon be empty and the upstairs would make a wonderful apartment and office space."

Wyatt stiffened. Emily hunched closer.

"The downstairs would really be better suited to a retail business than a law practice, but you could lease that space and make all kinds of return on your investment."

"But—but—" Wyatt was reeling. He frowned at Emily. She frowned back, then pressed the side of his head with hers.

Brynn didn't seem to notice his inability to speak. "Yes, the owner is highly motivated to sell. I guess she's going to be moving to Washington, D.C., to be nearer to the man she loves. So, if you're going to do it, move. The price is right, big guy."

"I'll take it," Wyatt shouted and high-fived Emily. "I'll take the whole damned thing. The upstairs, the downstairs and all the junk inside." He hung up and, as he and Emily stood staring at each other and breathing hard, his cell phone rang.

"Wyatt Russell here." He frowned, then grinned and held up a hand meant to stave off Emily who bounced around, made elaborate hand signals and whispered in his free ear, trying to get him to tell her who it was. "Yes. Right. Uh-huh, sure. Really? You're kidding! You sold it already? To whom? Okay. Okay, yes, I'll go talk to her immediately."

Still dazed, Wyatt snapped his phone off, tossed a handful of bills under his plate, shrugged into his jacket and headed for the door.

"Hey!" Emily shouted. "Get back here! Who did Annie sell her store to? Wait!"

"Okay. You, too. Thanks for the fries."

Annie knew he was in the room, even before she saw him. Her heart began to beat double time and suddenly, her lungs were starved for oxygen. Slowly, she turned from where she'd been polishing the stained glass shade of a Tiffany lamp and her gaze slammed into Wyatt's.

He'd come back.

Even after she'd run off, he'd come back. Tears burned the backs of her eyes, and her heart—in the tradition of the Grinch—swelled two sizes times two. Before she even paused to wonder if she should go to him, her feet were flying, carrying her across the room and into his open arms.

"Wyatt!"

He slipped his arms around her waist and, lifting her up, swung her in a circle.

"Oh, Wyatt! I've been such a fool. I have so much to apologize to you for."

"Isn't this where I'm supposed to say, 'love means never having to say you're sorry,' or something corny like that?"

Annie, laughing and crying, pressed a light palm over his mouth and rushed to spill everything she'd been wanting to tell him. "No. Because I *am* sorry. So very, very sorry. I should have let you finish. But I was so confused,

I just couldn't. But I'm better now. And I want to pick up on our conversation where we left off.''

Wyatt let her slide down his body and, cradling the back of her head in his hands, rained gentle, soft kisses across her lips.

"Wyatt, stop, please," she murmured. "You're making it hard to think."

"Don't mind me," he urged, still kissing her. "Go on."

"Mmm. Ah-hem." She cleared her throat and closed her eyes. His mouth moved to her neck and sent a cascade of wonderful chills sweeping over her body. "Okay. Now then, I want to ask you...I want to ask...I want...I... Mmmm." She allowed her head to loll back and thereby give him better access to that little spot in the hollow of her throat that had her pulses singing. "Uh, you know when you do that," she said, giggling and squirming, "I have a hard time concentrating."

"Me too."

"Now stop it and listen to me. Because I have something very important to ask you."

"Continue," he urged, moving his way up her neck and to her jaw.

"Okay. Where was I? Oh, yes. Wyatt Russell, I want to make an honest man out of you."

"That'll take some doing."

"Would you please be serious?"

"I'm being very serious." He took her earlobe between his teeth and growled.

"Wyatt! Quit it, or I'm going to get mad."

He dipped his tongue into her ear. "I love it when you're mad. You're beautiful when you're angry."

"Oh, I give up." Annie sighed and let him have his way with her, and when he moved his mouth over hers, kissed him back with all the desire that had been building during the years they'd been apart.

"Hey!" A youthful shout came from the playroom at the back of the store. "Alex! The space monster is back! And he's kissin' our mom!"

Alex whooped and the two boys came barreling out to greet Wyatt.

Wyatt caught them both up in a hug and for a few wild, noisy moments of reunion, chaos reigned.

"Watter ya doin' here?" Noah demanded.

"I'm here to answer a question for your mom."

"What question?" Alex wondered.

"I don't know. She won't ask it."

"Ask him, Mom," Noah instructed.

"If you'll all just be quiet for a minute, I will." Annie huffed and puffed and turned toward an antique dresser and straightened her clothing and hair in the mirror. When she felt that she was presentable, she turned to face her men. "Okay. Boys, I need you to be quiet for a few minutes here, okay?"

"Okay." They nodded.

"Okay. Wyatt?"

"Yes?"

"Will you marry us?" She gestured first to herself, then to her boys.

Wyatt grinned from ear to ear.

Before he could answer, the boys went berserk. "Wyatt's gonna be our dad! Wyatt's gonna be our dad!"

"I'm gonna go pack," Noah screamed.

"I'm gonna call Sean Mercury," Alex shouted.

They dashed off and it was eerily quiet.

"Well?" Annie asked, her mouth suddenly dry, her palms suddenly clammy.

"Yes."

"Oh, my."

"Something wrong?"

"Suddenly, I can't breathe."

MaryPat and Brynn were right behind Emily as she burst through the door. "I'm on a break! I can't stand the suspense. Annie! Who did you sell your store to? And why are you turning blue?"

Frowning with concern, Wyatt patted Annie's back. "She says she can't breathe."

"What'd you do to her?" Brynn demanded.

"I accepted her proposal of marriage."

"Ah." MaryPat reached behind the counter for a paper bag. "Give her this and tell her to put it over her mouth. It's just a little case of falling in love. She'll be just fine in a few minutes. Used to happen to me with her daddy all the time."

Wyatt complied as Emily continued to pelt him with screechy, giddy questions. "You guys are getting married? How wonderful! So who bought the store?"

Whoosh, snap. Annie looked at Brynn. "Someone bought the store?"

"Yes."

Whoosh, snap, whoosh, snap. "Who?"

"Him."

Whoosh, snap! Whoosh, snap! "Him?"

Wyatt nodded. "I'm moving to Keyhole."

Whoosh. "You *are?*" *Snap.*

"Yep. I'm hanging my shingle out front and taking the space upstairs for my office. I have to have somewhere to transact business, if I'm going to practice law part-time."

Emily frowned. "But who just called and said the store was already sold?"

Wyatt glanced from Emily to Annie. "That call wasn't about the store. It was about one of Annie's paintings. I sold one of her paintings through a gallery in New York. And they want more.''

"You did? They *do?*"

"Yes. And that's why I'm only going to practice law part-time. The rest of the time I'm going to broker your art and help you run the store.''

"Well!'' MaryPat clasped her hands together. "Isn't that nice. Okay then. Em, let's get you back to work. Brynn, come along. I have a ham in the oven and you know how Toby hates to wait.''

MaryPat hustled the girls out the front door, then turned and winked at Wyatt. "You're a hell of a classy guy, Wyatt Russell. Welcome to the family. It's about time.''

Wyatt grinned. "Thanks, Mom.''

When the door slammed shut, Annie looked up at Wyatt with awe. "You're moving to Keyhole? Are you sure you want to do that?''

"Annie, my love, I've never been more sure of anything in my life. I already gave Rand my resignation, just this morning.''

"You did?''

"Yep. Told him I was getting married, taking on twins and wouldn't have time for the rat race anymore.''

"What'd he say?''

"Well, when he was done picking Lucy up off the floor, he congratulated me and wished me luck.'' He dipped his head and planted a kiss on her neck that thrilled her to her toes. "I'm a very lucky man, Annie Summers.''

"As lucky as Sean Mercury's new dad?'' she teased, hearing the happy hubbub coming from her office.

"Twice as lucky,'' Wyatt murmured, and covered her mouth with his.

Look for more of
The Coltons *in February 2002*
in Karen Hughes's
WED TO THE WITNESS

One

"So, here you are," she said after a moment. "Jackson Colton, who professes to have never wanted a serious relationship with a woman, claims to suddenly want one with me."

"I do—"

"Is it just a happy coincidence that I'm the *one woman* who can maybe prevent you from going to jail if I keep my mouth shut about where I saw you that night?"

He closed his eyes. As an attorney, he had anticipated her reaction. As a man whose feelings for her seemed to deepen by the minute, he'd dreaded it. He shifted against the rail, then settled back again to study her profile.

"I didn't come here to try to sweet-talk you into keeping me out of jail."

"Really?" She turned and gave him a steady stare. Her burnished skin carried a flush of anger, her mouth had thinned. In a slash of time, Jackson saw the full power of her heritage in her face. "A woman involved in a serious relationship might think twice before implicating her lover in an attempted murder."

"Am I going to be your lover, Cheyenne?"

Her chin rose. "That's exactly what you tried to become this morning. But you discovered I'm not a woman who's easily seduced. Your Plan A didn't work. You've had all day to come up with a new course of action. Is this Plan B, Jackson? Have you come here this evening, expecting to cajole me into not telling the police where I saw you?"

Understanding her reaction didn't stop anger from churning inside him. Jaw set, he pushed off the rail, walked across the porch to face her.

"Listen to me," he said, forcing a steadiness into his voice he was far from feeling. "I didn't want what happened between us this morning to stop with a kiss. I'm sure that was obvious. I want you, Cheyenne. Every time I see you, get close to you, *smell you,* that need deepens. Like now."

"I…" When she took a step back, he took one forward. "I don't want—"

"I do," he continued quietly. "I want to take you someplace quiet where the only light comes from flickering candles." Slowly, his eyes skimmed over her face, lingering on each feature. "I want to drink warm, sweet wine with you and listen to you sigh while I peel every piece of clothing off your body. Then I want to make love with you until I'm the only man who ever has, or will, exist for you. That's what I want, Cheyenne."

Her lips parted, trembled. "Don't. I can't think straight when you say things like that."

"Good, because I'm having a hard time thinking straight when I get around you, too." He blew out a breath. "My kissing you this morning had nothing to do with the problems I've got with the police. And I'm not here now to try to 'cajole' you into keeping quiet when Thad Law contacts you. I expect you to tell the man the truth about that night, just like I did."

She slicked her tongue over her lips. "You *want* me to tell him I can place you in almost the exact spot as the person who fired a shot at your uncle?"

"Hell, no, I don't *want* that." Jackson jabbed a hand through his hair. "But it's the truth, so there's nothing I can do to change it. I didn't try to kill my uncle that night— I was halfway to the bar when I heard the shot. I ran back into the courtyard where all hell had broken loose. It's my bad luck no one saw me in that hallway. Just like it was bad luck months later to be alone when the bastard took a second shot at Uncle Joe. Those are facts *I* have to deal with. Just like I've dealt for the past ten months with thoughts playing in my head of the time you and I spent together at the birthday party."

"Maybe I..." Her voice was ragged, unsteady.

"Maybe you what?"

Dragging in a breath, she wrapped her arms around her waist. "There's no maybes about it. Since that night, I've dealt with those same kind of thoughts about you."

Jackson acknowledged the streak of primitive male satisfaction that came with her words. "So, maybe you understand why I'm asking for a chance at a relationship with you?" he asked evenly. "There's a reason we've stuck in each other's heads, Cheyenne. Maybe you'd like to know that reason as much as I would?"

"Maybe. Maybe just the thought of knowing scares me."

Coming in January 2002 from Silhouette Books...

THE GREAT MONTANA COWBOY AUCTION

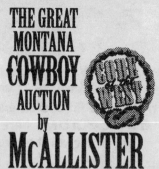

by

ANNE McALLISTER

With a neighbor's ranch at stake, Montana-cowboy-turned-Hollywood-heartthrob Sloan Gallagher agreed to take part in the Great Montana Cowboy Auction organized by Polly McMaster. Then, in order to avoid going home with an overly enthusiastic fan, he provided the money so that Polly could buy him and take him home for a weekend of playing house. But Polly had other ideas....

Also in the Code of the West

Available at your favorite retail outlet.

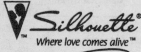

Silhouette®

Where love comes alive™

Visit Silhouette at www.eHarlequin.com

PSGMCA

THE COLTONS

If you missed the first seven exciting stories from
THE COLTONS, here's a chance
to order your copies today!

0-373-38704-0	BELOVED WOLF by Kasey Michaels	$4.50 U.S.☐	$5.25 CAN.☐
0-373-38705-9	THE VIRGIN MISTRESS by Linda Turner	$4.50 U.S.☐	$5.25 CAN.☐
0-373-38706-7	I MARRIED A SHEIK by Sharon De Vita	$4.50 U.S.☐	$5.25 CAN.☐
0-373-38707-5	THE DOCTOR DELIVERS by Judy Christenberry	$4.50 U.S.☐	$5.25 CAN.☐
0-373-38708-3	FROM BOSS TO BRIDEGROOM by Victoria Pade	$4.50 U.S.☐	$5.25 CAN.☐
0-373-38709-1	PASSION'S LAW by Ruth Langan	$4.50 U.S.☐	$5.25 CAN.☐
0-373-38710-5	THE HOUSEKEEPER'S DAUGHTER by Laurie Paige	$4.50 U.S.☐	$5.25 CAN.☐

(limited quantities available)

TOTAL AMOUNT	$ _____
POSTAGE & HANDLING	$ _____
($1.00 for one book, 50¢ for each additional)	
APPLICABLE TAXES*	$ _____
TOTAL PAYABLE	$ _____

(check or money order—please do not send cash)

To order, send the completed form, along with a check or money order for the total above, payable to **THE COLTONS**, to: In the U.S.: 3010 Walden Avenue, P.O. Box 9077, Buffalo, NY 14269-9077; In Canada: P.O. Box 636, Fort Erie, Ontario L2A 5X3.

Name: _____

Address: _____ City: _____

State/Prov.: _____ Zip/Postal Code: _____

Account # (if applicable): _____ 075 CSAS

*New York residents remit applicable sales taxes.
Canadian residents remit applicable GST and provincial taxes.

Visit Silhouette at www.eHarlequin.com
COLTBACK-7

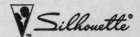